NOAH
COULD
NEVER

NOAH COULD NEVER

SIMON JAMES GREEN

■SCHOLASTIC

Scholastic Children's Books
An imprint of Scholastic Ltd
Euston House, 24 Eversholt Street, London, NW1 1DB, UK
Registered office: Westfield Road, Southam, Warwickshire, CV47 0RA
SCHOLASTIC and associated logos are trademarks and/or
registered trademarks of Scholastic Inc.

First published in the UK by Scholastic Ltd, 2018

Copyright © Simon James Green, 2018

The right of Simon James Green to be identified as the author
of this work has been asserted by him.

ISBN 978 1407 18002 1

A CIP catalogue record for this book
is available from the British Library.

Printed by CPI Group (UK) Ltd, Croydon, CR0 4YY

Papers used by Scholastic Children's Books are made
from wood grown in sustainable forests.

1 3 5 7 9 10 8 6 4 2

This is a work of fiction. Names, characters, places, incidents and
dialogues are products of the author's imagination or are used
fictitiously. Any resemblance to actual people, living or
dead, events or locales is entirely coincidental.

www.scholastic.co.uk

For Mum

CHAPTER ONE

"Uh, uh, uh, uh. . ."

"Come on, come on . . . *that's it. . .*"

"Uh, uh, uh, oh. . . Oh, oh, oh. . ."

"Harder! Harder!"

"Ah, ah, ah, ah. . ."

"YEAH!"

"AH! AH! AH! AH!"

"OH YES! OH YES!"

"AH! UH! AH! ARGHHHHHHH!"

"YEEEEAAAAHHHHH!"

"AHHHHHHHHHHH!"

"HELL YEAH!"

Noah sat frozen in the reception area of ActiveFit health club, staring in unmitigated terror towards whatever *depravity* was taking place in the gym itself. The only noises Noah had previously associated with any form of physical exercise were the words "No, I'm not doing it", "I'm not kicking that" and "I can't, I've hurt my shoulder." But *these* noises were different. Yes, they were sounds of pain. But a sort of pleasure-pain. Almost like … like the person making the noises *wanted* to be in searing agony. Like they were *enjoying* it.

Noah squirmed, sat on his hands and averted his eyes as two women, clad in spandex running tights, Asics trainers and sports tops walked across the foyer, their cheeks glowing, laughing and appearing generally fit, healthy and happy.

Noah, and Noah's life, was the antithesis of every*thing* and every*one* here.

He should probably go home. He couldn't go home.

He had to go through with this.

Because he couldn't unsee what he'd seen.

Noah wished he'd never clicked on that gay website's listicle, "Top 25 Christmas Gifts for Your BF". He'd subsequently fallen into a wormhole of washboard abs, perfect pecs, and frankly alarming information about "male grooming" that seemed to largely suggest removing all your pubic hair.

Was this what gay guys did? Was this the reality he must

now embrace? More importantly, *was this what Harry would want Noah to be?*

Noah was already painfully aware that Harry was, in every respect he could think of, *perfect*. Harry's height and weight were the perfect ratio, definitely falling into the "normal" shading on one of those puberty growth charts. And he was pretty sure that Harry wasn't working out in secret, yet he still managed to have muscle tone and definition. Noah had seen for himself, during a fraught ten minutes helping Harry struggle out of a polo shirt that was too small for him, *something that looked distinctly like some form of abs.* Just above the waistband of his boxers. Noah instinctively reached out to feel, to see if those formations were real, but just before contact he remembered himself and sprang back, as if he'd touched a hot stove.

And thank heavens! If he'd touched Harry there, it could totally have unleashed a sequence of events that might have resulted in Noah being expected to disrobe and BE NAKED.

In the two months since Harry had officially become Noah's "bae" (as popular culture would have it), Noah had managed to avoid this dreaded scenario. Sure, there had been assorted kissing, which had been *very* agreeable, and there had been a certain amount of low-level rubbing and stroking through clothes, which had once made Harry make a noise not dissimilar to those emanating from the gym right now, and once made Noah go, "Hahahaha – oh – wooooow, that tickles, nooooo! Stop! No, seriously, STOP. That's enough. Thank you. Oh. Oh dear." So, there had been *that*, but nothing else.

Noah had happily avoided further friskiness because of, well, the Christmas season. It's a time for family and children and candles, not *bow chicka wah wah*, because what would the little baby Jesus say?

And mock exams! The rigor of Noah's revision schedule would put Russian gymnasts to shame, and it had been planned long – long! – before getting together with Harry. He also had a v important speech to prepare, and that took, well, *ages*. So of course he didn't have time for *bow chicka wah wah* – only a cinema trip, perhaps, and some walks in the park to feed the ducks, and maybe sit on a bench there for a bit.

But who was Noah kidding? Even just thinking about it made the hair on the back of his neck stand on end and his stomach do little flips. Best friends for ever, sure. And holding hands, kissing ... those things were great! *But other stuff?* It was SO WEIRD. And if it went wrong, *everything* would be screwed up. "Let's just be friends," people would say, before never speaking again and slagging each other off to their other friends. Noah didn't really have any other friends. At best, he could phone his ex, Sophie, in glamorous Milton Keynes, but she wouldn't put up with him saying bad stuff about Haz ... or, if truth be told, put up with him ever describing her as an ex. They may have shared an experimental kiss, and he may have nearly pissed himself in front of her, but those two things didn't add up to a relationship.

Anyway! He couldn't imagine saying anything bad about Haz. Noah wanted Harry. He loved Harry. But what if, after trying to *do stuff*, it was *so bloody bad*, Harry realized he didn't want Noah? Noah could possibly deal with losing a *boy*friend. He'd seen people handle it in films by eating large tubs of Häagen-Dazs and curling up on sofas under duvets – no problems there, and in some respects, quite appealing. But losing his *friend*?

Harry, bless him, was respectful of Noah's need to revise as per the planned schedule and didn't try to interfere. But now, here they were in late January, mocks were over, spring would soon be upon them and ... the sap would be rising. Noah could only hold off the inevitable for so long.

And so, he had decided to take positive action! Noah Grimes would join the local gymnasium, work out, and become the sort of boy who was confident to whip off his boxers and say, "Come and get me, tiger! GRRRRRRR!" (He had already practised the growl, and it was really good, and v sexy, so he was halfway there, really.)

Determined to get a head start on the exciting "new him", Noah had booked a complimentary induction session with a personal trainer – or "PT", as they were known in the biz. A PT! For him! He was just like a Hollywood star, working out with his PT, like some sort of—

"Noah! *Dude!* What are the chances?!"

Noah's stomach sank.

It couldn't be.

Shit.

He narrowed his eyes at the muscular Adonis standing before him, wearing a T-shirt which bore the legend "Personal Trainer". *"Josh,"* he said. "Fancy seeing you here."

"Well, I work part-time here, so you'll probably see me a fair bit now you've signed up." Josh grabbed his right foot, stretching his leg back, whilst remaining balanced on his left, like some sort of Cirque du Soleil contortionist or something.

Noah considered his options because NO WAY was this happening. "Oh! You work at the osteopath's now?" he said, knowing even by his standards this was going to be a lame-arse excuse. Desperate times.

"Funny, dude," Josh grinned. "This is a *gym*, and I think you know that."

"Gym?" Noah said. "Oh dear, how embarrassing. I'm in quite the wrong place. I thought this was the osteopath's. I've slipped a disc, you see, probably from lifting all those textbooks and..." *Stop talking, get up and leave!* "Never mind, I'll just go and—"

"Always go to the osteopath in your PE kit, yeah?"

Josh raised his eyebrows, and folded his beefy arms across his bulky chest.

"Look!" Noah hissed. "I'm sorry, no, I don't have *Adidas* trainers, or *Nike* trackie bottoms, or a *Le Coq Sportif* T-shirt, or a *Puma* water bottle, or a *Reebok* sweat towel, or a—"

"Mate, let's just train. The kit doesn't matter and the rest . . . it's all water under the bridge, yeah?"

Noah glared at him. By "the rest", Josh was presumably referring to the small matter that he had spent a couple of ill-advised weeks SHAGGING NOAH'S MUM. An appalling act of selfishness, foulness and betrayal, now relegated to just being *liquid under some proverbial bridge*, even though it was about the worst thing to have ever happened to Noah. "Josh, I am still *reeling* from the events of last year," Noah said. "It has taken *months* to piece my life back together."

Josh put a heavy hand on Noah's shoulder. "I'm sorry, Noah, all right? Bro? I *am* sorry. I never meant to hurt you. You're all right."

"Well," Noah said, feeling the heft of that muscular hand and rather liking the fact that he was considered "all right" by a nineteen-year-old who happened to look *great* in gym shorts. "Thank you."

"I messed up, I admit that," Josh said, running his hand through his slicked-back hair. "But you gotta believe me when I say, I've changed. I've grown up a lot in the last

7

couple of months. Now I have Jess, and the baby coming, it's made me reassess my priorities. What I want out of life. I've knocked the uni idea on the head for now, and I'm working here. Earn some money and I can work towards a diploma too in a year's time. Be great if I had a few more clients, though," he said, looking hopefully at Noah.

"Look, I'm really not—"

"We can have you looking buff in no time, mate."

"Wha— *Really?* You think... Are you sure?"

"*Totes.* Little bit of cardio, work on those arms, legs..."

"I don't want to look like a bodybuilder," Noah said. "That would be ridiculous. But ... maybe like a footballer."

"Yeah, yeah, get a nice bod, ready for summer. All the boys will be beating a path to your door!"

"Boys..." Noah sniggered, "... my ... door. And you can... Those things are possible, you say?"

"Dude. It's what I do. If you're committed, it's possible. What the mind wants –" Josh tapped his finger on the side of Noah's head "– the body gets. You get me?"

Noah chewed his lip. "I have a Kangol headband – shall I put it on?"

"Go for it."

CHAPTER TWO

Noah was wide-eyed and quivering as Josh led him through the main part of the gym, with its contraptions, racks and stocks. A gigantic beast of a man, entirely made of muscles except for incredibly small hands, feet and a pin-like head, bellowed and roared as he heaved vast weights above his head, before crashing them back down on the floor with an almighty smash.

"GRRRRAAAAWWWGGHHHHH!" the big man boomed.

Noah rolled his eyes. Why did people who lifted weights have to make so much goddam noise? Sure, it took effort, but so did lots of things. Noah didn't roar every time he worked out the angles of a parallelogram.

They arrived on some exercise mats in the far corner

and Josh slapped Noah on the back. "All right, bud, let's get you warmed up first and see what we're dealing with. We're gonna do some *burpees*."

Noah frowned at Josh. "I'm not an infant, you know."

"Just watch," Josh said, squatting down. "You begin in a standing position, then drop down to a squat, kick your feet back into a plank while keeping your arms extended, then return your feet to the squat position and stand up into a jump on the final count. Got it?"

Noah looked at him blankly.

"Noah?"

"What was the first bit?"

"Standing. Like you're standing now."

"Then..."

"Drop into a squat," Josh said, demonstrating, his impressive thigh muscles bulging as he did so. "And into a plank."

"Plank," Noah repeated, trying to get used to this new word. "*Plank.*"

"This is a plank," Josh said, effortlessly kicking himself back into one. "See?"

"*Plank.*"

"Plank. That's right."

"And then up again into a star jump?" Noah said.

"*No,*" Josh said, patiently. "Back to the squat, *then* up to standing, finishing with just a jump. Not a star jump. Then you repeat the whole thing again."

"Wait. What do you mean?"

"That's just one rep. You're gonna do at least ten of these mofos, maybe more if you can."

"Surely one is enough, no?" Noah said. "How will I have enough energy for more?"

"Bro, you're young, you're... Well, you're *young*, innit? 'Course you'll have energy. You're reaching your peak physical condition at sixteen!"

Noah swallowed as panic welled in his stomach. *Shit.* Was this as good as it was going to get? After sixteen, was it basically a steady decline towards arthritis, mobility scooters and the grave? *Sodding hell.*

Josh slapped him on the back again. "Sixteen's the age, man! Peak physical and sexual condition at sixteen!"

Noah's eyes widened. *Oh great.* So he was now also at the age when he should be having the best sex and it would only get shitter and shitter from here on in. The clock was ticking and he hadn't got anywhere near doing it yet, and soon it would all be too late and he would only ever experience a skinny, runty body with saggy bits and crap, disappointing, flaccid sex, if he could ever get his head around engaging in any at all.

"Off you go," Josh encouraged him. "I'm gonna count your reps, and you're gonna keep going for as long as you can."

Noah chewed his lip. "Josh, can I just ascertain – are you first-aid trained?"

11

Josh nodded. "Basic level, yeah."

"What's that, just putting on a plaster?"

"My manager's done the full course and he's on duty now, so no worries."

Noah nodded. "OK. And is there a defibrillator on the premises?"

"Don't worry, Noah," Josh smirked. "If you collapse, I will personally give you the kiss of life."

Noah's face grew hot. With the antics Josh had engaged in with Noah's own mother, that was basically like suggesting incest. It would be wrong. Very wrong...

Anyhoo, he supposed he should at least give all this a jolly good try. After all, if he was going to be confident enough to do things with Haz, he needed to be confident in his own body. He was already in peak mental condition, he just needed the other departments to catch up, really. And then everything would be perfect and nice.

He could do this.

"Count me in, then," Noah said, shifting about on his feet in readiness.

"What do you mean, count you in?" Josh frowned.

"You know, like 'a five, six, seven, eight!'"

"It's not a dance routine!" Josh looked at an expectant Noah, and sighed. Then he glanced around, and said, "*Fine.* A five, six, seven, eight!"

Noah dropped down into a squat, thrust his legs back into a plank. "Now what?!" he squealed.

"Back into the squat!"

Noah thrust forward back to a squat.

"Up and jump!" Josh barked, like some sort of VILE ARMY MAJOR. "Lift your feet higher! Stretch the arms!"

Noah's wheezy chest tightened, as he sank back down into the squat position, his heart pounding, ears ringing, kick back into ... plank ... gasp for ... squat now ... and ... UP into the air ... air ... need more air...

"BACK INTO THE SQUAT! PUSH, NOAH! PUSH!"

Push indeed! He wasn't giving birth, he was ... squatting ... the mat was moving ... spinning ... vision blurred now, but OK ... push ... into ... gasp for ... need oxygen ... heart ... POUND PUMP ... plank ... into ... p-l-a—

SMACK! He collapsed face down on to the mat, spasming like a dying fish. He hoped whoever was in charge of the defibrillator would bring it quickly. Was that an ambulance siren he could hear, or just the ringing in his ears?

Noah felt a gentle pressure on his stomach, slowly opening an eye to see one of Josh's Nike Airs nudging him. "Up! Up you get, Noah! C'mon! Back on your feet, work through the pain, you need to FINISH STRONG!"

Finish strong? What the hell was this utter bullshit? He had nearly died! He was actually nearly dead!

"Right!" he said, scrambling to his feet, suddenly powered by raw indignation. "That's it! No! I don't care!"

Noah ripped the Kangol headband off, hurled it in a nearby bin and strode off towards the exit.

Josh grabbed a rucksack from the floor and hurried after him. "Bro! Mate!"

"I'm exhausted, Josh!" Noah said, wiping the sweat from his brow. "You've pushed me too far and now I've hurt my . , . nose a bit. On the mat. Very dangerous. I could probably sue."

"You didn't even complete one full set, mate!"

"No, Josh. No, I didn't, because *it was too difficult*! You made me do an advanced exercise that's probably for top athletes and now I've hurt myself and I look foolish. I'm going. Don't try to stop me. I hate this gymnasium. It's stupid and it's full of stupid people with NO BRAINS!"

The big man with the small head dropped the weights he was holding and looked pointedly at Noah.

Noah swallowed. "I should never have come here. *Goodbye*, Josh. You will never see me again."

Noah turned and headed back through to reception.

"Hold up!" Josh called, following him out. "I did not have Noah Grimes down for a quitter!" he said, just as Noah reached the main exit.

Noah stopped but didn't turn around. He was *not* a quitter. He was a survivor, as tenacious and dedicated as Jessica Fletcher on a murder case.

But Noah guessed that Mrs Fletcher never had to do a burpee, and it was worth noting that she ended up fine; elderly gentlemen were constantly courting her.

"Come on, mate," Josh cooed, edging towards a small table. "Come and sit down for a minute at least."

Noah weighed it up for a moment, then turned and joined him at the table. Josh reached into his rucksack and pulled out a large plastic sports beaker containing what looked like milkshake.

"Look, maybe you need a little extra help," Josh said, pushing the drink towards him.

Noah looked up with wide eyes. "Is this drugs?!" he said. "I'm not taking steroids!"

"Protein shake," Josh explained. "It's just a nice, big hit of protein."

"To help build muscle?"

"Precisely. Now, what about the rest of your diet? What's for dinner tonight, for example?"

Noah pursed his lips. "Hmm, well, it depends – maybe a pan-fried duck breast, potato rosti, with a port and plum jus." One could always *hope*, after all.

"No. Grilled chicken breast and cottage cheese."

"Well, that sounds ... a bit plain."

"Food is your fuel. It's not about whether it tastes good. Try some of the shake."

Noah indicated the sucky lid. "Have you..."

"I've not had any," Josh smiled. "The lid's clean."

Noah nodded and took a sip of the protein shake, screwing his face up as he swallowed. "Horrible," he muttered.

"Get it down you."

"How much of this do I have to drink?"

"The whole thing. Three times a day. It'll help bulk you up a bit. You up for it?"

"I don't know. Is this... How much is this?"

Josh leaned in and lowered his voice. "Well, now, here's the great thing. I've just become one of the sales reps for this protein shake and I'm making good money. *Great* money. I'm shifting fifty tubs of this baby a week, and that number's only gonna go up. I can let you have a tub for free, Noah. Normal price: thirty quid."

"Really?"

"Really." Josh shrugged. "I'm rolling in it, thanks to this little sideline. Shame, really; there's so much demand I can't actually service all the customers who want it. If you know anyone who's looking to make a bit of extra cash, push 'em my way, won't you?"

"Uh-huh." Noah nodded. "So, er, what does it entail exactly?"

Josh shifted in a little closer. "OK, so, it's *so* easy. The deal is, I recruit just two sales reps, who get their stock from me."

"And those reps sell it door to door?"

"Well, they *can*. Or they can then recruit two sales

reps each as well. Let's say, just for the sake of argument, you, Noah, *you* became my rep."

"OK, this is just an example, but OK," Noah said.

"So, you recruit two more sales reps, who get their stock from you, and you get your stock from me. And so it goes on. Your reps recruit two more reps each, and the chain fans out like a ... well, like a pyramid, I guess."

Noah nodded. He wasn't sure if Josh was deliberately trying to con him (quite possible), or whether Josh was just stupid (also possible), but this was quite obviously a pyramid *scheme*. As such, two outcomes were inevitable: (1) the business would eventually collapse because they always did, once there were insufficient people at the bottom to service those higher up; (2) various participants in the scheme would end up in prison for fraud.

"Know anyone who might be interested?" Josh said.

Noah sat back in the chair, stretched and yawned. "Sounds illegal to me, Josh."

Josh tutted. "What you chatting about?"

"Josh, it's a pyramid scheme. Google it! Google 'pyramid scheme' and see if you recognize the business structure."

"Yeah?"

Noah nodded. "*Yeah*, Josh. You need to knock this on the head."

"Well, guess what, dude?" Josh smiled. "I already Googled it. And what this company is, is *multilevel network*

17

marketing. Sure, there's a pyramid structure, but it's all above board and totally legal."

"Fine," Noah sighed. "Good luck with your pyramid."

"Not about luck. It's about *networking* and *positivity*. *People buying the dream*. And you could be part of the dream, Noah."

Noah got up. "Just remember, some pyramids have secret chambers, Josh. And some of those secret chambers have *curses*."

Josh screwed his face up. "I don't get what you're trying to say."

Noah put his hands on his hips. "I'm just saying … beware. Beware, Josh!" And he whisked away towards the exit, disappearing in a dramatic swirl of— "Um, the door won't open."

"You gotta press the green button."

"Green … button. . ." Noah said, trying to locate it.

"On the side! Left-hand side!"

Noah found it and gave it a press. The door slid open. "Beware!" Noah said, disappearing into the late afternoon gloom.

CHAPTER THREE

Noah hurried towards his house, the cold biting at his naked little legs, but stopped dead in his tracks when he saw what was parked on the driveway: a bright pink Ford Transit van with the words "Girlz on tour" painted on the side and fake eyelashes attached to the headlights.

What fresh hell was this?

He slammed the front door behind him, walked through to the lounge and froze. "Bambi Sugapops!" he said, recognizing her immediately.

"Hiya, Noah!" she cooed, coquettishly.

Noah took a deep breath but couldn't stop the rise of panic in his chest, couldn't stop the flashback playing in his brain. His thirteenth birthday party. His hopeful, boyish face as his mother announced a "surprise". The promise of bowling, or a trip to Pizza Hut ... and then in she comes.

Bambi Sugapops. The morally bankrupt stripper with the terrifyingly massive breasts that couldn't possibly have been the result of natural development. She had gyrated in close proximity to Noah's tear-stained face (an image that had been captured on camera, uploaded and become impossible to get rid of), whilst his mother clapped and cheered and said things like, "You're thirteen now, you're supposed to love stuff like this!"

He didn't sleep for five whole nights afterwards – something his mother, rather appallingly, put down to nocturnal activities connected with Bambi's erotic extravaganza. But she couldn't have been more wrong. It was because of the *trauma*.

"Who's a big boy now, then?" Bambi purred, giving him a little wink from where she was sitting on the sofa. She was a tall woman, black, quite broad, with great poise and elegance. If only she'd shown a bit more of that three years ago!

"I'm going upstairs," Noah said.

"Noah," his mum said, "manners, please! Haven't you got anything to say?"

Noah glanced at his mother, sitting on the sofa in her bright pink velour tracksuit which had "Gold Digga" written across the arse. She stared back at him and cocked her head in a way that Noah knew meant she was serious.

He sighed and looked at Bambi. "Hi, Bambi," he muttered. "Nice to see you."

"Ooh, he's got a voice almost like a man now!" she said, pouting her bright purple lips a little.

"What do you mean, *almost*?" Noah said.

"And I've heard all about your new BF," Bambi continued.

"Thanks, Mum." Noah grimaced.

"Always said you were gay, honey!" Bambi said. "Didn't we always say, Lisa?"

"Well, with a mother like me!" his mum snorted.

"Ooh, she knew all the gays back in the day, hun!" Bambi added, like this was some sort of achievement.

Noah nodded and gave a tight little smile. "Well, that's brilliant."

"Everyone used to come to our shows. Talk of the town, we were!" Bambi adjusted her fringe, her whole scalp seeming to shift.

Odd.

"Ooh, my poor feet!" Bambi continued, kicking her heels off. "Right! I've gotta get out of this gear!" And she stood up, all six feet of her, and pulled her hair off, revealing a shaved head underneath.

Noah stared, unblinking.

That tall, elegant woman with poise was suddenly a man in a dress and some rather excessive make-up.

Oh good God.

The outfit ... the mention of "shows" ... the "gay scene"... Bambi Sugapops wasn't a stripper; she was a drag queen.

"How's things with you, Noah?" his mum was saying. "Tell us all about your day!"

He stared wildly between his mother and Bambi, not wanting to give away his rather late revelation. How had he been so utterly clueless and stupid? *Keep a poker face*, he told himself. He couldn't show any weakness or surprise. *Do not provoke the drag queen.* "Nothing to report." He swallowed and attempted a smile. "I'm going to go up to my room now. Where's Dad?"

"He's popped out to book a table at the Indian," his mum said. "It's date night tomorrow!"

Even in the midst of his hurricane of horrified emotions, Noah felt a flash of irritation and ground his teeth. His dad had been AWOL for years. Noah had even been allowed to think he was dead! As a kid, all he'd wished was for his dad to come home. But now he had, Noah realized that his memories of this man were all some fantasy, possibly based on films like *Finding Nemo*, where fathers were heroic and actually cared about their kids. Gah! He couldn't believe he'd once hoped for his parents to get back together! Why couldn't they be like the parents of people from school, desperately attending marriage counselling whilst shouting, calling each other selfish and then packing bags, storming out, and spending the night in a Travelodge in order to make some dramatic point? God, his life could never be normal, could it? "You do know that restaurants accept bookings via phone and the internet these days?"

"He wants to secure a good table." His mum smiled. "And you know when your father turns the charm on, he usually gets his way! Silver-tongued!" She emitted a cheeky little giggle that made Noah feel sick.

"Brian's always been good with his tongue, or so you say," Bambi said, winking at Noah's mum.

Noah was literally about to explode into actual vomit. Oh-my-God.

"Hush!" his mother giggled. "Not in front of Noah!"

Noah snorted. "Not in front" of him? It had been *perfectly fine* for Noah to witness all manner of terrible things (e.g., her *kissing Josh*) up until a couple of months ago. Now, with his dad back, his mother had become some sort of manic 1950s-style housewife: doing housework, baking, and making regular contributions to Mumsnet.

Bambi passed a weary hand over her cheek. "Ugh, I really gotta take this slap off."

"Mick had to leave Stoke-on-Trent in a rush," his mother said to Noah.

"Who?"

"Me, babes," Bambi said. "Call me Mick. Unless I got me hair on, in which case, I'm Bambi."

Noah nodded. "*Fine.*"

"Not gonna lie, honey, I literally had to run for my

23

life from a rehearsal just four hours ago," Mick continued. "A turf war's broken out on the Stoke drag scene. I've had a bit of trouble with this tired old has-been, aka my former business partner..."

Noah zoned out as Mick rambled on. *What would be for dinner?*

"Ditched me and Polly Esther, she has, and joined forces with this bitch who showed up last month, fresh from some shitty season in Las Vegas, or so she claims!"

Should he do as Josh suggested and consume vast amounts of dreary protein?

"Of course, she wants me to pay her back for what she claims is 'her share' of our tour van, but screw that!"

...He just fancied a nice slice of Battenberg cake, truth be told...

"I won't play ball, so now she's trying to force me out! Trying to snaffle all of Bambi's best clients. There's been threats."

"Threats? And you came here?" Noah said, his disinterest shifting quickly to alarm.

"Someone dropped *something* through my letter box," Mick said, eyes full of meaning.

"A letter?" Noah said.

"Max Factor foundation. Everyone knows I wouldn't touch that shit. It's them basically saying, 'You're cheap! Worthless! A Max-Factor-wearing slag!' That's what they're saying."

Noah nodded. "Awful."

Noah's mum nodded, solemnly. "So Mick's going to be kipping here for a bit, just while he gets himself together."

The blood drained from Noah's face. "But my French exchange student is coming! Tomorrow!"

"I'll be fine on the sofa, babes. Mickey ain't grand!"

Not grand, but he refers to himself in the third person! "Mum!"

"Noah, Mick is practically family!"

"Mum!" Noah hissed. "I've met this person once before, under circumstances no one would describe as family friendly."

"You mean your birthday party?" Mick smiled. "Tears of joy rolling down your face, as I recall, hun!"

"They were tears of pain and humiliation!" Noah snapped. He turned to his mum. "I can't have a drag queen on the sofa – what will our guest think?"

Mick put his hands on his hips. "When did you become such a little puritan?"

"I'm not," Noah said. "I'm merely wishing to make a good impression."

"Stop being a sourpuss, Noah," his mum chimed in. "Lighten up!"

Noah glared at her, tight-lipped and wide-eyed.

His mum held her hand up. "My house, my rules. Besides, Mick's already got a trial gig lined up in London next weekend, so things are already looking up. And in the meantime, I'm sure your French boy will love it. They're all into that Moulin Rouge stuff over there."

"Oh, that's right, just stereotype an entire nation!" Noah hissed.

"Anyone mind if I use the bathroom for twenty minutes? If I don't get this slap off, Bambi's gonna have the face of a zombie."

"Noah? Do you need a wee before Mick uses the bathroom?"

Noah smarted. "Mum! I'm not *five*!"

"OK, fine." His mum shrugged.

"Yes, I do," Noah conceded. "I'll be two minutes." He glanced over at Mick. "Right, well, I shall see you later," Noah said, stomping through to the kitchen, grabbing a peach yoghurt from the fridge because he was sodding starving, and swiftly exiting again up the stairs.

"You bet, hun!" Mick shouted after him. "We've so much catching up to do! And I want to know all about your love life! Sounds like you've bagged yourself a right hunk. You go, *gurl*!"

"Fucking nutter," Noah muttered to himself as he snapped his shorts back up, splashed some water over his hands and dried them on his bare legs. He paced across the landing and pushed his bedroom door open. "ARGH!"

"All right, Noah?" said Harry, looking up from

Noah's bed, where he was lying down, apparently having a snooze.

"How did you get in?"

"Your mum?" Harry said, sitting up against the pillows, rubbing his eyes, his blond hair sticking up in tufts. "Why are you in your PE kit?"

Noah blinked at him. "Look, I haven't had an accident."

"No," Harry said. "Good."

Noah nodded, tore the lid off his yoghurt and put it on his bedside table. *Just act normal!* he told himself. *Harry must not suspect you've visited a gym — it might draw your lack of muscle tone to his attention!* "So, it's a nice day. How are you? I'm fine," Noah said, dipping his spoon in the pot.

"Why are you in your PE kit?"

Noah blew out a breath. "Mum ... forgot to wash my clothes. I didn't have any clothes. It's winter, and I had to go out like this. *Criminal.* Heartless old witch."

Noah followed Harry's glance as he looked across at the pile of freshly laundered and neatly folded clothes on top of Noah's chest of drawers. He took a breath, and then had another mouthful of yoghurt, because he really wasn't sure what else to say about that. Noah turned back, to see the yoghurt lid on his bedside table had been *licked clean*. His eyes widened at a patently guilty Harry, who had a bit of yoghurt on his top lip. "Um ... Harry? Have you just eaten my lid yoghurt?"

Harry stared at him for a moment. "I thought you didn't want it."

"*Didn't want it?* Haz, everyone knows the lid yoghurt is the best bit of the whole yoghurt. I was saving it till last! It's the creamiest part, why *wouldn't I* want it?"

"Um," Harry said. "Oh, right. Well ... *sorry?*"

Noah considered him a moment. He supposed this was one of those times – you know, when you had to *forgive* the person you loved, because sometimes people you loved did silly things, but you had to say, "That's fine, it's OK, you ate my lid yoghurt but I will forgive you."

"That's fine, I will forgive you," Noah said. "Although if you do it again I will literally commit some form of violence on you."

"Ha ha!" Harry chuckled.

Noah wasn't joking.

"Cool." Harry patted the bit of bed next to him and smiled. "Come here, then."

Noah put the yoghurt down, scooted over and plopped himself down next to Harry.

Harry put his hands on Noah's hips, leaned in, and gave him a peck on the lips. A small act, but Harry, *so close, so intimate*, still made Noah catch his breath, even now, even after *quite a bit* of kissing over the last few weeks.

"Are you *trembling?*" Harry said.

"No, not..." *He was, he could feel it.* "I'm a bit cold," Noah offered.

Harry smiled and wrapped his arms around Noah. "Come here, it's OK."

And it was OK, as Noah sank into the blissful cuddle and the warmth of Harry's fluffy, baby-blue jumper. "I got you something," Harry murmured.

"Oh?"

"Here," Harry said, breaking away and pulling a carrier bag out from behind him.

"But it's not my birthday. Or Christmas," Noah said.

Harry smiled. "I know. I was just buying my boyfriend a little present."

"Oh." Noah swallowed. *Shit. He was a terrible boyfriend — why hadn't he ever thought of doing something like this?* Instead, there he was, making a huge issue over a bit of lid yoghurt! "Oh! That's... *Thank you*, Harry. That's lovely! A lovely thing! Thank you. I... This is so nice. It's the best thing ever. You're so lovely."

"You don't know what it is yet."

"No. No, I don't, but you got it for me, so I'll love it whatever it is!"

"Have a look, then."

"OK," Noah said, peering inside the bag and pulling out a beautifully soft, grey hoodie.

"Do you like the colour?" Harry asked.

Noah nodded, rubbing the fleecy interior against his cheek. "Oh my God, it's so soft!"

Harry grinned. "Glad you like it."

"Thanks, Harry. This is so lovely," Noah said, putting it on. Warm and soft and perfect – just like the person who gave it to him. He did the zip up. "Ta-da! I am literally going to wear this everywhere. And if I'm not wearing it, like because it needs a wash or the thing I'm doing requires a different sort of outfit, then I'll still have it with me. Because it'll remind me of you."

"Cute," Harry said, pulling the hood over Noah's head. "You look really, really good. And now you'll be warm too."

They both leaned forward at the same time and fell into a long kiss, the hood falling away again as Noah wrapped his arms around Harry, whilst Harry nuzzled kisses into Noah's neck and rubbed his hand up Noah's thigh, his fingers gently tickling under the leg of Noah's PE shorts.

"Aww," Harry sighed, "wish your mum wasn't downstairs."

"And if you don't already know, I have to tell you: there's also a drag queen on the loose."

Harry shook his head. "Your house is crazy." He planted another kiss on Noah's lips. "Maybe ... if we're quiet?"

"There's no lock on my door, though!" Noah said, pulling back a bit. "And Mum ... well, you know what she's like."

"Yeah. Of course." Harry nodded.

"I do want to, though," Noah added, quickly. "Just to confirm that. I would definitely, absolutely, like to do things. With you."

Harry smiled. "Me too."

"We'll plan it!"

"OK, fine, we'll plan it," Harry chuckled.

This was good, Noah considered. Having a plan was an excellent thing to have. And it would give him a bit of time. To work on his abs and down protein shakes, so he wouldn't be all skinny and awkward. He could plan for shadowy lighting, and various sexy garments to strategically obscure as much of his body as possible.

"Just probably not at either of our houses," Harry continued.

Granted, this was a problem, albeit one that was happily buying Noah a bit more time. Noah's house was becoming increasingly impossible by the day. With Dad back and sleeping in Mum's room, his half-brother, Eric, regularly staying the night in the spare room – which would shortly be occupied by Noah's French exchange student – and now Mick or Bambi on the sofa, the house was bulging at the seams. Harry's house was a calmer affair, but was policed twenty-four-seven by his manic mum, who was still getting used to the idea of Harry being gay, to put it charitably. There was currently nowhere for them to have sufficient privacy to do anything – and whilst the patch of wooded scrubland off the A631 was popular with many people their age (for reasons not connected with an interest in forestry), those kids were basically asking to be murdered by a serial killer/escaped genetic experiment by going there. If American movies had taught Noah little else, they had taught him this.

"We'll work something out," Noah said. "And in any case, I do of course have to rehearse my welcome speech for the French tomorrow!"

Harry gave a little smile. "Why are they making you do that?"

Noah sighed and looked heavenwards. "Because you know how the school works! 'Oh, look, we've got something shit that no one else wants to take responsibility for – I know, we'll get Noah to do it!' God, I'm so, so, so, so sick of always being the one who they make do everything, just because I have good microphone technique and know about puns."

"You volunteered, didn't you?" Harry grinned.

Noah moistened his lips. "Only partially."

"How do you partially volunteer?"

"Long story, long story," Noah sighed.

"Uh-huh?"

Noah stifled a grimace. "OK, so the signing-up sheets on the noticeboard were partially obscured. I thought I was putting myself down for ... Model Club, but—"

Harry snorted. "*Model* Club? What's that – a guy in CK's parading around on a catwalk?!"

32

Why was Harry thinking about guys in underwear on catwalks? "*No*, Harry, not that, Airfix model aircraft. Point is, there was confusion, misunderstandings, it happened, no point crying over spilled milk, best to just get on with it, yes?"

Harry smiled. "And you're ... you're keeping it ... er, simple, I hope?"

"I actually read it out to Sophie over Skype a few days ago," Noah said. "She said most of it was great."

"*Most* of it?"

"Yeah, yeah," Noah said, "I mean, she wanted me to make a couple of minor editorial changes, but I think she's wrong, so I haven't."

Harry stared at him. "You thought Sophie might have been *wrong*?"

Noah screwed his face up. "Er, Harry," he said, pointing to himself. "County debating champion last year! Think I can put together a little speech!"

"Sure." Harry nodded. "Of course."

"It's going to be ace. You'll see. Got a few public speaking tricks up my sleeve. They'll be eating out of my arse."

"Hand."

"That's right. *Hand*."

CHAPTER FOUR

"I'm doing a speech," Noah said, glancing at Connor Evans as they waited next to each other in the playground for the French bus to turn up.

"Yeah? That's great," Connor muttered, clapping his gloved hands together to stay warm.

"No biggie," Noah said. "Just a few words to welcome them to the UK – someone's gotta do it."

"Cool," Connor said. He looked at Harry. "You helping with the speech too, Haz? Little joint effort?"

Harry shook his head. "Some things are best left to Noah."

Connor chuckled. "Damn right."

Noah nodded and gave a polite smile. He wasn't massively keen on the fact Harry and Connor were still so matey with one another. How, when Harry had blatantly dumped Connor for Noah, were they still such good friends, able to exchange conversation and have a laugh? A laugh that felt like it was, quite possibly, at Noah's expense?

Worse, Connor was positioning himself as some sort of alpha gay within the school. He'd dyed his quiffed hair peroxide blond, his trousers had got tighter, his muscles bigger, and Noah had no doubt his body hair situation would be completely in line with what the gay websites said it should be. Rumour had it, Connor was seeing a boy in Year Thirteen – two years his senior! How very edgy. That meant Connor was also probably sexually experienced now, taken under the wing of this sugar daddy in the sixth form, who would have doubtless shown him exactly what to do and when to do it. If anything did ever happen with Noah and Harry in that department, Noah was going to have to rely on playground banter, dubious websites and his book on puberty (that didn't mention anything about being gay in it) for guidance. Some people had it so easy.

All the more reason for Harry to see that what Noah might lack in the GAY SEX KNOWLEDGE department, he more than made up for with public speaking skills. And, after all, which was more important?

"Hey, booooys!" Jess Jackson sidled up to them. Her little baby bump was beginning to bulge under her school shirt, but in every other respect, she was the same old

Jess: dressed for a night out rather than a day in school, manicured and perfect, with her silky hair and flawless make-up.

"Noah's doing a speech, Jess," Connor said.

Her eyes lit up. "Are you doing a speech, Noah?"

"Yes, I'm doing a bit of a speech."

"What about?" Jess grinned, like this was somehow the most exciting news she'd received for months.

"Just stuff." Noah shrugged, picking some imaginary lint off his blazer. "Just about welcoming them to our humble country. It's not like I want to do it, but the school asked."

"Mmmm," Jess giggled, "that's so cool. I love that." She looked over to where Melissa was standing with some of the other aloof and possibly mean girls. "Hey, Mel? MEL?! NOAH'S DOING A SPEECH!"

"NO SHIT, YOU DOING A SPEECH, NOAH?!" Melissa shouted back.

Noah grimaced. "Just ... yeah, a bit of one."

"WHAT?!"

"YES! A BIT OF ONE!" Noah shouted back. "God, why's everyone going on about it so much?"

Connor gave him side-eye. "You mentioned it, mate."

"Just in passing, though—" Noah stopped as the coach pulled into the yard. "Oh goodness, they're here, I'd better go and stand near Mrs Stirling so I'm ready."

Noah pushed through the crowd as everyone

descended into hushed anticipation. Noah knew what that was about. His peers might be mildly curious about what the French students would be like, or who they would each be assigned to, but the big question most of them were asking was *would any of them be fit?*

Noah cleared his throat, straightened his school tie, brushed a bit more imaginary lint off his blazer and glanced at Mrs Stirling for his cue. Across the playground, Jess Jackson blew him a kiss. "I'm *hot* for your speech, Noah!" she called out.

Noah gave her a brief nod. He had worked out the best approach with Jess was just to go along with it – not fight.

The coach opened its door with a hiss and the French students made their first steps on to UK soil. Thirty or so students gradually spilled out. Boys, girls, short, tall, some with spots, some with braces – despite the reputation of their provenance, they were, in essence, *just like them*. Noah straightened his tie again. Mrs Stirling was busy looking at her clipboard, but he supposed she would give him the signal for his speech any second now.

"SPEECH!" Jess Jackson shouted.

Noah looked over and scowled. Jess should realize that these things were properly stage-managed – official speeches didn't just happen willy-nilly. He had to wait for the cue.

Mrs Stirling raised a loudhailer to her mouth. Noah

frowned. Was he to do his speech through *that*, like some sort of fire marshal? Didn't this school have a proper PA system?

"OK, everyone!" Mrs Stirling began. "Let's give a warm British welcome to our guests from France!"

Cheers and whoops erupted from the crowd, at a level and intensity completely at odds with the thing being celebrated.

"OK, OK," Mrs Stirling boomed, "it's very cold so we'll crack on..."

Noah cleared his throat again. This was surely the moment. He glanced over at Harry, Connor and Jess. Harry gave him the thumbs up.

"Give it to us, Noah!" Jess shouted, to laughter from her mates.

Mrs Stirling was looking at her clipboard again, apparently unaware of the disruption. "Right, if you can all form an orderly queue, Mr Baxter will be introducing you to your new French *ami*..."

Noah looked at her with wide eyes.

"The luggage needs to go to reception until you take your student home with you later on..."

Should he say something?

"And don't forget our very own England versus France football match this afternoon. And just to remind everyone, it's a *friendly* match, not an opportunity, as I overheard a certain individual in Year Twelve mention, 'to

38

remind them who won the Napoleonic Wars'. Thank you, and behave responsibly."

No, no, no, no!

Everyone started to shuffle off, forming a queue to collect their French student. Noah stood, wide-eyed and going red, at the apparent fact he'd been forgotten.

What. About. His. Speech?!

He glanced over at Harry, Connor and Jess. Connor was in hysterics, loving every second of it. Harry was as wide-eyed as Noah was, watching open-mouthed as Mrs Stirling disappeared into the crowd. Jess looked *delighted*.

Fine, it was fine, Noah thought. He didn't care about the speech anyway. It was fine that he'd spent *weeks* writing and rehearsing it, even whilst revising for mocks, and that was all now time wasted. The next time Mrs Stirling, or anyone, asked for his help, he would politely decline – then they would be sorry. Who would run the tombola at the summer fair? *Not him.*

Noah bowed his head and surreptitiously started to skulk away from the small podium, pretending like he was just a normal part of the crowd like everyone else, and he'd had no special duties he'd been meant to perform that day.

Jess collapsed into him with breathless excitement. "It was epic, Noah! So good! Best speech I ever heard!"

He glowered at her. "Thanks," he muttered, through gritted teeth.

"My favourite bit was the part where you literally

said nothing and didn't even make a speech. It's like you subverted the whole concept of public speaking!"

He wasn't going to rise to it. Maybe acting like she was genuinely giving him a compliment would confuse her. "Thanks, Jess."

"That speech will definitely get you head."

Or possibly not.

She winked at him and flounced off through the crowd. Noah took a deep and calming breath before Connor tumbled into him, all smiles and laughter. "Fuck me, Noah," Connor said, slapping Noah on the back, "that was hilarious, mate."

Noah forced out a laugh. "Yeah. Dodged that bullet!"

Connor guffawed. "We gotta hang out more often. Actually, we *gotta*, 'cause have you seen the *little fitty* that Harry's been paired with?"

Noah looked around just as Harry pushed through with the second most beautiful boy Noah had ever seen in his life.

"Hey, guys!" Harry chirped.

Noah understood why Harry was so goddam chirpy. With his chiselled jaw, smouldering dark eyes, roguish smile, lightly tanned skin and deep brown, tousled hair, this boy was mesmerizing. This boy looked ready to film a perfume commercial.

"I'm Pierre," the boy said, in smooth, silky tones. "Pierre *Victoire*."

CHAPTER FIVE

Noah glanced between Pierre and Harry and loosened his tie a little. "So. You two are paired up. That's nice. Very nice."

"Yeah, it's gonna be cool," Harry said, with a little too much enthusiasm for Noah's liking. "Pierre's really into films, so I've said we'll go to the cinema one night."

Noah nodded. "Uh-huh. You found that out quickly. Been talking, I suppose?"

"Right," Harry said, brow furrowed. "That's kinda the idea."

"No, totally. *Totally*," Noah said. "Cinema, huh? That's not actually on the official itinerary, of course."

Harry shot Noah a look. "No. It was just ... you know, an idea."

"Very spontaneous," Noah said.

"You two are lovers?" Pierre said, wiggling his finger between them both.

"Noah's my boyfriend, yeah," Harry said.

Pierre nodded. "That's nice. Me, I am also gay."

Of course you bloody are, Noah thought, while nodding politely, like this was all really pleasant news and not at all an issue.

"Nice," Pierre said again. "We are gay together."

Noah gave a nervous laugh at this suggestive faux pas and glanced at Harry. Noah could only hope that Harry would never be persuaded to be gay with anyone other than him. Even if that other someone was SO INCREDIBLY ATTRACTIVE IT WAS BEYOND BELIEF. No. Their gayness was exclusive.

"Ah, Mr Grimes," said Mr Baxter, sauntering over with a ridiculously tall girl, who seemed to be entirely arms and legs. "This is Eva. Eva – this is Noah."

Eva flicked her depressed eyes momentarily up at him from under her blonde fringe.

"All right?" Noah nodded.

Mr Baxter rubbed his hands together. "Excellent. I'll let you two get to know one another, then!"

Noah grabbed Mr Baxter's arm like he'd just been tasered. "WHOA! Whoa, whoa, whoa! What's that? You're not suggesting she's my exchange partner?!"

Mr Baxter nodded.

"But I'm a boy? I'm supposed to be paired with another boy!"

"Well, we don't have equal numbers of boys and girls," Mr Baxter explained, like this was a totally reasonable solution to the problem.

"Yes, but—" Noah pulled Mr Baxter to one side and lowered his voice. "Eva is a girl and *I* . . . *I* am a boy! It's surely not allowed for us to share a house! What if. . ."

"She's in a separate room, Noah."

"Yes, but what if. . . I don't know, surely it's tempting fate or something?"

"That's why we put her with you."

Noah smarted. "But . . . well, all I'm saying is, if she gets pregnant or something, it's not my fault."

"No," Mr Baxter said. "I don't imagine it would be."

Noah turned back to Eva and managed a monumentally disappointed smile. There she was, all tall and wan, with a battered guitar case, small holdall and a sullen attitude. Noah hoped she wasn't planning on playing that guitar. The last thing he needed was some miserable girl strumming out old Radiohead tunes whilst he was trying to sleep.

"Is that a *German* flag on your guitar case?" Noah said.

"Yes."

"*Why?*"

"I am from Germany."

Noah stared at her while he computed this information, and then stalked back to Mr Baxter, taking him aside again. "She's German."

"Yes."

"But this is a *French* exchange programme."

"She lives in France."

"But she's German!"

"Yes, well, her parents moved to France from Germany to work. You can ask her all about it yourself."

"But this is a *French* exchange trip. They're meant to be French."

"They're all *from* France."

Noah glared at Mr Baxter. This was a disaster. He had been promised a French *boy* who was supposed to have been all poetic and soulful, and ideally just as goddam sexy as Pierre. Pierre *Victoire*.

"Oh, Noah, stop being ridiculous. Eva knows French too. She's trilingual. These kids put our own language skills to shame."

Noah nodded, tight-lipped and furious. If Mr Baxter wasn't so adult and so *teacher*, he would have told him exactly what he thought.

Mr Baxter said, "Crack on, kiddo," and walked off, discussion over.

Noah rolled his eyes and rejoined the group, where Pierre and Harry were talking animatedly. "All right, Harry? Pierre? What's happening?"

"Pierre was just saying how much he likes pizza and that maybe we could go for some Italian food sometime," Harry said.

Noah shrugged. "Sure. Pizza's cool. I like pizza. Love it."

Harry furrowed his brow. "Last time I suggested it, you said pizza was lazy food, which the Italians had ripped off from the British cheese on toast."

Noah laughed maniacally. "Don't be silly, I wouldn't say that."

"What's your favourite topping, Noah?" Pierre said.

"I tend to go tropical," Noah said. "Ham and pineapple. The classic *Hawaiian*."

Pierre chuckled. "You British are so funny with your flavours."

"What about you, Eva?" Harry asked. "You like pizza?"

Eva sniffed and pulled a pack of cigarettes from her high-waisted jeans pocket. "No. You have a lighter?"

"Oh, no, Eva, no! You can't do that! Smoking –" Noah frantically did a smoking mime in case Eva didn't understand "– is not allowed, NOT ALLOWED, on school premises."

"Cool. You don't need to shout," Eva said, shifting her weight on to one incredibly long leg and folding her arms.

"So, there's lots to look forward to," Noah said, "including a quiz night on Saturday that I'm in charge of – which is called –" Noah paused to heighten the sense of anticipation "– the Great British *Quiz Off*!" He looked between the parties. "Ha ha! Right?!"

Pierre and Eva looked blank. Harry nodded and smiled.

"Maybe we can get a coffee?" Pierre suggested, as the bell for class rang.

"Get a coffee? *Get a coffee?*" Noah said, screwing up his face. "This is a British secondary school; if you want refreshments, we'll all have to go and have a suck on the water fountain. Hopefully they've disinfected it after that Year Eight kid weed in it. This way, people!"

Noah strode off with the others in tow … all except Eva, who grabbed her guitar case and walked in the opposite direction.

CHAPTER SIX

Noah dallied about at the far end of the pitch, the mirror opposite of where the ball was, and, he was pretty sure, at the greatest possible distance from the action, as the crow flies. He had to appear willing and participate in this ridiculous football match, but why they couldn't have had a pleasant afternoon doing something like a nature trail instead, he didn't know. It would have been interesting for the French students to spot British wild flowers and native birds and moss and stuff.

"Grimes!" Ms O'Malley shouted, blowing her whistle at him. "The ball's over there! Do you need new glasses?!"

"No, I'm in defence!" Noah explained. "I'm a defender!"

"You're a *slacker*, that's what you are! Get stuck in!"

Noah made a half-hearted two-step jog, then looked down. "Oh – my lace is undone!" he said, bending over, untying the lace on his football boot and starting to retie it again, slowly. "I'll just be a second!"

He needn't have worried. Ms O'Malley's attention was drawn by a sudden cheer from the crowd as a majestic Pierre suddenly surged forward with the ball, deftly kicking it around five of Noah's teammates and gliding across the pitch as if it were ice. Pierre was fast. In no time he'd broken through and left the entire team in his wake, unable to catch up.

And he was heading right towards Noah.

Ms O'Malley blew her whistle again. "Grimes! This is your time to shine!"

Noah had precious moments to develop a strategy. Everyone was watching as Pierre hurtled towards him like a Japanese bullet train ... but one that had a really charming grin and surprisingly muscular legs.

"Noah! Noah!" people were shouting.

Shit.

"Get him, Noah!"

Oh God!

"C'mon, Noah!"

Noah swallowed. There was no avoiding this. He set off towards Pierre, charting a course of imminent collision. He looked directly into Pierre's smouldering eyes as they ran towards each other. Oh God, he was going to be flattened! His delicate bones would be shattered into a million pieces!

Noah crumpled into a heap on the ground, about three metres from Pierre, who simply skipped around him. "Ahhhh!" Noah said, weakly.

The crowd groaned.

Pierre smashed the ball into the net. The French side all cheered.

"For God's sake, Noah!" someone shouted.

"Frickin' useless!" a girl screamed.

"You tosser!" said a Year Nine boy, making a wanking gesture with his hand. "He never even touched you!"

"Cramp!" Noah explained to the braying mob, clutching his leg in a vague, non-specific way.

"Bull-*shit*!" several people chorused, before starting up a chant. "Bull*shit*, bull*shit*, bull*shit*. . ."

Noah strode up to Ms O'Malley, remembering to limp at the last moment. "They're chanting at me," he complained.

Ms O'Malley shrugged. "Don't like it? Don't let them down."

Noah sighed and turned around to see Harry running up to Pierre, laughing and hugging him, congratulating Pierre on his bloody amazing goal.

Hugging him! A hug! They didn't even know each other three hours ago, and now they were intimately hugging. God only knew what they would be doing by tonight... Pierre, sneaking into Harry's bedroom ... and probably:

> HARRY: Oh, Pierre, that goal was so good, I
> can't stop thinking about it.
> PIERRE: I did it for you, Harry.
> HARRY: For me?
> PIERRE: Yes. And I want to score again.
> HARRY: (giggles) Oh ... Pierre!
> PIERRE: I will bypass all your defences and
> shoot it into your goal, Harry.
> HARRY: Take me in your French arms and
> French kiss me!

That's *exactly* what would happen. Good-looking, gay *and* great at sport. How could Noah compete? And Harry was clearly loving it ... was clearly *impressed*...

Noah clenched his fists. He would show Harry. He would show everyone. If he put his mind to it, he too could score a goal. He could be just as majestic and ... *smouldering* as Pierre.

Ms O'Malley blew the whistle.

His time was now.

Everything became a blur, except his pin-sharp tunnel vision on the ball. He charged towards it, his legs taking on a life of their own, surging forward with an energy he hitherto didn't know he had possessed... Just him ... and the roar of the crowd as he took possession of the ball, swinging around and breaking through the French team's centre forwards, his path ahead towards the goal remarkably clear ... the crowd cheering ... calling his name... Glory would be his... Harry would see he was just as good – nay, *better* – than Pierre!

He had a clear run at the goal ... just a solitary girl standing in his way... Damn her... Why did she have to be there, ruining his chance? No ... keep running ... gather speed ... hurtle towards her ... hurtle ... and...

He started swirling his arms around like a crazed helicopter ... it would be a fearsome sight ... she would move out of sheer fear!

Swirling! Hurtling!

Noah sat on the edge of the pitch with his head in his hands as the ambulance crew stretchered the stricken French girl away.

"It's possibly broken," a paramedic was saying to Ms O'Malley. "We'll get her over to the hospital and see what's what."

Noah looked up as they loaded the girl into the ambulance, immediately feeling everyone's eyes flick from the stretcher to him, and burying his face back in his knees.

"Right, everyone!" Ms O'Malley shouted. "Obviously because of certain *irresponsible actions* –" she caught Noah's eye just as he snuck a surreptitious glance at her "– the match is over."

Groans, boos and jeers from the crowd.

"There's no point in booing. If you've got any complaints, speak to Noah Grimes in Year Eleven." Ms O'Malley hopped in the back of the ambulance, and they slammed the door shut behind her as the vehicle drove off the sports field.

Noah longed for a rock he could crawl under and die.

"Way to go, Noah," Jess Jackson smirked as she walked by, raising a perfectly manicured middle finger at him. "Pushing an innocent girl to the ground and stamping on her legs. You *hero*."

Maybe he could just die *next* to a rock. Maybe a full-on rock wasn't necessary. It could be a small piece of gravel. Like the one he was focusing on right now.

"Hello, little white piece of gravel," Noah muttered. "Is life better as a stone?"

Noah nodded at the stone's response. "Oh, how I yearn for your simple life, stone. Just doing your thing, year in, year out..."

"You OK, Noah?" said a voice that was ninety-nine per cent definitely Harry.

Noah nodded, still keeping his head buried between his knees.

"OK, well, we're going to get changed, then, I guess," Harry said.

"Mm," Noah muttered, not looking up.

"You coming?"

Noah vaguely shook his head.

"You all right?" Harry said.

"Uh-huh."

"Sure?"

"Uh-huh." Noah could feel Harry looking at him.

"Go ahead, I'll catch you up," Harry said to someone else.

"OK," answered a sexy, French-accented voice, as Noah watched a pair of football boots jog off towards the changing rooms.

Harry sat down on the ground, next to Noah. "I'm not sure what the hell you were doing out there," Harry said.

"Nor am I," Noah said, finally lifting his head.

"It's like you were suddenly possessed by some sort of demon. A PE demon. You were crazed."

Noah sniffed and rubbed his freezing-cold nose. "Yeah."

Harry put his arm around Noah's shoulders, pulling him close. "I'm sure she'll be fine. It's probably just a sprain – happens in football all the time. Come on. Let's go and get changed, you'll freeze out here."

"Maybe that's the best thing now."

"*Fine*," Harry said, "then we'll die together." He fell backwards, spreading himself out on the ground. "Come, cruel winter! Show me no mercy!"

Noah managed a half smile. Harry looked adorable – rosy cheeked from exercising in the cold and cute in his football kit. It fitted him perfectly, like the person who designed it used Harry for all the measurements. Nothing ever fitted Noah like that. He always felt like his clothes actively hated him. "Anyway," Noah sighed, "I've ... got to take all the equipment back to the PE office."

"You mean the football?"

"That, yes," Noah said.

Harry sat back up. "Cool, well, I suppose..."

"It's fine. You go ahead. Go and ... get changed with Pierre," Noah said, trying to keep it light.

Harry looked at him and bit his lip. "What's the matter? Why are you being weird?"

"Weird? No. I'm not being weird."

"Do you think I fancy Pierre?"

"WHAT?!" Noah made a good show of spluttering, to highlight how totally ridiculous he thought that statement was.

Harry wiped the spit from his cheek. "Uh-huh. Fine, then."

"Wait. *Do you* fancy Pierre?"

"No. I don't fancy Pierre."

"It's just odd that you would say that, just out of the blue like that. That's all."

"I don't fancy Pierre."

"You don't fancy Pierre?"

"I don't fancy Pierre." Harry rolled his eyes, gave Noah a quick peck, then jumped up and brushed the wet grass off his bottom. "See you in a bit, then," he said, heading off towards the changing rooms.

Noah watched him go.

Oh my God. *Harry fancied Pierre.*

Noah pushed the door of Ms O'Malley's disgusting PE office open and was immediately hit by the sour stench of musty socks, sweat and humiliation. He looked around: how was it possible that so much misery-inducing stuff could be in one room?

There in the corner was the javelin some bigger boys had once forcibly inserted down through a leg of his PE shorts, spearing him into the ground, so he couldn't move. Those Year Sevens who found him during the next band had pissed themselves laughing.

Oh, and there was the rugby ball that once accidentally ended up in his hands during a lesson, prompting some bigger boys to charge at him, tackling him to the ground and piling on top of him, writhing around like the big, hairy, muscular beasts they were, pressing against him, grinding into him... Yes, it was terrible... Just terrible...

He plonked the wretched football down in the middle of Ms O'Malley's desk.

Why does Ms O'Malley even need a desk? he wondered.

What paperwork could she have to do? Lesson plans? What would they possibly contain? He let his eyes sweep over the papers – not being nosy or anything, it was definitely more to check the football wasn't damaging anything important...

Oh!

What juiciness was this, poking out from under a folder? He gently pulled the paper out: a money transfer confirmation ... direct to "Ms B O'Malley's" bank account ... for *ten thousand* Great British pounds ... from someone in *Russia*!

Noah stared hard at the paper, knowing it was none of his business but massively intrigued. What could this possibly be about? Large sums of money! From Russia! Since when was that *ever* a good thing?

"Oh, you *bad* boy."

Noah froze and looked up. *Shit.* Busted.

CHAPTER
SEVEN

"I was putting the football away!" Noah bleated.

Eric shook his head. "Shit, man, you are *such* a bad liar."

"No. Not a liar. *Truth teller*," Noah said, eyes wide in panic.

Eric snorted and ambled into the office, glancing around at everything like a detective walking into a murder scene. "You're behind her desk when you don't need to be, and you've got a piece of paper in your hand. What is that?"

"Paper?" said Noah, looking at the paper he was holding. "Oh, this? This paper? Oh, no, I was just ... moving this paper so I could put the football there. It was in the way, is all." Noah put the paper back on the desk.

"There we go. It's back now. I've no idea what it was about anyway."

Eric smiled. "She's got secrets."

"Oh?" Noah said.

"I think you've just found one, haven't you?"

Noah shrugged. "No, because I didn't look at the paper."

"How do you know I was meaning the paper?"

"I ... didn't. It was a guess."

Eric scratched his mop of greasy black hair as if he had some sort of infestation. Noah wrinkled his nose. The boy had a permanently red and sweaty face – probably because he was constantly thinking about sex and depraved things, Noah considered.

"I've been meaning to talk to you, actually." Eric perched on the edge of Ms O'Malley's desk, his tight trousers riding up his legs to reveal his dirty white socks and pale ankles. Shit, he was brave. They totally shouldn't be in here, casually sitting about, chatting. If they were found – trouble!

Noah swallowed. "Should we not talk later, like, at home?"

"Nah."

"Why not?"

"This is about home."

"OK." Noah's heart rate increased. Eric's half-brother status was still a secret, known only to a small handful of people. Apart from wanting to avoid the gossip, their father had decided it was best not to incur the wrath of the guy who *thought* he was Eric's biological dad – Mad Dog Razor Jaws Smith. "Keep it on the down-low, 'cause if Mad Dog finds out the truth, we're all for the mincer," Dad had said, giving Noah visions of their lifeless bodies being fed into some huge meat-processing contraption. Considering how terrifying and dangerous Mad Dog Smith was, it was probably the wisest thing Noah's father had ever said. Eric came around from time to time, but infrequently enough that it didn't raise any suspicions from Mad Dog, who didn't keep careful tabs on Eric anyway.

"I've been hearing some stuff," Eric sniffed. "Little things between our dad and your mum. I reckon there's troubles."

"Relationship troubles?" said Noah, hopefully.

Eric shook his head. "Money."

"How ... how bad? What sort of thing?"

"A letter came," Eric said. *"Bailiffs."*

"What do they want?"

Eric gave a little chuckle. "Oh, you know, just asking how everyone was, telling us about their trip to Barbados over the summer." Eric's face dropped into a frown. *"Money*, dickhead. And if they don't get it, they'll take stuff instead."

Noah's mouth dropped open. "Like my computer?!"

"Sure." Eric shrugged.

"My complete Agatha Christie collection?"

Eric looked more doubtful.

Noah ran his hands through his hair. "How much do they want?"

"From what I reckon," Eric said, giving his balls a scratch, "in the region of fifteen grand."

Noah stopped breathing.

Dear God, how the hell had his parents managed to rack up that sort of debt?

No. This could not be allowed to happen.

He fixed Eric with a steely stare. "You're telling me this, so what's the plan? You must have a plan."

"Empty the shed."

"What?"

"That was three words, Noah. Which one didn't you understand?"

"You want me to empty our shed? What, to sell the contents?

Eric raised an eyebrow. "Valuables in there, is there?"

"I'm not sure... I mean, there's my old bike from when I was ten..."

"Not even," Eric said, shaking his head. "The only bike in there is a pink one with silver streamers and a Hello Kitty basket... *Oh.*"

"My loyal steed," Noah said. "It served me well."

"Look, I ain't got time for this. Just shift your shit out of the shed. I don't care where and I don't care what you do with it."

"That's it? That will solve our financial crisis?"

"It'll help," Eric said.

"But how?"

Eric slid off the desk and came round to where Noah was standing, so they were almost nose to nose. "You don't want to know —" Noah could smell Eric's Monster Munch breath — *vile* "— because the less you know, the more you can stay out of trouble."

He did have a point: whatever Eric was up to, Noah wanted no part of it. He stared into Eric's dark brown eyes, then down at the light fuzz that was blooming on his top lip. *Huh.* How come Eric had some facial hair coming, and not Noah?

"Fine," Noah said. "I'll do it at the weekend."

"No. *Tonight.*"

"Fine! Tonight! God! I love how you think I can just clear my schedule to accommodate your whims! Some of us are actually trying to complete coursework whilst entertaining French exchange students, you know?"

"Speaking of which, you should probably get over to the changing room," Eric said.

"Why?"

"Because Pierre Victoire will probably be just getting out of the showers by now. Don't want Harry's eye to wander, do we?"

"What?! It wouldn't!" Noah cried, outraged — *outraged!* — at the preposterous notion.

He casually stepped back towards the door. "Nevertheless, I probably should head over there anyway. Change out of these clothes and all."

"See you later, Noah. Can't wait to see my nice empty shed later tonight."

"You're not going to do something . . . *criminal* there, are you?"

"Just go."

CHAPTER EIGHT

Pierre stood in the middle of the changing room, a towel dangling from the fingers of one hand and the rest of him completely naked.

Noah hovered in the doorway, appalled. There wasn't a scrap of clothing on the Frenchman. Not a thread. Not so much as an atom of cotton was attached to his nubile and toned body, which was also glistening from having recently emerged from the showers.

And yet Pierre was totally OK with that.

Intolerable.

"Yes," Pierre was saying, gesticulating with his hand that wasn't holding the towel, "although my favourite ballet is *La Bayadère*, of course. Considered by many to be Petipa's greatest work."

Noah glanced across to where Harry was sitting on the wooden bench, already back in his uniform and rooting inside the rucksack on his lap.

Noah narrowed his eyes. *Oh yes, he saw this for what it was, all right!* Noah had used that strategic rucksack trick several times! And was it just a coincidence that Harry was using it now, with a naked and moist Pierre parading around in front of him, his boy bits on display for everyone to gawk at?

"Huh, I've not been to the ballet," Harry said. "My parents have. They went down to London to see something at the Royal Opera House..."

"Ah! A beautiful place!" Pierre said, languidly drying his testicles with the towel.

"Uh-huh..." Harry muttered.

Noah saw red. "Right, everyone!" he shouted, striding towards them. "I'm back and here. Hello, Harry. Hello, Pierre. Pierre, I see that you are naked. *Very* naked. That's fine and au naturel and all, but I think you should aim to put some pants on."

Pierre laughed. "Noah! It is good you have come, we were just talking about the ballet."

"Were you?" Noah nodded. "Were you, indeed? Well, that's all very nice." Noah allowed his eyes to drift down, past Pierre's abs and shaved pubes to his absolutely enormous... Noah swallowed hard. *Gosh, really, now?* That was ... my goodness.

"All very nice," Noah repeated absent-mindedly. "Um... Harry, can I help you find what you're looking for in there?" Noah panic-sat next to Harry on the wooden bench, pulling the bag over his lap, ostensibly to help the search.

"I know I left it in here," Harry said into the bag.

"Are you dry yet, Pierre?" Noah said, also staring into Harry's bag. "If so, please put clothes on. *Please.*"

Pierre dropped his towel on the floor, stretched, and walked over to where his clothes were hanging. "I am sorry," he said. "My parents are naturists. They brought me up to have no shame about my body. No embarrassment."

"Well," Noah said, "that's all very hip, I'm sure. And certainly there's no shame in a little flash of ankle, or a saucy bit of wrist, but here in the United Kingdom, we are taught that being naked is sinful and wrong. Or hilarious. So we never, ever do it. This is an important cultural difference to learn."

"Hahahaha!" Pierre laughed, grabbing his T-shirt and pulling it on.

Noah turned to Harry. "He's putting his T-shirt on *before* his boxers!" he whispered.

"Oh? Weird..." Harry said, distractedly

"It's like he's keeping it out for the maximum amount of time possible!" Noah hissed.

"Found it!" Harry said, pulling out his phone with a grin of triumph and quickly scrolling through his notifications. "I knew I didn't leave it in the box – I threw it in here!"

Noah glanced at Pierre again, who appeared to be preoccupied pulling his socks the right way out, before producing a pair of AussieBum boxers with a flourish.

"Finally!" Noah breathed.

Noah shifted uncomfortably on the bench and considered the situation. Just because handsome, toned, moist Pierre was staying with Harry, and just because he was comfortable with being totally naked all the time and had above-averagely-sized boy parts, didn't mean that anything would happen between Pierre and Harry, because Harry was loyal and reliable and a *good boy*.

There was nothing to worry about.

And yet, somehow, there was everything to worry about.

What if Harry, sick of waiting for Noah to finally have the sort of body where some form of *bow chicka wah wah* was acceptable, simply lowered his defences against the impossibly French and aggressively naked Pierre?

There was a risk.

And risk had to be managed.

"So, I've had an idea," Noah began. "And the idea is that my parents will be going on a date –" bile rose in his throat "– tonight, so you and Pierre *must* come round to mine for dinner!"

"Oh, right," Harry said, finishing off a message and sending it.

"So, yes, I'm doing something special. Very special. It's a tasting menu, exploring everything the UK has to offer in terms of culinary excellence. Very exciting!" Noah said, immediately starting to regret the ambition of the proposed event. A tasting menu?! How the merry hell was he going to put that together?

"Sounds fantastic," Pierre said. "I hear your food has improved a lot over here in recent years?"

Noah arched an eyebrow, sensing an insult hidden in Pierre's words. "Even the *Guide Michelin* considers us world leaders in cuisine, and tonight, I shall demonstrate to you the full spectrum of our accomplishments." *Shut up, shut up, why are you building this up like this?!*

Pierre pulled his boxers up, snapping the waistband against his abdomen. "I am gagging for it," Pierre said, with a wink.

"Sounds delicious," Harry chimed in.

"So, that's fine. In a minute or two I will put my own clothes on and then I shall see you both later. Seven o'clock for an amuse-bouche." Noah smiled, even though he had no idea what that was; he'd heard the term on *MasterChef* once.

Pierre pulled his jeans on. "See! I am dressed!"

"Congratulations," Noah said.

"OK, let's go. See you later, Noah," Harry said, standing up, slipping his phone in his pocket and plucking his bag off Noah's lap.

"Love you," Noah said, deftly sweeping a nearby soggy

towel that someone had abandoned on to his lap instead.

"Love you too," Harry replied, bending down and giving Noah a peck on the cheek. "Aww!" He smiled, seeing what was in Noah's open bag on the floor. "You brought the hoodie to school!"

"I told you," Noah said. "It'll be with me always."

"Awww!" said Pierre. "Watching you two makes me wish I also had a boyfriend!"

Noah rolled his eyes as Pierre and Harry walked out. *Great, Pierre was single too.* Single and "ready to mingle", no doubt!

The changing room now deserted, Noah flung the towel aside and picked up his phone out of the "valuables box" (that had just been left on one of the benches for anyone to steal, so good on Harry for avoiding it), and texted his mother:

MOTHER, I KNOW MONEY IS TIGHT RIGHT NOW, BUT I REQUIRE THESE URGENT INGREDIENTS FOR A HOSTED DINNER TONIGHT: SCALLOPS, PANCETTA, CAULIFLOWER, LAMB, MINT, PEAS, POTATOES, TRUFFLE, BERGAMOT, STUFF TO MAKE MERINGUE, DELICIOUS PETIT FOURS, AND SOME CHEESE.
   Sincerely,
   NOAH (YOUR SON)

OK, he knew it was a long shot his useless mother would get everything on the list, but even with most of these ingredients, he could whip up the dining event of the year ... if not the decade!

He could do this. He could bloody do this!

CHAPTER NINE

"So, this is my street," Noah explained to a morose Eva as he led the way back to his house. "It's part of a council redevelopment project from the early 1980s, encouraging young families to move into affordable homes in the area in an attempt to rejuvenate it. Sadly it all backfired in the early nineties when it was discovered the water company had illegally pumped thousands of litres of raw sewage into the River Fobb, and the town became synonymous with corruption and environmental catastrophe, but we are a proud people, us Fobbers, and we got through it ... well, I didn't, I wasn't born then, this was all in the olden days." Noah gestured at the houses. "I suppose I would say it's designed in a modernist architectural style, not ornate, but certainly practical. The white PVC double-glazing is a more recent addition."

Eva's eyes swept over the identikit homes on his street. "It is not nice, is it? It is like Le Corbusier took a shit here."

Noah gritted his teeth. Normally he would have agreed, but this was *his street* she was talking about. But he couldn't allow this German *imposteur* to ruin his dinner tonight, so he had to keep things light and happy.

Light ... and ... happy...

"Fuck!" Noah suddenly said. Outside his house, the lurid pink van was still there. Would Mick be around during the dinner tonight?

Noah took a deep breath. Light! Happy! He extended his arm towards the house and beamed. "Ta-da!"

Eva glanced at him. "Great," she said, frowning.

"So, come inside!" Noah chirped, opening the front door and leading Eva through the hall, into the lounge. "This man –" Noah waved at his dad, who was sitting in his joggers and a ketchup-stained T-shirt watching television, having failed to shave "– is my father. Dad, this is Eva."

"Eva!" His dad grinned, suddenly coming to life and bouncing over to shake her hand. "Nice to meet you, darlin'!"

Noah flinched at the "darlin'".

"Hallo." Eva shrugged.

"Good trip over, I hope? I'm sure Noah's got lots of –" he made quote marks with his fingers "– 'fun' planned!"

Noah resented the fun in quote marks. The Great British Quiz Off was certainly going to be fun – not that his philistine father would appreciate any of it.

Eva was looking at his dad. "Have we met? You look familiar."

"Never tried to buy timeshare in Spain, have you?" His dad laughed, hollowly, suddenly on edge.

"HA HA HA HA!" Noah screeched. "Moving on, on, on!" He whisked Eva around, away from his father. "This person," Noah said, turning to Mick, who was stretched elegantly out on the sofa, painting his nails, "is a man who likes to dress up as a woman for entertainment purposes. When he doesn't have two kilos of polyester hair on his head, his name is *Mick*."

Mick extended his hand. *"Enchanté*. And don't listen to him, it's always *natural*."

"I have a friend who does drag in Berlin," Eva said. "Actually, it's genderfuck performance art, but I'm sure they are similar."

"Sounds kinky," Noah's dad smirked.

Eva looked at him with unimpressed eyes. "Actually, it's my view that genderfuck empowers artists to explore and comment on binaried gender through performance. Yes, it can be playful, but it is *always* political."

Mick gave her look that was either admiration or

contempt – Noah couldn't quite place it. His dad, meanwhile, whose face had been totally blank, finally muttered, "Politics, huh? I don't bother voting myself. Crooks, every one of 'em!"

"Aaaaanyway," Noah said, "I'm sure you can discuss all this with Mick some other time." He looked at Mick and chewed his lip. "Do you have plans for this evening?"

Mick swiped his phone, smiled and looked up at Noah. "Actually, I think I have. Meeting a new friend – ScallyLad35."

"Odd name," Noah said.

"Yeah, it's not his name I'm bothered about," Mick said, giving Noah a wink and flashing his phone screen at him.

"Gah! Onwards!" Noah said, pulling Eva over to where his mother had emerged, in the doorway that led through to the kitchen-diner. Inexplicably wearing an apron, and with a cigarette hanging from her mouth, she looked like a character who might run a café in a soap opera – the sort with Formica tables, and ketchup in plastic bottles made to look like giant tomatoes. "My mother," he said. "Mother – this is Eva. She's German and a girl."

"Nice to—"

"So!" Noah interrupted, before his mother could say anything embarrassing, "that's everyone for now, please proceed to your bedroom, which is up the stairs and first on the left. Sorry about the box of Kleenex Mansize, but I thought you were going to be a boy."

"Cool," Eva said.

"Also, please note," he said, putting on his most apologetic face, "smoking is not permitted," he winced as his mother took a drag of her cigarette, "and you can only play your guitar between the hours of eight a.m. and eight p.m."

Eva stared at Noah.

"OK?" Noah said.

"Cool," Eva said, hauling her bag and guitar back through the door and up the stairs.

"She seems nice," his mother said.

Noah shook his head. "I'm pretty sure some of those symbols on her guitar case are satanic," he whispered. "Anyway, you received my message?" Noah asked, turning towards the kitchen.

His mum sighed. "Yes, Noah, I did."

"Good, where is everything?" He walked through into the kitchen-diner. "I hope you've refrigerated the scallops because—" He looked at the empty space in front of him, turned on his heel and came back through to the lounge. "Where's the table?"

"Sold it," muttered his dad from the armchair.

"You *sold it*?" Noah repeated. "Sold it? You've sold the dining table?!"

"We never use it," his dad said. "It's about decluttering!"

"Decluttering!" Noah shouted. "Have you gone entirely mad? Where are we supposed to eat?"

His dad looked at him like Noah was the mad one. "Trays on our laps, like normal?"

"I am having a *dinner party* this evening," Noah hissed. "What am I supposed to tell the guests?"

"Well, how were we meant to know? Go out and grab some kebabs. Now shush," his dad said. "I'm tryin' to watch the end of this *Antiques Roadshow* I recorded. The last thing they show is always worth a lot."

"We need the money, Noah," his mum said. "We've all got to tighten our belts a bit. Money doesn't grow on trees."

No, no, no, no! Not this, not now! Well, of *course* they didn't have any money: however much they wanted to play this "happy perfect family" charade, his father was a layabout thief who nobody in their right mind would employ, and his mother, his bloody useless mother, did a Beyoncé tribute act that had attracted not a single, solitary booking in the last three months. Mainly because, all things considered, it was SHITE. No money? How about taking some responsibility? How about, just once, his parents tried acting like adults and getting real jobs?

He pointed at his mum. "You do realize, don't you, that this country is in the midst of *historic lows* of unemployment, right? There is a *shortage of labour* in the market. You could literally walk into any shop – anywhere! – and—"

75

"Noah? I'm going for some air," Eva said, suddenly appearing in almost the entire length of the doorway.

"*Mais oui!*" Noah replied, suddenly sweetness and light, doing a small curtsy. "Please enjoy the surrounding English countryside and all that Little Fobbing has to offer. Sometimes I like to visit the park and look at the ducks. Oh, the one off Gordon Road is probably best; they found high levels of mercury in the soil of the one by the primary school."

"Cool," said Eva.

"Dinner will be served at seven. Please be punctual."

Eva shrugged and drifted out the front door.

Noah turned back to his mum, who was now sitting calmly on the sofa, a look of concern all over her face. "What's the matter, Noah? You seem on edge."

"Oh, I can't think why, Mother!"

"Are you being cyberbullied?"

Noah screwed his face up. "What?! No, I'm not being cyberbullied! God!"

"Do you want to speak with your dad about puberty?"

"I would rather orchestrate my own demise with a circular saw," Noah said. *Or possibly yours, Mother!*

"We're planning a family outing to Beaver's Garden Centre on Saturday," his mum said. "Eva's welcome, of course. And Harry. You could use some of your Christmas money to buy some seeds. You like seeds."

Noah blinked at his mother.

"Right, well," his mother sighed. "While you're here, we need you to move your stuff out of the shed."

Noah threw his hands in the air. "Eric's already asked me to do that!"

"Why does Eric want the shed empty?" his dad said.

"Why do you?" Noah countered.

His mother could barely contain her excitement. "Your father and I ... we're buying a tandem! Bike rides, Noah!"

Noah nodded, solemnly. "Yeah? How much is that costing?"

"It's from the catalogue, so it's paid over five years. Free, basically." His mum smiled.

Noah stared at her. The electricity company had recently transferred them to a prepay metre because of the unpaid bills, the bailiffs were sending threatening letters, *they'd just sold the sodding dining table*, but oh yes, there was still the cash to buy some stupid bike. Noah clutched his hands to his chest in mock glee. "Oh! It's so *wonderful* being wealthy! Mmmm! Rah, rah, rah! One may just bathe in some liquid gold this evening and then take the pony skiing, is that OK, Mother?"

"Noah, this is about your father and me reconnecting with our feelings for one another. It's about us, our relationship. Because what does our relationship make?"

"Me sick?" Noah suggested.

"A strong and stable family unit," his mum said, a

dreamy look in her eyes. "And that's what we are now, Noah. A strong and stable *family*, who love and support one another. So please, be supportive."

"Useless," Noah muttered to himself as he bashed about in the kitchen, looking at options for a five-course tasting menu, "selfish, mean, horrible old trout..." He reached up on tiptoe and flung open one of the top cupboards and was promptly hit by a bag of lentils, purchased when his mum went vegan for twelve hours last summer.

"Don't wait up for us," his mum shouted from the front door.

Noah kicked the lentils into the corner of the kitchen. He hoped they choked on their date-night chicken korma. He opened another cupboard and found some butterscotch Angel Delight. OK. This was dessert. And maybe, if he could find a tub, he might be able to put a glacé cherry on top, for extra poshness. He grabbed a carton of milk from the fridge that miraculously was in-date, poured it into a bowl with the powder and started whisking.

"Nice wrist action!" Mick grinned, appearing in the kitchen, dressed in jeans and a jacket for his night out.

Noah rolled his eyes and focused on the job in hand.

"Got a lot of strength in that right arm, haven't you?"

Noah dropped the whisk. "Any more? Let's get all the masturbation jokes out of the way, shall we?"

Mick stared at him. "Wow. If that's how you whack off, I think we need to have a chat."

"Oh, shut up. Why are you still here?"

"Grabbing a beer to take with me," Mick said, opening the fridge.

Noah grimaced and got back to his whisking.

"Slow and steady," Mick said, cracking the can open on his way out. "You don't need to go at it full throttle. Take your time. Enjoy it."

Noah tried to push his rage aside until he heard Mick go out the front door and he could breathe. Good. Now his full attention could be on this dining extravaganza. Deciding the mixture was probably thick enough, he hunted around for four appropriate receptacles that he could serve the "delight" in. He would have to make do with one teacup, two wine glasses and a mug emblazoned with "I heart Scunthorpe". He found some cherries and ran them under the hot tap to remove the light bloom of fungus on them, popping one atop each portion. Delightfully, he had also found a tub of hundreds and thousands that he would sprinkle over the dish just before serving. *Voila!* Dessert was prepared.

The main, courtesy of "some mate" of his father's, was to be the big fish currently residing on the bottom shelf of the fridge. Noah wasn't sure what type of sea beast it was, but it was probably a cod or something. This "mate" had apparently pulled it out of some reservoir on a fishing trip and given it to his dad, the latter assuring Noah that it was "only a few days old" and "probably still OK". *Fine.* What was not fine, though, was the beast's beady, glassy eye staring at Noah as he tried to work out how to fillet and portion it up, so Noah decided a better idea would be to cook the fish whole, in silver foil, with some herbs ... well, some dried oregano that he'd found in the cupboard, best before 1998, but it looked fine. He was *fairly confident* he had seen fish cooked like this on *MasterChef.* And with some potatoes and peas, it would be a "take" on the classic British fish and chips – which was *very, very* clever.

He turned the oven dial to the required temperature. *CLUNK.*

Noah froze. Everything had gone off. The lights. The oven. The dinner party playlist that Noah had rigged up to work through his dad's old hi-fi...

"No no no no no," he bleated. The credit on the prepay electric meter must have run out! *Arses!*

Noah felt his way through to the lounge, plunging his hands down the back of the sofa cushions, hoping to find a stray pound coin or two. A slice of toast, five crisp packets and a bra later, and still no joy. He flung the last cushion back on the sofa and breathed hard into the black void. No way was he going to let this jeopardize his chance to simultaneously impress Harry, make Pierre realize he could never compete with Noah, *and* ensure Harry and

Pierre didn't get off with each other. At least, not whilst they were at the dinner party, anyway.

No. The dinner party would very much continue.

The show must go on.

He would single-handedly put the *great* into *Great Britain*.

"Good evening, guests!" Noah said, standing before Harry and Pierre at the front door, wearing his special grey hoodie from Harry. This was a clever move, hopefully giving Pierre a subtle visual signal that Noah and Harry were very much together. Or at least, it might have done if Pierre could actually see it. "Please come through, as dinner is nearly served. I hope you enjoy the low-level lighting atmosphere I have *deliberately created* to enhance the mood."

Noah showed his guests through to the lounge, where he'd arranged an assortment of tea lights and an orange spiked with birthday candles, to provide a hint of something other than pitch-black *darkness*.

"It is certainly moody in here," Pierre commented, pretending to feel about in the dark with his hands. "Oh, what is this? Is this a cushion?"

"Hey!" Harry giggled.

"Oh!" Pierre said. "I am sorry. I thought it seemed very firm and pert."

"OK, right," Noah said, keen to move things on.

But Pierre seemed equally keen for more pretend "I can't see in this dark" comedy. "Oh, Noah, what is this sausage I seem to be holding?"

"OK, so just to confirm, he's not holding my penis," Noah said.

Pierre laughed. "I love this lighting. Anything could happen!"

"Well, what will be happening is some dinner and light conversation. That's what the evening has in store – nothing more, nothing less. Please help yourself to an amuse-bouche," Noah said, indicating the plate he had balanced on the side of the armchair. "These are a delicate crispbread with a pearl of soft cheese."

Harry picked one up. "Is this a sour-cream-and-chive Pringle?" he said, sniffing at it.

"Er, I guess you could say it's very similar," Noah said.

"With a dollop of Primula cheese spread on top?"

"Essentially, yes, that's what we're dealing with here."

Harry bit into it. "Awesome."

"I hope your *bouches* are *amused*." Noah smiled. "Please forgive me, I must away to my kitchen duties, but will return at unexpected intervals to make sure nothing is happening... I mean, that everything is all right. Harry, you sit down on the sofa, and Pierre, you could have the armchair?"

"Or both of us on the sofa?" Pierre suggested.

"No, because, *no*, because the other guests ... when

they come… That's the seating plan. OK? So. I'll be back in a minute. Or maybe thirty seconds. Or who knows!"

Noah disappeared into the kitchen, only to be confronted with drizzle on the window. "Arses," he muttered, dashing outside to where he'd set up the barbecue and was currently cooking the big fish. He was confident this arrangement would be fine – living in this sorry excuse for a home, he'd learned that most foods were improved, taste-wise at least, by barbecuing. Refusing to be outmanoeuvred by the weather, Noah dragged the patio umbrella over to the barbecue and positioned it overhead. *Perfect.*

The doorbell rang.

Noah darted back through the kitchen and lounge, glancing to make sure Harry and Pierre weren't too close to each other (approximately two metres apart – not ideal, but OK), and opened the door to Eva.

"I forgot my guitar," Eva explained, pushing past Noah. Three bedraggled, feral creatures were standing in the drive, eyeing Bambi's van. Noah recognized them immediately. They were drug addicts. Or rather, Noah was pretty sure he'd seen at least one of them smoking a cigarette in the park, so they were *probably* drug addicts.

"Oh, Eva?" Noah said, closing the door and calling up to her. "You can't bring your friends to dinner, I'm afraid. There won't be enough food."

He paused in the darkness, not hearing any response.

"Eva? Where are you?"

"Here."

"Oh, sorry, I couldn't see you. Look, those people outside, Eva. I know you're new here and don't have a read on the social situation, but you don't want to hang around with them. Trust me, those guys are trouble. OK?" He placed reassuring hands on her shoulders.

"Those are my breasts."

"I'm so terribly sorry!" Noah sprang back. "In this low light, *which is deliberate*, I couldn't see. It was a mistake, and just to reassure you, I have little to no interest in your breasts."

"Cool."

"Sit down next to Harry, who is on the sofa, which is five steps to your left and one back. I shall return presently with the first course!"

Noah felt his way back through to the kitchen, now lit by an odd orange glow. At the doorway, he froze in horror at the flames licking at the kitchen window.

"SHIIIIT!" he squealed, darting outside, to where the patio umbrella was inexplicably ablaze because it's not like the coals were actually on fire, they were just white hot, so why—

Oh, it didn't matter! What to do?! Naturally his parents wouldn't have spent money on a fire blanket or a responsible range of extinguishers (water, foam and carbon dioxide) so he was going to have to deal with this the retro way. Noah ran back into the kitchen, filled the bowl in the sink with water, darted back with it slopping about all over him and tripped over a bag of lentils which some halfwit had left lying about on the floor. Noah crashed on to the unforgiving vinyl as the water drenched him from top to toe, and outside the patio umbrella creaked and snapped, collapsing to the ground in a shower of sparks.

"FIRE! FIRE! CALL THE ENGINES!"

CHAPTER TEN

Noah sat cross-legged and silent on the floor of the lounge, the faint whiff of burning patio furniture hanging in the air as he half-heartedly tried to navigate eating some takeaway with a pair of chopsticks. He didn't want food now anyway. He really wasn't hungry.

"Dickhead," Eric muttered, spooning some noodles into his mouth with a fork.

The stricken patio umbrella had also knocked the barbecue over on its way down, meaning dinner had been entirely ruined. Putting out the flames had required all of the guests (except Eva, who had taken advantage of the commotion to slip out, presumably to join her junkie cohorts) to form a relay-style line, passing saucepans and bowls of water along in an attempt to avert further disaster.

Noah ignored Eric and angled his chopsticks at the sweet-and-sour chicken before him. Now he looked like a fool in front of Pierre. Would he and Harry laugh about this later tonight, when they were back at Harry's house together? He could picture it now:

PIERRE: Oh, Harry, your boyfriend is such an
    idiot, setting fire to everything.
HARRY: Yes.
PIERRE: And he's really poor and doesn't have
    any electricity.
HARRY: I know!
PIERRE: Ha ha ha ha! It's so funny.
HARRY: Ha ha ha ha!
PIERRE: Now we shall kiss and make love, the
    French way!
HARRY: Ooh la la!

Noah dropped the piece of chicken for the fifth time, sighed, and put his plate on the floor beside him. Screw this. Maybe he should just make some excuse and cut the whole thing short...

"I need to go to bed; my liver has just prolapsed," Noah said.

"This is delicious, cheers, Eric," Harry said, at exactly the same time. "Huh? What was that, Noah?"

"Nothing," Noah muttered.

Harry wiped his mouth with his napkin. "Very, very tasty."

Noah grimaced. Oh yes, Eric was the hero now, wasn't he? Noah had pushed the boat out big-time to welcome their international guests; he hadn't resorted to a takeaway, but had tried to cook a really big, mysterious fish. But all that meant nothing after one little house fire.

"Yes, Eric!" Pierre said, slurping up some noodles. "This is fantastic. Thank you!"

Noah sipped a little of the green tea he had requested as his drink. It was horrible, but it was sophisticated and cultured. *See, Pierre Victoire?* Even in Little Fobbing.

"No worries, no worries," Eric said, clearly thinking he was quite the man. Although, Noah had to concede, it *was* lucky Eric had turned up. Eric had walked into a scene of utter mayhem, but had calmly exited and then returned ten minutes later, having been to the corner shop and purchased *more electricity*. Lights restored, he then produced a further thirty quid from his wallet (and he had even more cash than that in there too!) and ordered them this takeaway.

"Would anyone like dessert?" Noah asked.

"Actually, Noah, we ought to make a move," Harry said. "It's getting a bit late and Mum'll start to panic."

Noah nodded at him. Probably for the best. If he did go and bring the Angel Delight out, something would only go wrong. He'd drop it, or accidentally hurl it in someone's face, or—

"Noah?"

"Huh?"

Harry was smiling at him. "You OK?"

"Yes. I'm just thinking about the dinner thing."

Harry nodded. "The food doesn't matter — it's the company that counts. Pierre? Grab your coat, I'll meet you outside, yeah?"

"Sure!" Pierre said.

Harry pulled Noah through into the kitchen. "You don't have to worry about Pierre."

"I'm not worried about Pierre," Noah lied. The very fact Harry had said he didn't need to worry clearly meant he absolutely *did* need to worry. It meant it had crossed Harry's mind. *Oh God.*

Harry stared at him, like he was totally reading Noah's mind. Just in case, Noah made sure he was only thinking of dolphins, mushrooms and the hits of ABBA. That would confuse him! "Then, cool. That's good," Harry said, stepping towards him, putting his arms around Noah's waist and his hands on Noah's bottom.

"I mean, Pierre does seem to have a very good body," Noah said. "Lots of muscles."

"Hmm," Harry murmured, into Noah's neck.

"Quite charismatic and charming..."

"Sure."

"You know, all said and done, he's got a lot going for him."

Harry delicately kissed the side of Noah's neck, causing a little shiver to run up his spine. "I'd better go."

"OK."

"Don't do anything I wouldn't do."

"Oh, what, with Eva? Pretty sure I won't," Noah said. "But, you know, same goes for you, Harry Lawson. You and Pierre."

"Ooh, yeah!" Harry chuckled. "Gimme! Gimme! Gimme!"

Noah's eyes widened. "Haz."

"See you tomorrow," Harry said, rolling his eyes, just a hint of irritation in his voice, as he headed out.

See? This was exactly what Noah meant. Now Harry was annoyed with him. Annoyed because Noah had hit a nerve, even if Harry denied it.

And it was odd. Harry used to read Noah's mind all the time when they were "just friends", and Noah used to love that. Harry would know what Noah wanted from the café, without even having to ask (toasted teacake and English breakfast tea); Harry knew what Noah would want to do on a Saturday night (play 3D Cluedo, eat cheesy Wotsits, have a debate about whether Joan Hickson or Geraldine McEwan was the best Marple); so why didn't Noah want Harry to know his thoughts now? How was being boyfriends, something that surely meant you were *closer*, making him feel like they were further apart?

Sometimes, having something really nice in your life was worse than not having it, because it made you worried you were going to lose it. And losing something is worse when you know just how wonderful that thing is.

"How's the shed looking?" Eric said, appearing in the doorway with his laptop under his arm.

"Ah, so here's the thing," Noah said. "Mother and Father have now expressed an interest in the shed themselves – to store some vile tandem bicycle."

"Fuck's sake," Eric muttered.

"So, my hands are tied."

"Those two are doing my head in. Last weekend, when I stayed over, did you hear them?"

Noah looked blank.

"Uh, uh, uh, UH! UH! OH! OH! YEAH!" Eric offered, by way of explanation.

"Weightlifting?"

"Shut up, bellend. Empty the shed. Do it tonight. Now." Eric's face turned from sly to evil. "I'll sort Dad and Lisa out."

CHAPTER
ELEVEN

Noah stared into his gran's empty room, chest tightening. She was *always* in here. *Always*. Where the hell was she?

He turned as he heard Matron clumping down the corridor, stoically maintaining her course despite Tabatha, the resident silver tabby cat, zigzagging in front of her. She was a relentlessly no-nonsense sort of woman, who seemed permanently hot and was fiercely practical. Noah had once heard her say she "never wore make-up" because it was just a "silly trifle" before going outside to chop a tree down in the garden.

"Where's Gran?" he asked.

"Ah," Matron said. "You haven't heard."

Noah's heart skipped a beat. "Heard about what?" He looked at her, eyes pleading. "Is she OK?"

"Noah, she's fine. She's..." Matron sighed, wearily wiping the sweat from her forehead and undoing the top button of her blue regulation tunic. "She's formed a ... musical group."

Noah raised his eyebrows as the opening chords of "Wind of Change" by the Scorpions drifted through the building.

Matron rolled her eyes. "See? That's them rehearsing. She won't thank you for interrupting, but she's in the Mayflower Lounge. Look, I'd love to stay and chat, but we're short-staffed. Plus the boiler's on the blink." She looked down at Tabatha, who was winding herself round her ankles, said *"I will feed you in a minute!"* then turned and continued on her way. "Oh, and Noah?" she shouted back as she was about to go through the fire door. "We love to support our residents in their artistic endeavours, but maybe you could persuade her to change the name?"

Musical group? Noah thought, walking off in the direction of the lounge as he heard his gran starting to sing an approximation of the lyrics down the mic.

He stopped in the doorway to the lounge. Most of the chairs had been shifted to the edges of the room, much to the obvious annoyance of one resident who was stoically knitting in the corner with a face like she was sucking a lemon. Gran was centre stage, mic in hand, wearing leather trousers, a pink tutu, a ridiculous silver metal tiara that she'd had for years, and a ripped T-shirt that bore the slogan "Never too old to rock". Surrounding her, Noah recognized her mate Dickie, who was sitting on a chair with a small Casio keyboard on a wheely table; Vera, who had worked at Bletchley Park in the War, but who was now standing with an electric guitar in her hand, in front of a music stand; and a woman Noah had never met before, who was sitting precariously on a stool, holding two wooden spoons, surrounded by a table of pots and pans and a portable commode.

"No, no, no!" Gran stopped singing and dropped the mic. "Vera? That's not the tune!" She stomped over and ripped the sheet music off Vera's stand. "This here is the sheet music to 'It's a Long Way to Tipperary'!"

"Oh," Vera muttered, "that must be from when those bloody awful kids came to sing at us..."

"And who's this?" his gran said, looking at him. "Are you from the record label?"

"It's me, Gran. Noah."

"Everyone," Gran shouted, "this is Noah. He's my manager."

"I'm her grandson," Noah corrected her.

Gran rolled her eyes. "I'm just kidding, Peanut. Lighten up. This is my band; what do you think?"

"Great," Noah said.

"Dickie on keyboard, Vera on guitar, and that's Babs on drums. Well, they will be drums when the kit arrives."

"Aye, lad!" said Dickie. "Rock 'n' roll!" He accidentally

hit the "demo" button on the keyboard, and a clunky version of "Happy Birthday" started playing.

"On keyboards" indeed, Noah thought. The only thing Dickie was on was his heart meds.

"Let's take five, everyone," Gran said, grabbing her stick and hobbling over to Noah. "I need to shoot the shit with ma gnomie."

"Gran, really now..."

"'Sup, Elena!" Gran said, seeing one of the younger staff members hurry in. "We'll take a couple of beers in the conservatory!"

"Actually, can I just have an Earl Grey?" Noah asked.

Elena looked utterly exasperated. "You know where they are," she snapped. "I need to take Dickie's blood pressure and give Vera her insulin – this isn't a hotel!"

It certainly isn't, Noah thought, as he watched Elena scoop up some teacups, dish out some pills and wrap a blood-pressure armband around Dickie.

Gran tutted and led Noah through an archway into the adjoining conservatory, where they both sat down on the wicker furniture. "So, *wassup*?" Gran asked.

"Gran, why are you speaking like that?"

Gran leaned towards him. "Noah, if this band stands a chance, and maybe it does, maybe it doesn't, I have to live the part, make the dream manifest. You get me?"

Noah frowned. "I see."

She picked a bag of Skittles out of her bag. "Want a little pick-me-up?" She tipped a good handful into his palm. "Now, tell me, what's on your mind? There's clearly something, else you wouldn't have come to see me."

"That's not true, Gran!" Noah said. "I come to see you all the time, not just when I have troubles!"

"So, there's no troubles?"

Noah chewed his lip.

"I knew it!" Gran said. "Speak!"

"It's about Harry—"

"*Lovely* Harry?" Gran smiled. Gran was Harry's second biggest fan, after Noah. They'd totally bonded whilst she was in hospital last year, especially when Harry smuggled a miniature of Scotch in, for her tea. "Harry who loves you?"

"And I love him!" Noah said.

"All's well, then!" Gran chirped. "I hope you've both kept it in your pants?"

Noah flinched. "Yes. Affirmative. But I think that Haz might quite like to... There could come a point, Gran, where, um..."

"Mutual masturbation?"

"Er, well..."

"Oral?"

"Gran, I..." He was bright red. "I'm worried I won't know what to do anyway, whatever we do. Or that it'll go badly, I'll mess it up, or he'll ..." He pulled the zip of his new hoodie up to his neck. "... see how skinny and awkward I really am, under my clothes, and go off me."

Gran leaned across and placed a hand gently on his knee. "You're a very sweet and handsome boy, Noah."

He pulled his hands into his sleeves and looked down at his shoes. "Sure."

"You should remember, there's no rush, no pressure. When the time is right – go for it, certainly, if you want to. After completing a full risk assessment and embracing all possible protection, of course. Do you want to?"

Noah looked up at her. "Yes?"

"Yes?"

"Doesn't... I mean, everyone wants to?"

Gran shook her head. "No, Noah. Some people don't. And you know what, Peanut? It's all fine. And the thing with you and Harry, you can work it out together. When, and if, you're ready and you want to. No rush."

"Yes, but what if Harry gets sick of waiting for me to be ready? There's this boy called Pierre and—"

"I'll tell you a story," Gran said. "Back in my youth, this new boy moved to town. I forget his name, but he caused quite a stir, as new boys often do. Anyway, it turned out he was really into –" Gran leaned forward and lowered her voice "– *mischief and tomfoolery*."

"Mischief and tomfoolery?"

"*Mischief and tomfoolery*." Gran nodded, imbuing every

word with *meaning*. She pursed her lips at Noah. "Are you reading me?"

Noah flicked his eyes to the floor. He guessed the sort of mischief she was referring to wasn't letting off stink bombs, or hilarious pranks with itching powder.

"Insatiable, he was!" Gran said, staring out of the window. "He'd have *mischief and tomfoolery* with anything that had a pulse – turned out that's why he'd had to move house. There'd been some unpleasantness with a young filly called Mary."

"Gran, calling a young woman a 'filly' is offensive."

Gran looked at him quizzically. "I agree," she said. "But Mary was a horse."

"Oh."

"It was just a shameful rumour, but the mud stuck and he had to get out of town."

"God," Noah said.

"Anyway, he was mad keen on me, let me tell you!" Gran smiled. "Always asking me out, he was. Leaving me roses, chocolates, stockings and the like! Oh, he tried it on, let me tell you, but I didn't give in. And the longer I left it, the more his desire grew. But it become more than desire... It became love. He got to know me for who I was, not just the sexy young woman I at first appeared."

Noah shifted uncomfortably. This wasn't the kind of advice he was hoping for. "Right."

"Want to see a photo?" Gran said, pulling a

yellowed scrap of paper from her handbag and handing it to Noah.

"This is a picture of Granddad."

"That's right!" Gran said, remembering. "He's your granddad, that's right."

Noah gave her the photo back. "So, Granddad was a horse shagger? Brilliant."

"No, I told you, it was a rumour," Gran scolded. "And that incident with the sheep a few years later was just a misunderstanding."

Noah's eyes widened.

"Anyway, my point," Gran said. "What is my point?"

"I don't know," Noah sighed. "I feel a bit sick now, to be honest."

"My point is, no rush, take your time. There are more important aspects to a relationship than sex. And sex doesn't prove love, Noah. That's the thing! Lust is transitory. Love *lasts*."

Noah nodded. That was an idea he could definitely get on board with. Relationships were about lots of things, all far more important than sex. Shared interests, support in times of crisis. But that sounded a lot like *friendship*, not boyfriendship. What was being boyfriends really about? Because at the moment, it just felt like endless paranoia that everything brilliant might end.

Noah shoved the rest of the Skittles in his mouth. In times of doubt, *sugar*.

"How's everyone at home?" Gran asked.

"Ng…" Noah said, chewing the Skittles. "Nah ng noo, tah oloo gah."

Gran nodded. "Oh, yes?"

"Gah. Ng da muh dang –" he swallowed "– is a useless, financially inept hag."

"So you're all broke?"

Noah took a deep breath. "It's very hard to maintain any sort of standards with the threat of bailiffs at the door. Mother will probably suggest I become a lady of the night in order to pay the bills. I wouldn't put it past her."

"Well, don't worry, because there's always this," Gran said, touching her tiara.

Noah rolled his eyes. It was a running joke with Gran – every time he complained about money, she'd bring out the tiara and say, "This may look like a Kinder egg piece of shit, but the real story is" – and here her voice would drop into a conspiratorial whisper – "my grandfather stole this from a fancy jeweller a long, long time ago. It was made for some disgraced Danish princess, he said, who wanted to flee the country with whatever jewellery she could smuggle out. That princess knew there was no way of getting her valuable diamonds out of the palace, so she arranged for a jeweller to set them in two worthless metal tiaras that no one would suspect contained the valuable stones. But before the jeweller could deliver the tiaras to the princess, my grandfather, helped by his fairy godmother and some clever mice, stole them from his workshop. So don't you worry, Peanut; if things get really bad, we can risk selling it and live like royalty." It was obviously all bollocks, but Noah would play along, wearing the tiara around the house and enjoying the pretence of being rich and fabulous. Then Harry would come round, and they'd play a make-believe heist game, with Noah in role as a rich society heiress called Tilly DeVere and Harry as a naughty ragamuffin who would try to steal her diamonds in various cunning ways. If Tilly DeVere caught the ragamuffin, she would get to spank his bottom. If the ragamuffin was successful, he would get to marry Tilly DeVere, who would bizarrely fall in love with the wayward working-class thief and realize that money wasn't everything. It was all innocent fun, a bit of boyish horseplay.

It was good to see Gran back to herself again, trying to make him feel better with her toy tiara. "That's true, Gran. Thank you."

"Remember when you and that charming boy played your game with these?" Gran said.

"Hmm." Noah nodded.

"You used to dress up in my tweed two-piece, high heels and a pearl necklace!"

"Yeah," he said, dropping his eyes.

"How old were you?"

Noah shrugged. "I dunno, it was really, really long ago. Fourteen, maybe?"

"So sweet!" Gran said.

Noah stood. "And on that note, I must away. Thanks for the pep talk. And good luck with the band, Gran. Adieu."

Gran looked up at him, sharply, pain in her eyes. "Don't go," she said.

"Gran, I gotta—"

"*Please!* Please stay for a bit."

Noah looked at her, small and frail in her chair, and tried to smile. "I'll be back soon, Gran. I promise."

"I hate it here. Nothing good happens here. Let me come back with you. Let me come back home."

Noah sat down again and reached for her hand. "Gran, right now, that can't happen. I'm sorry."

Gran stared at him, her eyes draining of recognition.

"Gran?"

"Don't worry about it, Brian."

Noah shook his head. "*Noah*, Gran. I'm Noah. Brian is my dad."

"I don't know anyone called Noah."

His mouth went dry. "Yes, Gran, you do. It's me. Noah. Your grandson. *Peanut*, remember?"

"No. No, I don't know." Gran sniffed and pulled her hand away from him and started fiddling with the tiara. "Get out, then. Go!"

Noah stared at her, mouth open.

"And don't come back! GO!"

Noah jumped as she shouted. "OK, OK, Gran. I'll go now. Nice to see you. Nice to... I'll come back soon, I'll..."

He looked at her, but she was far away, staring out into the gardens. He wanted to bend down and give her a kiss, but he was scared it might upset her, make her shout again. He blew a little kiss instead, but she didn't see.

Noah left the conservatory and plodded back out through the lounge, where Matron was walking through with a gas engineer. "Um, Matron?" he said.

"This isn't the best time, Noah. I've got to sort this boiler out."

"It's just Gran seems upset today."

"She has good days and bad days, Noah. And at the moment, more bad than good, but just be there for her. That will mean a lot."

"But—"

Matron sighed. "Look, if you're worried, maybe you should talk to your parents – look at some options."

"What would they be?" Noah said.

Matron gave him a kindly smile. "Nothing bad. There's a new home recently opened in West Fobbing, for example. Kingfisher Meadows. They do specialist dementia care there. I'm not saying your gran should definitely go there, but it's something your parents could look at."

"OK, but—"

"I'm sorry, Noah – we can talk another time, but if we don't get this boiler back up we'll all freeze tonight."

Noah released an unsteady breath as he watched Matron go. So this was how it was. He shook his head and hurried out, along the corridor towards the entrance foyer.

"Oi! Watch where you're going, numbnuts!"

Noah looked up at the person he'd just collided with and narrowed his eyes. "*Eric.*"

"All right?"

"And what, prithee, are you doing here? And what's with the bouquet of flowers?"

Eric grinned. "For Millie and the dickheads?"

"I beg your pardon?"

"Millie and the— Oh, you don't know about the band?"

Noah cleared his throat. "Oh, I totally knew that. I know all about the Dickheads. I mean, she is my gran."

"She's my gran too."

"Yes."

Eric nodded. "Well then." And he walked off.

Noah watched him go. If there was ever someone up to no damn good, Eric Smith was it.

CHAPTER TWELVE

Noah weaved along the pavement, head down, deep in thought. The one person he owed most to in this world was Gran. If she needed better care, if her life could be made happier, then he had to do that for her.

He pulled out his phone and searched for the Kingfisher Meadows website. The Willows wasn't a terrible place, and the staff did their best, but now he found himself looking at the spa, the en-suite rooms, the expert nursing – Kingfisher Meadows was like a hotel! This was what it *could* be like for Gran. And didn't she deserve the very best? Didn't he owe it to her to at least try to get her in there?

But it was also expensive. The Willows was paid for by the council, but Kingfisher Meadows was a private place, charging bigger bucks. From what he could gather, the council might pay for some of it, but they'd have to pay the rest themselves. No point in having that discussion with his mum and dad – they were totally skint – so he was on his own again with this one.

Kids his age started their own companies. Made millions. He didn't need millions, he just needed a bit. Surely he could do that? Surely he was capable of taking control? Positive action. For Gran.

"Awesome, dude, stay cool now, yeah?"

Noah stopped and looked up at the front door of the house opposite, where Josh Lewis was handing over a tub of protein shake in exchange for a wad of notes. Josh was all smiles and cool, in his jeans and American college jacket – even though they were not in America. "Hit me up when you get low," Josh was saying to the young man in the doorway. "I'll sort you out with another tub, no probs." He tapped his nose. "Special price too, dude. Just for you, so keep it mum!"

Noah couldn't take his eyes off the cash. It did indeed look like easy money. Yes, it was a pyramid scheme, but maybe if he was quick, got in and out before the whole thing collapsed ... and even if it did, Noah would just be one of reps at the bottom. They were never the ones who got done for fraud – it was always the top dogs, the ones who set it up. Worst case, he'd waste a bit of time. Best case – he'd make some cash to help pay for Gran to get better at Kingfisher Meadows.

She'd do anything for him. He should do the same for her. For people you love, whatever it takes. He had to do this. He at least had to *try*.

Josh and the man did some sort of complicated handshake affair, and Josh turned, bouncing down the drive and out on to the pavement, counting his cash. "Duuuude!" he said, seeing Noah.

"Hello. Dude," Noah replied.

"How's it hanging?"

Noah shrugged. "OK, I suppose, just normal. How's yours hanging? I mean, *it*?"

Josh laughed and slapped him on the back. "Funny, man. Listen, I would love to stay and chat, but I got so much more money to make tonight. This shit is selling like lemonade on a *drrrrrrry*, hot day."

"Uh-huh?"

Josh riffled through a wad of tens that he pulled from his pocket. "Two hundred. Just from the last hour and a half."

Noah's eyes lit up and he gave Josh a playful little punch on his big, muscular arm. "You're so minted you could be herbal tea!"

Josh stared at him.

"Like, a *peppermint* tea," Noah explained. "Or an indigestion tablet?" Noah suggested, "That's another … minty thing. Erm. An After Eight?"

Josh looked him up and down. "What do you want, little dude?"

Noah blew a breath out. Eating humble pie did not come easily to him. "Nothing much," Noah said. "Just out and about doing some thinking, *man...*"

"Uh-huh?"

"Yeah, just alone with my thoughts ... thinking about you actually... oh! Not in a pervy way," Noah clarified, "just about your pyramid scheme—"

"Multilevel marketing company."

"Yeah, sounds interesting." Noah nodded.

Josh looked at him. "You want a piece of this, bud?"

"A piece of ... piece of what, Josh?"

Josh stepped close to him. "We both know what I'm talkin' 'bout. We both know the deal here. You ain't stupid, Noah. You know a good thing when you see it. You know you could have all this. The cash. The dreams. Hell, the celeb lifestyle. Business keeps on like this, I'll be living the high life in LA this time next year. Mansion with a pool. Pretty girls. Whatever I like."

Noah nodded, mesmerized by all the words and images. "Sounds ... nice?"

"So," Josh said, riffling the notes under Noah's nose again so he could sniff the money, "you in?"

Noah swallowed and stared at the cash. "I'm in."

CHAPTER THIRTEEN

Noah struggled along the street with the ridiculously heavy and cumbersome box that Josh had given him. A bead of sweat had formed on his forehead and he had chafed his wrist from the rough cardboard. He was pretty sure a blister was forming on his toe. Who would have thought that running your own business would be such hard work?

For Gran, he kept telling himself. *Anything for Gran.*

"Oh no," he muttered, as Harry and Pierre came around the corner and made a beeline for him.

"What's in the box?" Harry said.

"Just stuff." Noah shrugged. "How are you? I'm fine."

"Big box," said Pierre.

"Yes. It is a big box. I'm transporting some big stuff," Noah said.

"Is it my birthday present?" Harry asked.

"Your birthday's not until October."

Harry nodded. "I was joking. That's cool. You've got a big, secret box."

"It's not a secret box!" Noah insisted. "It's just stuff."

Harry crossed his arms. "We're off to the cinema. Coming?"

"What, now? This evening?" Noah looked sharply between Harry and Pierre. How could they arrange something like this with such short notice? Was Noah supposed to just drop everything and go along? Why hadn't there been adequate warning? If he'd had warning, he might have been able to get some cash together.

"Maybe get a pizza first?" Pierre said.

"This is all very last minute!" Noah protested.

"Got plans with your big, secret box?" Harry grinned.

"No. Maybe," Noah replied. He sort of *did* have plans with the box. He wanted to make a start shifting some of the protein powder. "It's only..."

"It's fine if you're busy," Harry said.

"We see the film without you," Pierre added.

Oh yes, Pierre would bloody love that, wouldn't he? Bloody love being all alone with Harry in a darkened, romantic cinema, sharing a bucket of popcorn and a vat of Coke, holding one another's hands in the scary bits, getting seats on the back row, because that's where people sit for extracurricular cinema fun.

"Eva's in the park, in case you were wondering," Harry said.

Shit. Eva. He'd forgotten about her. But that was mainly her fault, in fairness. She was proving to be a crap exchange student: sullen, moody and completely unforthcoming with interesting titbits about her culture. "Great, I'll check she's OK," Noah said.

"Cool," Harry said. "Well, Mum's taking us over to the cinema at six thirty, so be at mine if you want to come along."

"OK, so I will try to do that, if I can, but—"

"The box, I get it," Harry said. "Big, secret box." He patted Pierre on the back. "Come on, Pierre."

Harry grinned at Noah and sauntered off with Pierre. This was hardly an ideal situation, but needs must. This multilevel marketing scheme couldn't fail.

"Yoo-hoo! Eva!" Noah called across the park, as he struggled with his box towards the small group of depressed-looking teens sitting in a circle on the grass. "It's me! Noah Grimes! Your exchange host!"

Noah noticed a furtive shuffling between the young people. He knew what was going on, all right. They had probably been secretly smoking cigarettes!

"Hello, Eva," Noah said, reaching them. "I didn't know where you'd got to."

"Cool," Eva said.

Noah eyed the scene and recognized the three feral undesirables who came to his door yesterday. "I see you have a two-litre bottle of 7 Up," Noah commented to one of the youths. He raised his eyebrows a little, just to show, whatever the reply, that he knew that bottle probably contained some form of alcohol. He knew what was what. He was streetwise and hip too. "That's cool."

The kid took a defiant chug of 7 Up – straight from the bottle, didn't even decant it into a little plastic cup first. Noah smiled to himself. Four people sharing a bottle? Not an antibacterial wipe in sight? It could only end one way. *Rhinovirus.* It spread like wildfire.

Noah turned his attention to Eva. He couldn't allow her to languish here, amongst such types. It was his duty, as host, to save her from these people.

He squatted down so his eyes were level to hers. He'd seen this technique on *Supernanny.* "Eva," he smiled. "I like to play ping-pong at the youth club. *Et tu?*" Noah nodded. He couldn't think of anything more hateful, but maybe it was different in France – the language textbooks at school might have been a bit dated, but the kids in those dialogues always liked to play ping-pong in youth clubs for some reason, and he couldn't see why it would be any different today. Plus, a girl like her, who was predominantly limbs, would probably excel at ping-pong, being able to dart effortlessly around the table, like a daddy-long-legs.

Eva shook her head and appeared to be laughing.

Fine. Laugh at me! Noah thought. *Go ahead and contract lung cancer or a runny nose in a crap park in England.*

He stood back up. "Right. Fine. But I'm locking the front door at ten sharp tonight, so you'd better be back by then." He picked up his box and started backing away from the group, not trusting he could turn his back on them until he was a little further away. "I know you're immature and will now do rude signs at me when I turn my back, but just to let you know, I don't care about that. OK? Just because you make a wanking gesture at me doesn't mean anything, so do it because I don't even care."

Noah turned his back on them and defiantly walked on.

The next thing he knew, an empty two-litre bottle of 7 Up collided with the back of his head.

He stood there, frozen, shocked.

Took a deep breath.

Counted to ten.

He didn't look back.

Just walked stoically on.

He would not dignify their actions with a response. No! That's what they wanted!

Walk on. Be proud. Be—

A pine cone clipped him on the back of his head.

Fine. That was fine. It stung a bit, but—

Thwack! Another direct hit by a cone! And then *whack!* A hail of pine cones was fired from the direction of the feral kids. Noah was under attack! He clutched his box tightly to his chest and struggled out of the park, heart pounding, keeping his head low.

Perhaps that's why he didn't see the man and woman sitting in the car watching him.

CHAPTER FOURTEEN

Noah had tried really, really hard the previous evening. And yet, on every single one of the three doors he'd finally plucked up the courage to knock on, he'd had a negative response, namely:

"No."

"Piss off."

"Pete, bring her down, he's here! She seems to have got something stuck up her anus— Oh, sorry, you're not the vet, are you?"

But it was a new dawn, a new day, and he was feeling ... mildly confident. He had a plan. Selling the shake yourself was one revenue stream. But the more lucrative one was recruiting others to sell *for you*. It was simple psychology – people didn't buy products, they bought *people*. Part of the reason Noah was even involved with this was that, deep down, a little part of him still looked up to Josh. The looks, the cool, confident persona – it was appealing. Noah wasn't buying protein shake, he was buying Josh. And now, Noah needed to find someone who would buy *Noah*. Noah needed to find someone who would be equally impressed with *him*. Someone who would look up to him; see him as a mentor. The Year Eights were a bunch of gobby shits, already too big for their boots. But the Year Sevens were a different matter. Barely four months out of primary school, these nervous little kids would surely be easy pickings for Noah. As a Year Eleven, they would naturally hold him in high esteem – maybe even be a little bit scared of Noah, just like he was of Josh.

And Noah had his sights firmly on one kid in particular. *Jack Hooper*. The kid had just been elected as Year Seven rep to the school council, ergo he must be both ambitious *and* have the respect of his peers. These were exactly the qualities Noah needed in one of his sellers.

"Good afternoon, Jack!" Noah gave a confident, wide smile as he approached the bench where Jack was lounging, baby-faced and barely four-and-a-half feet tall, but legs apart and chewing gum like a really much older boy, like a Year Ten, maybe. He was surrounded by what appeared to be a group of Year Seven henchmen – but that was clearly ridiculous because they were just Year Sevens.

A *very tall* girl swaggered up to Noah. "Who's this joker?"

"I wish to speak to Jack." Noah swallowed. "It's school council business."

Jack looked up (*finally!*) and gave Noah a lazy glance up and down. "It's Noah, yeah?"

"Yes, it's me," Noah said.

"Cool," Jack sniffed. "Guys, I need some space," he said to his goons.

Noah waited patiently as the gang of eight kids collected their bags and slunk off to the other corner of the playground. "So!" Noah began. "This is nice. I thought it might be—"

"Why are you here?" Jack interrupted.

"Right, OK, yes. So . . . may I sit?"

Jack nodded his consent and Noah perched down next to him, got his phone out and passed it to Jack. "You seen this stuff?"

Jack glanced at the picture on the screen. "Protein powder? Yeah, I've seen it. What about it?"

"It's a real growing market, Jack. Everyone wants to get their hands on it. Everyone wants to look good, right?!" Noah laughed, loud and hard, for way too long.

Jack gave him a withering look. "It can fuck up your kidneys, that stuff."

"Wha— *Can it?*" Noah said.

Jack nodded. "If you take too much." He chewed his Wrigley's Extra for a bit. "Anyway, what about it?"

Noah leaned into the boy. "This stuff is selling like ... lemonade on a *drrrrry*, hot day."

Jack screwed his face up. "Right?"

"I'm helping to sell this stuff and, let me tell you, I'm making good money."

"How much?"

Noah nodded. "Three hundred a week, not gonna lie," he lied.

Jack handed Noah the phone back. "It looks like low-quality shit."

"No! No, Jack, it's *high-quality* shit. I mean, not even shit. *Nectar.* It's the protein powder of the gods. And this is a brilliant *multilevel network marketing* opportunity."

"You mean it's a pyramid scheme."

Noah's leg started bouncing up and down. "No. No, no, no. It's just a simple network of sales reps, all working for the common good. No pyramid in sight. Look, do you want in? There's money to be made. Good money. Think of all the Lego you could buy."

Jack snorted. "*Lego?* Fucking *Lego?*"

Noah sighed. For a Year Seven he was certainly very confident with swear words and alarmingly clued up about the world. Kids grew up fast these days. "Or whatever. You can buy ... sweets, then!"

Jack laughed.

"Football cards?"

Jack guffawed with what appeared to be a vast amount of contempt.

"Listen, you can buy hard drugs and pay sex workers for all I care, *do you want in*?"

Jack shook his head. "Not really, Noah. Like I said, it looks like low-grade powder, with an unknown brand. It'll be a tough sell."

"You can get thirty quid a tub for it."

"And how much would I have to buy it for?"

Noah stifled a smile. He had him hooked. Now for the price! Josh sold it to Noah for a tenner a tub. If Noah sold it on for twenty, he could make a tidy ten-pound profit per sale. "Twenty."

"Make it six and we have a deal."

"Six fifty!" Noah blurted out, immediately realizing he should have come back with nineteen.

"Done!" Jack grabbed Noah's hand and shook it. "Nice doing business with you."

"No, wait, I made a fatal error because—"

Jack brushed Noah away. "You need to go, mate, I've got a date with my girlfriend."

Noah stared at him for a moment. How could this kid, who was *twelve* tops, have an actual, living girlfriend? Why was everyone so much more advanced than Noah was? "Look, of course, but when I said six fifty, what I meant was—"

"She's in Year Eight, just to warn you."

"Oh God," Noah said.

"I'll come find you when I've got my leads confirmed," Jack said.

"Uh-huh, lovely." Noah nodded.

"And you'd better have a reliable supply, because I'm gonna shift a metric fuck-tonne of this shit!"

"Cool, cool, everything's cool, it's just, I really need—"

Jack tossed him a two-pound coin. "Do us a favour and grab a can of KA from the canteen, will ya?"

Noah missed the coin, scrambling around on the ground to retrieve it. "Um, I'm kind of busy, though."

Jack held his hand out. "Get one for yourself, obviously."

Noah nodded. "Oh, well, that's kind – thank you. Thanks. I'll..."

"Be back soon. I'm thirsty."

"I'll ... sure. Right now, then. Great. So..." Noah smiled at Jack, but he was already busy texting on his phone. "OK, back in a minute, then."

Noah scuttled off in the direction of the vending machines in the main hall. "Hellfire and damnation," he muttered to himself. How had he allowed this to happen? Why was Jack so intimidating? Should he tell a teacher?

"Oh, hi there, No-ah!" Jess Jackson cooed, as she turned around from the vending machine, a Cadbury Flake in hand, as Noah hurried up.

"Jess." He squeezed past her and inserted his coin into the slot.

"So. Harry and Pierre," Jess said.

Noah froze at the machine and took a breath. Whatever bullshit she was about to spout, he didn't want to hear it.

"Mmmmmm," she purred. Noah glanced to the side, catching sight of her caressing the Flake with her parted glossy lips. "I love Flakes."

Noah rolled his eyes. "Oh? Are you still here, Jessica?" He gave her a tight smile and pressed the buttons for his can.

"That's cool, Noah. You're clearly fine with the whole cinema thing, so my work here is done."

THUD. The can hit the bottom of the vending drawer. Noah grabbed it and darted after Jess as she strolled away, gently stroking her baby bump.

"Wait, Jess! What do you mean the 'cinema thing'? How do you ... how did you know about the cinema?"

Jess took another languid bite of Flake, brushing some stray flecks of chocolate from her lips with her little finger. "I was at the cinema last night. I saw Harry and Pierre."

Noah swallowed. "Yes, they went to the cinema. I couldn't go."

"Exactly. That's why you didn't see."

"See what?"

"You didn't see Pierre all snuggled into Harry, resting his head on Harry's shoulder. You didn't see how cosy it looked, Noah. Maybe it means nothing. In fact, I'm sure it's totally innocent. I just thought I should say something. Josh says we gotta look after the employees, so, I guess that's what I'm doing. It's just, you have to admit, you do have this habit of somehow *repelling* people, don't you?" She smiled at him, a sad sort of smile. "I hope I'm wrong, Noah. I really hope I'm wrong. But, let's face it, you know I'm usually right."

CHAPTER FIFTEEN

"It's not true, she's winding you up, it's all lies," Noah repeated to himself as he walked towards the Willows. He'd spent the rest of the day acting normal around Harry, determined not to give in to the paranoia. Of course Harry didn't cuddle with Pierre – why would he? Harry was loyal and lovely and sweet. Definitely. And it wasn't as if Noah could delicately enquire anyway. There was no way of doing that without it sounding like an accusation.

He signed his name in the visitors' book and gave a cursory nod to Tabatha, who was sitting by the fish tank, one paw on the glass, watching the guppies with a wired look in her eyes. *It's not true. She's winding you up. It's all lies.*

Gran and Dickie were standing behind two keyboards

that had been set up in the lounge. Dickie had a streak of white make-up running across his nose and under his eyes; Gran two red stripes on her right cheek. She also had a colander on her head.

"Change of plans," Gran explained, seeing Noah. "We've ditched the bitch, aka Vera, and gone solo."

"Duo," Dickie corrected.

"Three-o?" said Babs, shuffling in with a tambourine.

"Right." Noah rolled his eyes. "And the colander?"

"Pet Shop Boys tribute," Gran sniffed. "Now, what's up with you? Need to talk?"

"Yeah," Noah said.

"Let's have a nice sit-down in my room," Gran said, coming over to Noah and leaning on his arm. "Which way is that?"

"This way, Gran," he said, leading her off.

"Sometimes I don't know which is left or right, up or down!"

Noah swallowed. "I know, Gran."

"Hold up, there's only *two* members of the Pet Shop Boys," Noah heard Babs say as they left. "*So where does that leave me?!*"

"I'm worried that I've got competition in the Harry department," Noah said as Gran settled herself into her armchair.

"Tea?"

"No thanks, Gran."

"Jack Daniels?"

"No. I'm fine."

Gran adjusted the cushion and sat back. "What about some nice tea, then?"

"No, I'm fine for tea."

"Or some Jack Daniels? Nice drop of JD?"

"Gran, I just wanted to talk to you about Harry."

Gran nodded. "You know who's a no-good man who's only after all my money?"

Noah sighed. "Uh-huh. Dad."

"*Your father!*" Gran said. "I've always had to watch him. Ever since he was a baby. He'd steal anything. Not six weeks old and he nicked some other baby's dummy." She leaned towards Noah. "He wants to get his hands on my property portfolio!"

"Right..." Noah said, humouring her. "Well, don't worry, I'll make sure he doesn't."

"Or my diamonds!"

"Or your diamonds, Gran," Noah said.

"Do you promise me that?"

"I promise, Gran. Of course I won't let him."

"You're a good boy, Noah. You've always been my favourite. You and I, we've always understood each other, haven't we?"

Noah nodded, pleased. At least she could remember who he was today. And he *was* a good boy. At least someone appreciated it. And being Gran's favourite? He'd always thought he probably was, but now it was confirmed. Excellent. People like Eric might, technically, be grandchildren too, but Noah was the preferred choice. He was number one. Even more so once he'd secured her place at Kingfisher Meadows! "You can rely on me, Gran."

"So! Where did those Cosmos get to? The staff here are *awful*! Slack as you like. They're all stupid young girls who just go around talking about their men troubles. Don't care about us!"

"The staff seem nice, Gran."

"They put that on! To fool visitors!"

"Gran, I just wanted to talk to you about Harry, you see—"

Gran put a finger in the air. "You and Harry need an activity! Something you can do together!"

Noah raised his eyebrows. Actually, it wasn't a bad suggestion, and it was clearly backed by relationship science – like Mum and Dad's tandem bike rides idea, although he and Harry would do something less smug and vomit-inducing.

"Like your granddad and me," Gran continued. "We were really into ... oh, what was it now?"

"You're probably going to end up saying 'bonking' or something," Noah muttered.

"Oh, you dirty little tyke!" Gran said. "I was not going to say that! Really, now, Noah! Sixteen and sex on the brain!"

"Sorry, Gran."

"*Beekeeping*, it was. That's how your granddad died in the end – stung by the very bees he cared for. Very sad."

Noah screwed his face up. "Um ... Granddad died of a heart attack in his sleep, Gran."

"No, no, you're getting confused," Gran sniffed. "Ask Mother."

"My mum would probably say the same thing, though."

"Not *your* mother, *my* mother!" Gran said. "You need to ask her!"

Noah swallowed and nodded. "OK, Gran. I will, but just to say, FYI, I haven't actually got 'sex on the brain'. I mean, I hardly ever think about it much. And I definitely think about other stuff, like exams and becoming a prefect, so it's hardly 'on the brain'. I'm not a sex maniac."

Gran nodded. "So you say, but I know what you boys get like! One minute you're all sweet and well mannered, and the next you're humping and bumping..."

"Gran!"

"Grinding and writhing!"

"GRAN!"

"Getting down and dirty with all and sundry!"

"I'VE ONLY EVER DONE IT WITH MYSELF!"

Gran stared at him and Noah looked back at her, open-mouthed and mortified. "Sorry, I didn't mean to shout," he muttered, as his cheeks started flaming. *Bloody brilliant.*

Noah cleared his throat. "What I meant, just to clarify, by that last thing I said ... was, that I've only ever ... um... I have some hobbies that I do by myself, like building Airfix models, for example, but I don't have hobbies that I do with other people. Just in case ... because you might have thought that what I just said sounded like..."

"Like you masturbate," Gran said.

"Uh."

"Which is fine, Noah, and perfectly normal, so I don't know why you're getting all hot and bothered about that."

"Well, ah..." *Could this get any more awful?*

"I would much rather you masturbate than engage in any irresponsible intercourse with another person."

"Please can you stop saying that word?"

"What word, Noah?"

For once, Noah's further embarrassment was saved by a commotion outside the door, as a flash of fur ran past the door, with Matron in hot pursuit. "NO! TABATHA! NOOOO!" Matron shouted.

Gran shook her head. "Not again. Noah? Go out and help, will you?"

He was only too pleased to. Noah walked out into the corridor to find Matron, red-faced and puffing, at the far end by the fire exit, cornering Tabatha.

"Bad Tabatha!" Matron shouted.

Noah edged closer and saw a dead, brightly coloured

fish on the floor, which Tabatha was prodding with her paw. A murder! And one that Tabatha wasn't even trying to conceal. She seemed almost proud.

Matron turned to look at Noah. "Doris keeps leaving the lid of the tank open, so Tabatha gets in," she explained.

"Very sad and upsetting," Noah said.

"I found a guppy in one of my orthopaedic sandals yesterday."

"Disgusting," Noah agreed.

"One thing's for sure – the tank's gonna have to go!" Matron said, whipping the dead fish off the floor and waddling back down the corridor.

Noah's brain spun. *Maybe this could be the joint activity that he and Harry needed!* He hurried after Matron.

"Oh, Matron!" he called.

"What is it, Noah?" she said, not looking at him. "I've got the supper to cook."

"Matron, if you're getting rid of the tank, maybe I could have it?"

Matron turned and crossed her arms.

Noah cleared his throat. She was clearly dubious about his credentials. "See, I have been considering taking up tropical fishkeeping for some time. I have studied widely around the issue, consulting textbooks and expert websites, and feel that I have accumulated a vast body of knowledge that makes me well-placed to take this responsibility on. I am a kind, intelligent boy, and I would make sure the fish were well cared for, attending to their needs and—"

"Yeah, fine, take it," Matron said. "Can't be bothered to sell it online. I'll have Bob pack it all up and drop it round to you in his van later."

"Oh. Right."

"Be a weight off my mind, truth be told."

"Great!"

"They're an absolute bugger to maintain, but if you've got the time, that sounds grand to me." Matron nodded and waddled off.

Good. Now Noah had a thing to do with Harry. A nice joint activity, a shared responsibility that would tie them closer together. They could keep it in Harry's bedroom, so it would always be a constant reminder of Noah, bubbling away in the corner, watching Harry... Which would work out well, because Noah didn't have the remotest clue about keeping tropical fish or, indeed, the time to do it himself.

CHAPTER SIXTEEN

Harry was kneeling next to him, looking at the tank on Noah's chest of drawers in his bedroom.

"What's its name?" Harry asked.

"Haven't given him one yet; I thought we could name him together," Noah said.

"Okaaay," Harry said. "It's a he? And he's a *fish*?"

Noah rolled his eyes. "He's not simply a *fish*, Harry! He's a *Poecilia reticulata*! The jewel of the rivers of South America!"

"Oh. Is that a... What's that?"

"A guppy."

"He's very pretty," Harry said.

"Yes," Noah said. "He has style."

Harry stood up. "So, er, what made you decide to take up fishkeeping?"

Noah stood up too. "Well, you say 'me' but I prefer to say 'we'."

"What do you mean?"

"I got him for us, Harry! I thought it would be nice for us to have a thing we could look after together."

Harry stared at him. "Okaaaay."

"It'll be fun! What shall we call him?"

Harry sat down on Noah's bed. "Did we discuss this?"

"It's a surprise."

"Yes. It is."

Noah swallowed. "Do you love it?"

Harry cleared his throat. "I suppose."

"You *suppose*?!"

"I mean, if it makes you happy, then ... it's great," Harry said.

"It's not about *me*, Haz. It's about *us*."

Harry took a breath. "Um ... OK!"

"OK." Noah nodded. "It'll be nice."

Noah looked into the tank, watching the guppy swim about, as Harry got up and paced over to the window.

"I mean, and hear me out here, Noah," Harry said, turning back into the room, "I'm just speaking my thoughts out loud, really, but have we... Do we really have time for this? This sort of thing? I mean, GCSEs are coming up. There's stuff to think about. And now this."

"*Fish*, not 'this'," Noah snapped.

"You wanted that sentence to be 'And now *fish*'?"

Noah glared at him.

"Right. *Fish*. Fine," Harry said. "But, you know, had you asked me first, all I'm saying is..."

"What *are* you saying?"

"I mean, it's fine now, because it's done, and that's OK, but had you asked me, I probably might have suggested we wait for a bit. You know? We're young, we've got time. It's nice to enjoy ourselves without being burdened with responsibilities."

"So now he's a burden!" Noah said, throwing his hands in the air.

"Well, you must admit..."

Noah couldn't believe it. Oh yes, Noah saw the sort of person Harry was becoming, all right! It was all fun and happiness at first, but now with a bit of commitment, it had all turned sour. Harry just wanted to sow his wild oats, probably with Pierre, just like Jess Jackson had told him. Harry didn't want to be troubled with changing ... tank water and ... feeding in the early hours of the morning, when fish woke up crying.

"That's fine, Harry. I will rear the fish alone."

Harry blinked at him. "I can help."

"Oh, that's good of you."

"It's just, it seems weird to share a pet when we don't even... It's not like we live together or anything... So, I mean, it seems strange to jointly have responsibility for him."

Even though it was true, and even though it was a completely reasonable thing for Harry to have said, especially when they'd only been a "thing" for a couple of months, those words still sent a cold tremble through Noah's stomach. He busied himself folding some clothes. "Fine. So, what, you'll visit at weekends, will you? Spend some time with him then? I mean, I wouldn't want to get in the way of your life, so you just say what works. We'll fit in around you."

"I can't work out if you're joking."

Noah wiped his brow. "Look, I'm sorry, I thought this might be a fun thing for us to do together. But if you don't want to, you don't have to. Don't worry about us, we'll be fine. I haven't got a lot of time, either, but that's OK. I don't mind making sacrifices for Timothy. That's his name, by the way. *Timothy.*"

"Well, that's a nice name."

Noah shrugged.

"It's almost five. Pierre wants to go to the roller disco in the sports hall. You coming?"

Noah froze at the mention of Pierre's name.

"What?" said Harry.

Noah gestured to the fish tank. "I have to set up Timothy properly."

"Yeah, but—"

"And I need to check over all the questions for the quiz night, so..."

Harry nodded. "Sure."

"Have fun, though," Noah said, tight-lipped. "Both of you."

"I'll buzz you later."

Noah turned back to the tank and fiddled around with the wires at the back. "Let yourself out, yeah?"

Noah waited until he heard the front door click shut, then turned back into the room. Matters were more serious than he could have imagined. And now, this whole pet thing had made him look like an utter fool. Worse, he was now burdened with this ridiculous, stupid fish.

And all this, all of it, was because of Pierre.

Pierre had waltzed into town, with his suave attitude, good body, and oversized boy parts, and he had ensnared Harry.

This was war.

CHAPTER SEVENTEEN

"I don't see why the French lot got to go to Fun Kingdom in Cleethorpes while we had to stay in maths," Harry complained as he and Noah left the room for lunch.

"Well, I suppose they're not here to be in our lessons, and we do have GCSEs in a few months, so all things considered, Haz..."

"Sure." Harry shrugged. "Just would have been nice, that's all."

Noah's stomach knotted again at Harry's keenness to be with Pierre, but he held it together, giving a nonchalant "Absolutely" as they walked down the corridor. "Still, they're due back now, aren't they? So we can spend lots of lovely time with them this afternoon. *C'est formidable*, I'm sure."

Ahead, leaning coolly against the wall, Noah spotted Jack Hooper, beckoning him over with his index finger.

"Um, I think that Year Seven wants you," Harry frowned.

"Hm?" Noah said, playing innocent. "Oh. Oh yes, it appears he does. I think it's school council business; would you wait here? I won't be but a moment."

"I need the gear," Jack said, as Noah arrived by his side.

"How much?"

"Fifteen tubs so far."

Noah's eyes widened. "How... That's a lot!"

Jack looked mildly irritated. "Tip of the iceberg. You said you had the stock, so let's have it."

Noah swallowed. "Yes, I do have it. I have it, absolutely. But, you see, it seems I made a small mistake in the calculations. Six fifty just isn't—"

"Deal's a deal," Jack said. "You made me a promise, and I've made other people promises. Now get your shit together and get me the gear, else—" Jack reached into his trouser pocket and pulled out a Swiss army knife. "Victorinox Evolution S17," he smiled, gently caressing it whilst maintaining eye contact with Noah. "Thirty-two functions – compass, ruler, wire crimper ... and this!" He flicked one of the bits out. "Know what this is?"

Noah swallowed and shook his head.

"The hook disgorger!" Jack said. "You use it in

fishing, to remove a hook from deep inside the mouth. But useful in other surprising ways, too." He leaned in closer. "Get. Me. The. Gear!"

Noah's eyes nearly bulged out. "Oh!" he gasped.

Jack reached up and gave him a friendly pat on the shoulder. "Good man. I know you're reliable. That's why you're on the school council, right? Trustworthy. No bullshit."

Noah nodded. "Mm," he squeaked. What the hell was he going to do? No way would Josh Lewis sell him the tubs for anything less than ten. At that rate, Noah was going to make a loss of three fifty per tub!

"All right?" Harry said, arriving at Noah's side.

"This is my boyfriend, Harry, he's my boyfriend," Noah babbled.

Jack pocketed the Swiss army knife and extended his hand. "Nice to meet you. Hey, we should go on a double date sometime, you two and me and Hannah. Be nice."

"Uh-huh," Harry said, clearly dubious.

"Ha ha ha!" Noah laughed, stopping when he saw Jack's expression of thunder. "No, but seriously, that would be ace."

Jack nodded. "Don't keep me waiting, Noah."

Noah nodded back, manically. "Bye, Jack, I love you... I mean, bye *lovely* Jack, it's been lovely, and I love this chat ... you're lovely."

Jack sauntered off down the corridor and Harry turned to him. "What the hell is going on?"

"How do you know anything is going on?" Noah said, smiling weakly.

"I'll tell you how," Harry said. "Because whenever you get nervous and are clearly bricking it, you start to shuffle about on your feet, like you need a wee or something."

"Do I?"

"You do."

"I don't need a wee though."

"But you *are* bricking it. So that's how I know it's time to come to your rescue."

Noah blushed. Harry was his *hero*. But he wasn't about to admit what was going on to him. Embroiled in a pyramid scheme with a Year Seven? Harry would definitely think it ridiculous. "Everything is cool, Harry." Noah blinked. "Everything is cool and under complete control." He blew out a breath. "Haz, I'm just going to pop to the boys' toilets, but not because I need a wee, I'm going for other reasons, um… No, not to… I'm just going to hang out there… No, not that either, huh. Um, I'm going there to … literally, I just need some tissue to blow my nose. So. That's why. I'll join you in the canteen – save me a spot."

"OK," Harry said, looking at him with narrowed eyes.

"What? Nothing's weird, everything's normal," Noah told him.

Noah hurried into the toilets, straight into a cubicle, slammed and locked the door, flipped down the toilet seat and flopped down with his head in his hands. *Fuckety fuck fuck. How was he going to sort this mess out?* And then, just as quickly, he shook his head. What the hell was he doing? Hiding in the toilets, in turmoil, because of some stupid kid in Year Seven? No. Oh no. Noah could sort this out. He'd just tell Jack Hooper straight. Something cool. Something like, "Sorry, bro: no dice," whatever the hell that meant. He wouldn't be a victim. Not with Jack, not with Pierre...

He heard the bathroom door open, and the sound of footsteps making their way into the cubicle next to him.

"Yes, yes, I can talk," said a hushed voice. "I am alone, yes."

Noah froze. That voice had an unmistakable sophisticated French twang to it.

That voice ... belonged to *Pierre*, clearly already back from Fun Kingdom.

Noah knew that a hushed tone and a declaration of being "alone" almost always meant bad stuff was afoot. He stood motionless, breathing shallow, waiting for more ... waiting for—

Noah put the thought out of his mind. Pierre wouldn't be on the phone to *Harry*. He couldn't be. It just wouldn't happen...

"Uh-huh, *oui, oui*," Pierre was saying.

Noah narrowed his eyes. *Come on, say something useful!*

"Ah, yes!" Pierre laughed. "And it is better if people do not see!"

Noah held his breath. Something secret. Something people must not see.

"Is fine, I come to the shed at nine tonight. Yes, by the side of the kitchens, I know the one."

Oh my God. There it was. A *rendezvous*. It was there for the taking – and at nine tonight, the truth would be revealed.

Noah heard the toilet flush (had Pierre been speaking to someone whilst sitting on the lavatory? Disgusting! Unhygienic!) and the adjacent cubicle door open. Pierre started humming a jolly tune as Noah heard him step towards where the sinks were.

Noah waited for the sound of the tap to finish running and the piss-poor hand dryer to finish emitting its wheezing while the worst scenarios were playing out in his mind...

Noah squeezed his eyes shut and shook his head. *No, no, no! Get a bloody grip!* He was being paranoid and silly.

But there was also a sick heaviness in his stomach.

He wished he could talk to Harry about his fears, but wouldn't that make him sound weird? High maintenance? Insecure?

But then, in a relationship, talking was important. Vital, in fact. He'd seen a programme when he was off sick at the end of last term, about couples sorting out their relationship crisis by going on an outward-bound weekend, building a raft together and *talking*.

Screw the raft building, but *talking* he could probably manage.

He was going to talk to Harry.

Yes! They would talk!

Noah took a deep breath and bounced out of the cubicle, scrubbing his hands at the sink because he would be COVERED IN FOUL GERMS from the vile cubicle and he didn't want a nasty bout of CHOLERA.

This would all be fine. He too hummed a happy tune to himself ("MMMBop" by Hanson) as he turned the tap off with his elbow and held his hands under the tepid air blower.

"Gonna be much longer?" asked Eric Smith, suddenly materializing by Noah's side with dripping hands.

Noah jumped, then glanced over his shoulder to check they were alone. "Eric, I've got a question for you. What's your assessment of Pierre?"

"My assessment is he's up to something at nine p.m. tonight," Eric grinned. "I was in the other cubicle."

"What do you suppose it is?"

Eric shrugged. "Frying bigger fish right now, Noah. That's one you're gonna have to work out yourself."

"You mean you don't know? Not losing your touch, are you, Eric?"

"How much longer you gonna be?"

"It's not my fault, Eric! This drying contraption is futile. My hands are still quite damp, I'm afraid. I won't be rushed."

"Screw this," Eric said, wiping his hands down his trousers instead. "I'll tell you this, though – that quiz night you're arranging for the exchange students?"

"My Great British Quiz Off, you mean?" Noah said. "You didn't hear it from me, but there's a whole section on the musicals of Andrew Lloyd Webber!"

"Uh, great. Well, I overheard Pierre and Harry talking, and they're planning on doing something else."

Noah dropped his hands and stared at Eric.

"Yeah," Eric said. "I just heard it, is all. Don't know why, don't know what else they got planned. I'm just telling you. And I ain't got no agenda 'cause we're— Noah? You OK?"

Noah stared hard at the brick wall in front of him, breathing, his blood coming up past a simmer to a violent boil. "Bastard!" Noah hissed, suddenly pushing past Eric and charging out of the toilets.

CHAPTER EIGHTEEN

Noah homed in on Harry and Pierre sitting in the corner of the dining hall, apparently enjoying some sort of cosmopolitan French stew that the canteen had made in honour of their visitors from France. *Oh, sure, for them the kitchen can source saffron and langoustines, but the minute they bid us adieu it'll be back to square pizza with baked beans and bananas with pink custard!*

Noah slid into a chair opposite the pair of them. "Hello, Harry. *Pierre.*"

"All right, Noah?" Harry said, mopping up his stew with some of the French baguette the canteen had also somehow magically been able to bake. "This isn't bad, actually."

"Really." Noah nodded. "How interesting. So, a little

bird tells me you are planning on *not coming* to my Great British Quiz Off, even though it has taken me weeks to prepare the questions. But you're not coming, so that's fine, don't worry about it."

Harry looked up from his bowl. "Ah, well, I was going to talk to you about this, see——"

Noah held his hand up. "No matter, Harry. No matter. You'll miss the British nuclear power-station visuals I put together on PowerPoint, that's all. But that's fine."

"Pierre was just really wanting to go clubbing, and the only day is Saturday, that's the thing," Harry said.

Noah stared at him, unblinking. "What?!"

"Clubbing?" Harry repeated.

Noah's eyes nearly popped out. "Oh, sure, clubbing at our age. I mean, what next? *Crack cocaine and MBMA?!*"

"MDMA."

"You even know the lingo!" Noah gasped.

"Look, relax, it's a nappy night."

"Nappy night?! *Nappy night?!*" Noah spluttered. "What the hell even are these words you're saying?! Is that a depraved fetish thing?"

"No," Harry said, patiently. "It's a night for under eighteens that they run once a month at Sindy's in Lincoln. It's just, this month, it happens to clash with the quiz night on Saturday. I mean, *what I was going to say* is that quite a few people are saying they're going to the club, so maybe it would be best to rearrange the quiz?"

Noah took an unsteady breath. "So, what you're now telling me, at the eleventh hour, is that everyone is sodding off to some training pants night at some shitty club in Lincoln? And nobody thought to let me know so I could rearrange the quiz in reasonable time? Great. That's just *great*. You know what? Maybe I'll just burn the quiz. If no one's interested and no one wants to bother coming. It's taken me days, nay, *weeks*, but I'll burn it. Burn the quiz down."

Harry gave Noah a hopeful smile. "Come! It'll be fun!"

"No, I don't think so," Noah sniffed. "Besides, I've nothing to wear and I don't like gyrating on sticky dance floors, you know that."

"Well, that's fine," Harry said. "I mean, normally I wouldn't either, but—" He cocked his head towards Pierre. "And maybe Eva would like to come? We do kind of have to entertain them."

"Entertainment had been arranged," Noah said, his eyes darkening. He glanced across to Pierre, who was happily lapping up his stew like Noah's obvious hurt and distress meant nothing to him. Like nothing in the world was going to change Pierre's mind about going to the potty night. He would just spoon up his stew, happy as you please, shutting Noah's humiliation out and acting like he knew he'd get what he wanted because boys like him, all handsome and muscles, always did.

"I can pay for you," Pierre muttered, not even looking up from his bowl.

Oh my God.

Oh my actual God.

Harry had told Pierre that Noah didn't have any money.

Harry had shared PRIVATE and BOYFRIEND-ONLY information with a third party!

That was it.

That was a red rag to a bull.

And Noah was more than ready to gore both Pierre and Harry on his word horns.

"You *weasels!*" Noah snarled, in both their directions. "Bloody little WANK WEASELS!"

Shocked silence in the dining hall.

Noah slammed his chair back so it fell over and stormed out of the canteen.

Harry and Pierre could get married and buy a fitted kitchen for all he cared.

He really didn't care.

He really, really didn't.

CHAPTER NINETEEN

"Noah?! What on earth's the matter?" his mother said as he stumbled through the front door, engulfed in the tears he'd been holding in since lunchtime.

"Yup hu over hi ween he n Harry!" he sobbed, slumping down on the sofa.

His mother screwed her face up. "What?"

"Babes?" Bambi said.

Noah looked up through tear-blurred eyes at Bambi, who was dressed in *very short* denim shorts, a gingham blouse that was tied at the waist, and a cowboy hat and boots. Noah heaved back tears. "Yup ha ... Harry!" he babbled.

His mother shook her head. "I'll put the kettle on."

Bambi popped herself next to Noah on the sofa. "Hun?"

Noah edged away from Bambi. "Go ... Ha ... away."

"Oh, babes. Bambi's seen it all. She's been hurt so many times by men, she's lost count. She's had it all: betrayal, lies, infidelity..."

"Herpes?" Noah snarled.

"Hush your mouth, filthy child!" Bambi scolded. "Bambi's a good girl, and if she can't be good she always takes protection. Now, you tell her what's happened."

Noah wiped the tears from his cheeks. "I think me and Ha ... Harry are over. Another boy called Pierre came along and he's better than me ... and ... and ... and then Jess said she saw them embracing at the cinema and now they're not coming to my quiz because they want to dance together all night long and ... and Pierre's got a big willy."

Bambi put an arm across Noah's shoulders. "And did Harry tell you it was over?"

Noah shrugged. "They're going to buy an integrated dishwasher and wine cooler, I bet!" And he started crying all over again.

His mother came in and perched on the sofa on the other side of Noah. "We'll get through this," she said, placing a hand on Noah's arm.

Noah snatched his arm away.

"We'll have a girls' night in," his mum suggested. "I'll run you a bath, and we'll watch a movie – I've got a pirate copy of *The Notebook*, and we can all have a big old cry!"

"I don't want a cry!" Noah cried. "I want..." He wiped all the tears from his face with his palms. "I want Harry."

"Well, OK, of course you do," his mum murmured. "But here's the thing, Noah: there are more fish in the sea! We'll sign you up on a dating app—"

"Mum, I'm sixteen!"

"And don't forget there's always Angie Parker's son, he's gay and—"

"MUM, HE'S FORTY-EIGHT, OH MY GOD!"

"Jesus Christ, here we go. I was only trying to lighten the mood, Noah! God, it's just like the Scouts all over again – when you were convinced you weren't going to be patrol leader – and look what happened!"

Noah looked up sharply. "Yeah! They made me quartermaster!"

"See, a master!" his mum said. "Just as good! That's my point!"

"It's not 'just as good'! Quartermaster is just a glorified dogsbody who has to keep the patrol kit box clean. I spent six months on my knees with a Handi-Vac!"

"Well..." his mother said.

"Well *what*?" Noah replied.

"Well, don't you think you should have talked to Harry about all this? Maybe he doesn't know how you're feeling?" she said. "You're a teenager, you're all emotion and no perspective."

"What? I'm all perspective! I have so little emotion

I'm practically a sociopath!" Noah hissed. "I don't need to *talk* to him. It's perfectly obvious how he feels. He knows how important the Great British Quiz Off was to me, and yet he was prepared to sacrifice all that because of Pierre!"

Bambi nodded. "I suppose actions do speak louder than words."

Noah burst into tears again.

"Oh dear, there, there," his mum said. "Do you want Bambi to do the tarot? We could see if fate has a solution for all this?"

"I'm at one with the cards, babe," Bambi said. "It's like I have a direct portal to the other side."

Noah heaved himself up. "I'm getting some air," he said, stopping at the raised voices emanating from outside the back door. "Who's that?"

"Oh, your father has surprised Eric with a fishing trip, you know, to bond? Seems Eric isn't too keen, but he's just pushing back because he's scared, Noah. Scared of being hurt again."

Noah stared at his mum. "Where's *my* fishing trip?"

"One, Noah, your dad's been around more for you than Eric, so they've got more catching up to do. And two, is fishing really your thing? I thought you could stay here with me, and we'd do something nice."

"Oh really, Mother? Like what? Bury you under the patio in several hundred litres of cement?"

His mum smiled. "I know you don't mean that, Noah, you're just upset."

"GAAAHHH!" Noah screamed. Why was she carrying on with this intolerable charade of being a reasonable, understanding mother? Noah didn't buy it for one second.

There was a knock at the door. Bambi looked around, wild-eyed, and flung herself down on the carpet.

"Get that, would you, Noah?" his mum whispered.

"You get it!"

"Bambi's in hiding and some of her enemies may well remember me from our days at the Pink Carnation!"

"If it's someone calling herself Mi-Chelle Sea Shells, tell her I'm not here, you've never heard of me!" Bambi hissed. "And get rid of her pronto – I'm doing a gig at the Red Lion tonight to try out some new material for London. I need to get on!"

Noah shook his head. What the hell was Bambi involved in to warrant this sort of reaction? How bad could a business disagreement between a few drag queens get? He walked through to the little hall and opened the front door.

CHAPTER TWENTY

"I come to say sorry," Pierre said, leaning against the door frame.

Noah crossed his arms and shrugged. "Fine."

"You have been crying."

"No," Noah lied. "That's not true, it's just my early-onset hay fever."

"I say a thing that upset you, I am sorry for that."

"Fine." Noah shrugged.

"We got off together . . ."

"*What?!*"

". . . on a bad start. So, let us go out to the park."

"Why, but it's nearly four o' clock! It's getting dark, and I have to do homework."

"No. We go to the park and I apologize."

"Did Harry put you up to this?"

Pierre shook his head. "I told him, and he thinks it is a good idea."

"I see."

"I have treats!" Pierre said, indicating a large wicker picnic basket on the ground next to him. "We should be friends. Come."

Noah hesitated, painfully aware that even if the picnic basket contained dog shit and barbed wire, it would still be more palatable than whatever his mother was planning on cooking tonight.

Noah grabbed his coat. "Yeah, come on, let's go."

The park was deserted. Why wouldn't it be? It was a chilly, and increasingly dark, January weekday afternoon. Noah was beginning to wish he'd worn his thermal vest. He could only hope that Pierre had the foresight to bring a thermos of tea – or anything, really, just to stave off hypothermia.

"Here looks good," Pierre said, setting the picnic hamper down on a patch of grass near one of the larger oak trees.

Noah patted the ground with his hand. "Bit damp."

"I have a travel rug!" Pierre said, snapping the clasps of the picnic hamper open and pulling it out.

Noah watched, possibly semi-impressed, as Pierre unfurled the rug and put it on the ground. It was lambswool in some sort of tartan design, with a waterproof liner. A quality rug, anyway.

"Sit!" Pierre said, patting the rug. "I just set things up here."

Noah did as he was told, but remained silent. He wanted Pierre to know that it was going to take more than a trip to the park and a sit on a posh travel rug to win him over.

Pierre struck a match and lit a candle nestled inside a lantern, which he placed in the middle of the rug. "And there was light!" Pierre smiled.

Noah twitched his mouth. "Is the rug fire retardant?"

"Yes, of course," Pierre said.

Noah nodded. "Fine."

Pierre returned to his basket, from which he pulled a disposable barbecue. Noah watched in horror as Pierre pulled the plastic wrapping off and set the thing up a short distance from them. "Er! No!" Noah said. "Barbecues are against park by-laws! They're forbidden! You can't light that!"

"No one knows!"

"They will!" Noah pleaded. "No, Pierre! You cannot light it!"

Pierre struck another match and lit the barbecue.

"Pierre!"

"Is fine."

Noah watched, wide-eyed, as the flames started

licking at the charcoal. His recent dinner party catastrophe had reminded him how hazardous barbecues could be – you were literally one step away from death with a barbecue – but death would be nothing compared to incurring the wrath of the park warden if he caught them with this PROHIBITED GRILLING APPLIANCE.

"Relax," Pierre said, producing a bottle of red wine from the basket, pulling out the cork and pouring two glasses. "Here we have a lovely French Merlot."

Pierre handed a glass to Noah. "Um ... I'm not sure about this, haven't you just got an Orangina? That's French, isn't it? Couldn't we just have that?"

"Try some. A little sip."

Noah did so. It was OK ... quite smooth ... buttery, almost, Noah considered. He took another sip, feeling the silky warmth in his throat. Was this what wine was meant to taste like? The wine he'd always tried before, stuff that his mother had purchased for Christmas and the like, was akin to drinking a glass of battery acid. But this wine... This was very special. Noah took another sip, the blackberry sweetness exploding in his mouth, sliding down the back of his throat like silk and enveloping his whole body in a sort of velvety warmth against the bitter winter air.

"Good, huh?" Pierre chuckled, placing a small bowl of olives and a plate of cured meats in the middle of the rug.

"Not at all bad," Noah admitted.

"These are Nocellara olives," Pierre said. "They are actually Italian, not French, but I like them. You will like them too. Some antipasti, and I cut some bread," he continued, pulling a baguette from the basket, a bread knife and wooden chopping board.

Much as he was battling against it, all of these things pleased Noah. Finally, he was enjoying the high life! Olives from Italy! An antipasti platter! This was how people from London, Paris and Milton Keynes lived!

Also, there was little doubt that Pierre had gone to a lot of effort. He hadn't just turned up with a vague apology and a small box of Nestlé Quality Street.

Pierre handed him a piece of buttered bread with a very thin slice of meat on top of it. "Jambon de Bayonne," Pierre explained. "The most famous of French hams – air dried and salted near the Pyrenees."

"Thank you," Noah said, popping it in his mouth. This was like nothing he'd ever experienced. The meat was fabulous. The bread was fabulous. Even the butter, which was presumably also French, was fabulous. Noah took another sip of wine. The wine, meat, olives, they all worked perfectly together, the flavours balancing in harmony. Noah was in clover. Pierre was ace.

But then he checked himself: Pierre was also a snake in the grass! He clearly had designs on Harry, had maybe already even carried those designs out! Pierre also had a secret rendezvous at the shed later this evening.

Noah had to be on his guard. This was nice, but Noah wouldn't be tricked into thinking Pierre was a friend.

"To friendship," Pierre said, offering Noah his glass to clink.

"Um, yes," Noah said, clinking glasses, supposing it was OK to lie. Keep your enemies close, that sort of thing.

They both took a sip of SUPER DELICIOUS AND FABULOUS wine.

"So," Pierre said, "I am sorry if you got the impression I don't like quizzes. The truth is, in fact, very different. I love quizzes."

"You love quizzes?"

"Noah, I *fucking love* quizzes!"

Noah laughed. "Oh, well, that's ... that's a surprise, Pierre. But a nice surprise. I love quizzes too."

"I know. I know you do. And that is why, both me and Harry, we *will* be coming to your Great British Quiz Off."

"Oh!" Noah said, clasping his hands together and nearly spilling his wine.

"I am looking forward to it."

"But then why did you say you wanted to go clubbing in the first place?" Noah asked.

Pierre shook his head. "Sometimes, I say the wrong thing. It comes out wrong, I don't know. Sometimes, everyone else is saying they want to do a thing, and I say I do too, even though I do not."

Noah nodded. "Peer pressure. Very dangerous."

"Sometimes, you may not think it, but I get nervous and everything gets mixed up."

"Well, I understand that," Noah said.

"Yes?"

"Sometimes, I'm the same."

Pierre smiled and looked down at his glass shyly. "You're so sweet."

Noah shrugged it off. "Oh now, that's very kind of you, but really. It's just true. And you've no reason to be nervous, Pierre. You're a very ... you know, you're a very nice guy and you've got a lot going for you, in all sorts of ways, so you should be confident, you know?"

"You're a very nice guy too, Noah," Pierre said, flicking his eyes up from his glass.

"Oh, phooey!" Noah giggled.

Pierre giggled back and glanced behind him. "Ah, now the flames have died down, I warm this cheese on the barbecue."

"Barbecued cheese?" Noah said, lifting an eyebrow.

"More baked, really. Just for a few minutes, you will enjoy."

"*Mais oui*," Noah said, having another sip of wine.

Noah watched as Pierre busied himself placing a boxed Camembert, studded with rosemary and garlic and wrapped in foil, on top of the barbecue. This was shaping up to be an excellent little evening of sophistication and glamour. *If,* and it was still a fairly big *if,* but *if* Pierre turned out not to be trying it on with Harry, and *if* Pierre turned out not to be up to no good with his secret shed meeting later that evening, and *if,* when Noah had had a chance to think about all the events and weigh things up, and on balance Pierre was in positive friendship figures, then maybe things could be nice between them. Maybe Pierre could become Noah's pen pal, and they would write to one another from their respective far-off lands: tales of exotic places and unfamiliar foods.

Pierre turned back towards him. "So, Noah, now you tell me more about you."

"Hmm – what like?"

"Like anything!" Pierre said. "What do you do for fun?"

Noah blew out a breath. "I like reading, especially mystery novels. And I watch TV – especially mystery shows. And now I'm also a fishkeeper – *poisson,*" Noah clarified.

"A geeky boy!" Pierre grinned.

"Well, maybe…"

Pierre waved his hand. "Ah, it was not a criticism. Geeky is good!"

"R-really?"

"Really. I like geeky boys. Geeky boys are cute."

Noah laughed. "If you say so."

"Sexy."

160

"Now you're just being –" Noah swallowed "– silly."

"Ask me what I like about geeky boys," Pierre said.

Noah moistened his lips. "What ... um, what do you like about ... geeky boys?"

Pierre shifted slightly so he was a little closer to Noah, drawing little circles with his finger on the travel rug. "I like their gentle nature, their innocent little ways. I like their intelligence." He looked up, directly into Noah's eyes. "I like them. I want to do things with them. I want to take the balloon of their virginity, and burst it. Pop!"

Noah jumped. There was a sizzling from the barbecue. Noah swallowed, hard. "I think the cheese has bubbled over."

"Oops," Pierre said, turning to the barbecue to sort it out. "I hate it when it bubbles over before you want it to."

"Huh. Yeah," Noah said, breathless. He swallowed again. Shifted his position on the travel rug. This was intense. But fine. It was fine because Pierre was talking about geeky boys in general, not specifically Noah. He was making generalized comments, in a general way, generally about geeky boys. It was just chance that Noah had a gentle nature, innocent little ways, and swollen virginity.

"Open your mouth," Pierre said, now coming at him with a dripping piece of baguette, oozing unctuous molten cheese.

Noah just did as he was told; it was only polite. He parted his lips as Pierre slid it in. The warm gooeyness filled Noah's mouth. The cheese was out of this world. "Oh . . . oh God," Noah muttered.

"Mmmm," Pierre cooed.

"That's so good."

"It is unpasteurized."

"Is that . . . bad?"

"It could be. Are you pregnant?"

"No," Noah giggled, blushing. "I couldn't possibly be. . ."

"Then . . . more?"

"Uh-huh," Noah said as he swallowed down the first mouthful. Yes, more. More, more, more. He could eat this all night long.

Pierre fed him another slither of crusty baguette, topped with more meltingly creamy cheese, which dripped on to Noah's lips and down his chin. Pierre caught the trickle of warm, thick goodness with his little finger, scooping it back into Noah's mouth. "Too good to waste," Pierre said.

"Uhhhh," Noah groaned, sucking it off Pierre's finger.

"This cheese is *fantastique*, huh?"

"Yeeeeahhhh. . ."

"I get you more cheese?"

"Just a little more," Noah said, wiping his mouth with the back of his hand. Noah leaned forward as Pierre presented another piece of baguette, piled extra high with a bubbling mound of molten cheese.

"Open wide. Take it all at once," Pierre suggested.

"Ug," Noah muttered, as he greedily gobbled the lot.

"Look at you!" Pierre laughed.

"I love your cheese!" Noah said, swallowing and taking a sip of the red wine. "I love it."

Pierre nodded. There was a brief moment of silence between them. "And I love you," Pierre said.

And Pierre leaned forward, put his hand behind Noah's head, and kissed him full on the lips.

CHAPTER
TWENTY-ONE

"Oh my God, what are you doing?!" Noah said, springing back from Pierre.

"I kiss you."

"No! No, Pierre! You can't! I have a boyfriend. Harry!"

"Yes, he is very nice."

Noah stared at him. This whole lovely picnic wasn't an apology at all. It was a seduction!

"We are having a good time, no?"

"A good time?!" Noah spluttered.

"Noah..."

Noah stood up and brushed himself down. "No. No, I'm sorry. So very sorry, but this can't happen. It must not happen. This is bad, Pierre. Harry is your French exchange host – you can't just try to snaffle me from under his very nose."

Pierre stood up too and edged closer to a very skittish Noah. "It is fine."

"It is *not* fine!"

"We are both hard. You know it."

Noah swallowed. "No. No, that's not ... entirely true. Maybe you. Not really me. But look, this has been nice, and I am flattered, I really am, but—"

Pierre stepped in and kissed Noah again, Noah immediately de-suckering himself from Pierre's lips. "OK, thank you. I should go."

"I upset you?"

"No. Not upset. Just bad. *Wrong.*"

"How can love ever be wrong, Noah?"

Noah flapped about, doing his coat back up. "Look, right, wrong, I don't know. But Harry is my boyfriend and I love him. And now you've tricked me with fancy wine and lovely cheese... You created an atmosphere with your lantern and ambushed me!"

Pierre dropped his head. "I am sorry."

Noah nodded. "Fine. Good."

"I should have known."

"OK."

"I am stupid. So stupid!" Pierre slapped his hand against his forehead a few times. "I made a fool of myself."

"Noooo..."

Pierre looked at him. "You are good boy, Noah. Harry is lucky. You are both lucky. I have made mess of this. I was thinking that the three of us... Oh, never mind. I mess it up now."

Noah frowned. What *had* he been thinking?

"You go. I pack up here," Pierre said.

"Alone? By yourself in the park?"

Pierre shrugged.

Noah swallowed. He knew he should talk to Harry about all this, but in doing so he would have to tell him what happened, and he had no way of knowing how Harry might react. He knew how *he* would react, if it was the other way round. And that would not be good.

Plus, thinking about it, it *looked* terrible. A picnic. A lantern! Wine and baked cheese! Noah might as well claim that Pierre turned up with a packet of condoms and a sex manual, but he was still surprised when the kiss happened. How stupid would Harry think he was?! It might be best ... to bury this.

"Um ... about what happened, though?" Noah said.

"Huh?"

"We should... I mean, obviously you made a mistake, and you weren't to know. What I'm saying is, I don't think Harry would be happy if he found out what you did, you know? So, what I'm saying is, I would be prepared not to say anything about it? You know?"

"Thank you."

"OK, good. So, just to confirm, we will both say nothing? Pretend nothing happened? We came out, had a nice, basic picnic, chatted ... and went home. That's all?"

"Yes."

"OK. OK, then. Right." Noah shifted about awkwardly on the spot, wanting to go, but feeling a lot was now up in the air. "And, look, it was nice... The picnic, I mean. The picnic was a good picnic. Lovely, in fact. I liked it. So ... *thank you.*"

"You are welcome. We are friends?"

"Yes!" Noah said. "Friends, for certain!"

"We hug? As friends?"

Noah took a breath. Swallowed. "Sure. As friends."

With permission apparently granted, Pierre came up and enveloped Noah in his arms, pressing himself tight against him, breathing heavily into Noah's neck. They stood like that for what felt like minutes. But it was a "friends" hug, so it was fine. Just friends, saying goodbye. Just friends, who may totally coincidentally have had hard-ons, saying thanks for a nice evening, and I'll see you tomorrow. Totally fine.

Noah wriggled free. "OK. Right. Thanks. Bye, then." And he turned and scooted off. Heart racing. Mouth dry. Doing his best "trying to make it look like fast walking when you're really running" walk, perfected through years of hurrying along school corridors. He tried to rationalize what had just happened.

Why hadn't he just run away after Pierre first kissed him? Why did he let it happen a second time?

Shit, he hated himself.

How could he have been so weak and pathetic?

Was it because part of him was paranoid that Pierre had done the same thing with Harry, and Noah needed proof he was worthy of being snogged too? Like, some stupid game of boy one-upmanship?

Christ, what a mess.

He hurried towards the exit on to Gordon Road. He would make this up to Harry. He would redouble his romantic efforts with him. He would make it very obvious to Harry that he was the one for him. And by next week, Pierre would be gone, and with him, the horrible secret that must never be told.

He jumped when he saw her, looking like the Slender Man, lurking in the shadows by the street lamp. "Eva?"

"Hallo, Noah."

"You scared me, Eva. What are you doing here? It's late."

"Waiting," she replied.

"Well, I would call it *lurking*, Eva. *Lurking* is a criminal offence in England, did you know that? You must come home, Eva. Where it's safe."

Eva glanced at him. "Meeting a friend."

"What sort of friend?" He glanced down at her guitar case that rested on the ground.

"Enjoy your evening with Pierre?" Eva said, a twinkle in her eye, the merest hint of a smile playing on her lips.

Noah froze. "Just chatting."

"Nothing else?"

Noah felt his heart jump into his throat. He took a breath. "Er, bit of food. Some ... crisps. A Coke. Nothing major. Just catching up. Why?"

Eva shrugged and looked away. "Cool."

"OK, then. So, come on. I'll walk back home with you."

"Go away, Noah."

Noah gasped. "Eva! I am your English host! You must come with me!"

"I'll come back when I'm ready."

"Er, *no*, you'll come back now!"

"Or I'll tell Harry what you did with Pierre."

Noah stopped. "Didn't do anything."

Eva snorted. "Cool."

"OK. OK, then, *fine.* Do as you please."

"Leave the front door unlocked."

"OK."

"And don't wait up for me."

Noah looked her in the eyes – her stare was hard. Defiant. "Fine." Noah turned, plunged his hands in his pockets and walked off, deep in worry about what Eva might or might not have seen. Noah knew he hadn't actively kissed Pierre back, but what might Harry make of a maliciously presented report suggesting the contrary?

Also, was that what Jess Jackson had done, when relaying the information about Harry and Pierre at the cinema? Was it simply the case that Harry had been ambushed too, but had not responded in any meaningful way?

All these thoughts.

All these dilemmas.

He was lost in his own little world, but he still saw her. The lone woman, sitting in a black Vauxhall Astra, parked across the street, pointing a camera in his direction and taking photos.

He instinctively looked over his shoulder. What was so interesting and photo-worthy?

Nothing.

He stared in her direction, a tingle playing on the back of his neck. Something didn't feel right. He hurried off, but he needn't have worried. She started the car and pulled away, disappearing quickly up the road and round the corner, swallowed up into the night.

CHAPTER
TWENTY-TWO

Noah sighed and flicked off his anglepoise lamp, staring at the English homework he'd been unable to complete. Sometimes, being so au fait with *Murder, She Wrote* was a total curse, because there he was, stressing himself out, when there were probably a million and one explanations for the sinister mystery woman in the car taking photos. Like, maybe she was a professional photographer getting new pictures for her exhibition... Maybe it had a "night life" theme, capturing the nocturnal activities of a broad cross-section of people in semi-rural England. Sure, you usually needed some sort of legal waiver to have your image used, but...

Noah moved to the window, staring out across the back garden and into the dark field beyond the fence. The possibilities were gnawing at him, but he must not give in to yet more paranoia. Let's face it: it was probably just a misunderstanding. People take photos all the time. *It doesn't have to mean anything.*

He checked his Casio digital watch. Quarter to nine. Time to see what Pierre was really up to. He got himself together. Grey joggers, his hoodie from Harry (which he would burn if it turned out Harry was at the shed with Pierre – burn with the white-hot, anguished tears that would cascade from his betrayed eyes), espadrilles, a compass, binoculars and his lightweight, packable cagoule – perfect for unpredictable weather, with its tough nylon exterior, adjustable hood and drawstring waist. Finally, he pulled his pièce de résistance from his bottom drawer, last used on a two-day orienteering expedition with the Scouts. Yeah, his three-hole FlexiTog balaclava. Double knit, long neck, ten-gauge acrylic: you couldn't get better.

He was ready.

He would now be able to slip stealthily and unseen towards the school shed, operating in the shadows, off the grid and under the radar.

"What are you doing?" his mother said, standing immediately outside his door when he opened it.

Noah blinked at her through the balaclava. "I'm testing my outdoor wear for durability. I may leave online reviews."

His mother considered him. "Fine," she said eventually. "Don't walk my espadrilles through any mud."

"I won't," he muttered, trying to get past her.

"What was that?"

"I WON'T!" he repeated. "God, can I just go?"

She stepped aside. "Back before ten, Noah, and remember to use a condom."

"Will you please shut up?" he said, already down the stairs and out the front door before she could respond. They were surely both perfectly aware that no one had ever got laid wearing a cagoule and a balaclava.

He darted through the darkness towards the school, swift, stealthy...

"Who's the prick in the balaclava?" some drunk men shouted from across the road.

Noah grimaced and swung a left down Linwood Road. Fewer street lights. Now he really was invisible – a whisper in the wind! He had often imagined himself working undercover for MI5 ... in fact, he was expecting the tap on the shoulder from one of their recruiters any day now. He would be known as "The Ghost" – mysterious, unseen...

"Nice cagoule, Noah!" a pair of Year Nines, *who shouldn't have been out anyway*, said as he walked past them.

Noah ignored them. There was a possibility his cover had been compromised. Too bad. He had to check out what the "asset" was up to in the shed, like it or not. Yeah, "asset". He knew all the words.

Feeling particularly heroic and powerful, he hunkered down behind a bush located a good twenty metres from the shed and checked his watch: 20:56. The moment of truth would soon be upon him. Four minutes. Was that enough time to have a nibble on the Kendal Mint Cake he'd packed? Probably not. He should stay focused. He got his binoculars out and trained them on the door to the shed, heart in his mouth, dreading the sight of Harry appearing at this assignation.

The sound of a car in the distance, growing louder.

A flash of headlights. The crunch of gravel.

A car drove across the access drive towards the shed, stopping by the door and cutting the engine.

Noah swung the binoculars across, but he couldn't see who was driving, past the glare from the headlights. He swung his view back to the shed, and then towards a movement he saw off to the left. Pierre. Walking from the other direction, a holdall hanging from his right hand.

The driver got out of the car.

It was Ms O'Malley.

CHAPTER TWENTY-THREE

Noah watched as Ms O'Malley and Pierre exchanged a few words before Pierre opened his holdall and let her look inside. Ms O'Malley poked around, looking at the contents, looked back up at Pierre and said something Noah couldn't make out, then patted him on the shoulder (*very chummy!*) and led him around the back of her car. Noah couldn't see what they were looking at when she opened the boot, but whatever it was made Pierre laugh and say *"Fantastique!"* – so it must have been fairly good.

Although this was highly curious, Noah's main feeling at that very moment was one of relief. Pierre was not here to meet Harry. There was no secret love affair happening (well, not right now, anyway). The meeting was not about secret shagging, it was something else entirely. That was excellent news.

But now he also felt guilt, for thinking it in the first place. Because of course Harry wouldn't do something like that. Harry was too lovely and loyal and kind to do anything that would hurt Noah. And he also wasn't stupid enough to get involved in some sort of love triangle, nor fickle enough to get together and have a holiday-type romance with a boy who would only be here for a little over a week anyway. Noah could see that now. Why hadn't he before?

He sighed. When he next saw Harry, he *would* explain everything. He *would* tell him the truth. He would explain all his feelings and all his worries, and hope Harry would understand. And because it was Harry, he probably would.

Pierre and Ms O'Malley came back round the front of the car again, Ms O'Malley now jangling a set of keys from her fingers, which she used to unlock the shed. Then Noah watched as they unloaded two wooden crates from the boot of the car and went inside.

What the actual hell?

Noah kept the binoculars trained on the door to the shed, his mouth getting increasingly dry. There were two ways of looking at this situation:

1) Noah had read nearly all of Agatha Christie's novels, so was highly attuned to the possibility of wrongdoing, so much so,

he saw it when none actually existed and lived in a constant state of paranoia which was entirely unjustified. Or...

2) Noah had read nearly all of Agatha Christie's novels and therefore knew wrongdoing when it was staring him in the face – and this was what he had just stumbled across.

OK, there were some facts here. Noah knew that teachers were not supposed to meet up secretly with students. That was how teachers got their photos on news sites, shielding their faces from the camera, or leaving court with a towel over their heads. At least Ms O'Malley wouldn't struggle to find a suitable towel – there were loads of rank, minging ones in the PE lost property basket.

But before he had a chance to consider the clues further, Ms O'Malley had stepped out of the shed, now on her mobile. "Yes! The money has been received. Yes ... from Moscow..."

Moscow...

The money...

And then Noah remembered...

The Russian wire transfer that Noah had seen in her office!

Noah swallowed three times in quick succession. Oh,

the terrible burden of having a curious mind! It would have been better not to witness any of this, to have never tasted the forbidden fruit of Knowledge! Ignorance would have been bliss. Now, like it or not, he knew stuff. He had a responsibility.

Pierre came out of the shed. Ms O'Malley finished the call and took a bundle of cash out of her pocket, which she counted into Pierre's hand. A few more words, and then they nodded at each other and Pierre hurried away – the holdall still hanging from his fingers ... only now, it was clearly empty.

Ms O'Malley locked up the shed and glanced around. Satisfied they had worked undetected, she got in her car and drove back along the access lane, disappearing into the night.

Noah lowered the binoculars and stared towards the shed, shivering as an icy wind prickled the back of his neck: *who exactly was Pierre?*

Noah wanted to know.

And who exactly was Ms O'Malley?

Was she deep undercover for the KGB?

He pushed his way out from the bushes, on to the small path, and pulled his balaclava off as he rejoined the main road. Something was afoot; he could feel it. The clues were there, they always had been, he just couldn't see how they connected. He just—

"Have you got the time?"

"Um, yes, it's—" He looked up, and straight into a familiar face. A woman. *The woman from earlier. Taking photos from her car.* His chest tightened, as he shot a glance at his watch. "Ten past nine," he muttered.

She smiled. "Thanks."

Noah looked at the man she was standing with, tapping away on his phone, on the pavement ... waiting for a cab, maybe? Yes. That was probably it. The woman who had a perfectly good car was probably now waiting for a cab...

"Hope you're not only just leaving school," the woman said, cocking her head towards the sign that pointed to the gates from where Noah had just emerged.

"No, I haven't..." Noah swallowed, flicked his eyes towards her and then away, "I haven't..."

"Been at school?"

"No."

The woman looked at him for a moment, then nodded.

Noah gave a tight smile. "Good evening," he mumbled, hurrying away up the pavement. If he wasn't worried before, or had at least been able to think of a logical explanation, he couldn't now. Twice in one night wasn't coincidence – it was a sign. A sign that something was definitely up. And whether they were undercover police or secret government agents or plain old DANGEROUS UNDERWORLD GANGSTERS, they were on to something ... something in Little Fobbing...

Noah's mind raced as he hotfooted it back home. Dad,

Bambi, Eric, Ms O'Malley and the Russians, and whatever she and Pierre were up to . . . any one of those things.

And how could he be so sure?

That man had been using a mobile phone.

No one asks for the time when it's always on your mobile phone.

CHAPTER TWENTY-FOUR

Noah had taken the shortcut through the PE corridor in the hope of getting to Design Technology early and thereby securing one of the better soldering irons, but he now wished he hadn't. A mob of squirming, wriggling Year Sevens were swarming around the entrance to the changing rooms, and ahead, at the centre of it all, was Jack Hooper.

It was no good. Noah couldn't avoid him for ever. He was going to have to bite the bullet. Noah scuttled up to the boy. "Jack—"

"Too late. Found another source," Jack said, turning away from Noah.

"What? Who?"

"Can't reveal that."

Noah nodded, the tension in his shoulders subsiding. "Well, I wish you well, Jack." *Some other sucker can make a loss selling it to you.* Noah held out a hand to shake with Jack. "Good luck."

Jack stared at Noah's hand and shook his head. "No."

"What do you mean?"

An evil grin played across Jack's mouth as he stepped in close. "This is my patch now. There's not room for both of us, so you need to back right off."

"Look, I'm not going to be told what I can and can't do by – AH!" Noah gasped as Jack somehow pushed him face first into a Year Nine display entitled "How to Spot Bullying" on the corridor wall. "Jack – no! Please!" Noah said as Jack started pulling Noah's rucksack off. "No! You're being too rough! Ow! AHH! Stop!" Two lackeys pinned a squirming Noah still whilst Jack rifled through his bag.

"Nice! A Laughing Cow cheese triangle!" Jack said, triumphantly holding it aloft.

The lackeys released him, and Noah turned and brushed himself down. "That's part of my lunch, Jack. That's *my* Laughing Cow triangle. Put it back."

"Point is," Jack said, keeping his eyes fixed on Noah as he carefully peeled back the foil wrapper, "things will get a whole lot worse for you unless you agree to my demands and stop selling the shake. My territory, my rules." Jack stepped closer to a quivering Noah, waving the naked soft-cheese triangle under his nose. "Get me?"

"You won't get away with this!" Noah hissed.

"Oh," Jack said, smearing the Laughing Cow triangle gently over Noah's lips, nose and cheeks, "I think I will. I think you'll do exactly what's right. In the end." Jack stepped back and tutted. "Oh, Noah, you've got cheese all over your face. Cheese Face!"

"Shut up."

"Cheese Face! Cheese Face!" Jack started chanting.

"Jack, this isn't—"

But Jack's obvious popularity and influence meant the other Year Sevens started joining in the chant. "CHEESE FACE! CHEESE FACE!"

"SILENCE! ALL OF YOU!" It was Ms O'Malley – red and furious. "Grimes!" she said, spotting him. "What sort of message does it send our youngest students if you are playing with your food, like some sort of *pig*? Go and get cleaned up and think about your actions."

Noah glared at Ms O'Malley and then at Jack, who gave him the sweetest smile. "Yeah, that's really immature, Noah! You shouldn't waste food when there are people less fortunate than us who don't have enough to eat."

"Exactly right, Jack!" Ms O'Malley said. "Two merit marks for showing maturity and consideration."

Noah stomped off down the corridor, fists clenched, now forced to make a detour to the boys' toilets, dreams of the best soldering iron in tatters. How was he going to secure the funds for Gran's dream care home now? How dare Jack behave like this! How dare the little shit screw him over! How dare—

"You need to show kids like that who's boss!"

Noah turned as Connor strolled up to him. Huh. Easy for Connor to say. Connor was tall and packed a healthy nine-and-a-half stone of toned muscle in his uniform that somehow looked fashionable and cool on him. No one would mess with him.

Connor put his arm across Noah's shoulders. "How do you think you could do that, Noah?"

"Advanced weaponry?" Noah shrugged.

Connor shook his head. "Nah, carrying that sort of shit will get you arrested. You gotta stop them from even engaging; you've got to intimidate them with how you look."

"What, like, being bigger and stronger, you mean?"

"Sure." Connor nodded. "And hey, added bonus, bet Harry wouldn't complain either!"

"Huh," Noah said, flicking his eyes to the floor.

"I know," Connor said. "Big mountain to climb, right? Lots of hours in the gym, and gym sucks, right?"

"Pretty much," Noah agreed.

Connor sighed and shook his head. "Unless!" He jumped back, an amazing idea suddenly forming in his head. "Unless there's an easier way! A way to get bigger ... without so much effort..."

Noah looked up sharply. Surely this wasn't going the way he thought it was?! "What like?"

"Like this!" Connor said, whipping his rucksack off his back and pulling out a tub of protein shake. "Now, normally this retails at thirty quid a tub, but—"

Noah held his hand up. "Connor, I know about this. I'm a rep."

"A rep?" Connor spluttered. "This is my patch, mate! You back off and sell somewhere else!"

"I wasn't told anything about areas!" Noah protested.

"Well, you have been now." Connor shook his head and turned back down the corridor. "Jesus," Noah heard him mutter.

This was just brilliant. Who else was a rep for this sodding shake? His gran? Sophie in Milton Keynes? The Queen of bloody England?!

"Noah?"

"Not now, Harry!" Noah snapped.

"Why have you got cheese all over your—"

"BECAUSE I JUST HAVE, OK?!"

Harry looked at him with puppy-dog eyes. Eyes that seemed to be pleading, *don't be cross with me.* "Do you want a tissue?"

"Yes, please," Noah muttered.

Harry pulled one from a pack in his blazer pocket and handed it to Noah. "Um, I wanted to apologize for the whole quiz thing, so ... here I am. Saying sorry. I was wrong to even think the club was a good idea – I know how hard you've worked on the quiz and it was thoughtless of me. Sorry, Noah." Harry looked at him and chewed his lip. "And I only mentioned to Pierre that you had to be careful with cash because he was asking why you didn't want to come out and do stuff. So, again, I'm sorry."

"Well, I wish you hadn't, Haz. It's awful having no money. It's a horrible thing. I like nice things – you know I do. I like posh food and fancy restaurants. Well, I like the *idea* of them anyway, I've never actually been to any. I suppose it's stupid, really. There are plenty of people worse off."

Harry nodded. "I know. But I'm sorry for saying anything to Pierre. It's none of his business, and I didn't think."

"OK, well, I'm sorry too. For overreacting and ... calling you a wank weasel."

"That *was* a mean thing to call me," Harry said.

"Heat of the moment, Haz," Noah said. "But take comfort that I didn't call you a fap rat or a no-cock peacock, because they're worse, really."

Harry chuckled, took hold of the lapels of Noah's blazer and pecked him on the lips.

Noah flinched. "*Haz*. Not in the corridor!"

Harry nodded. "Not in school, sure. But we're OK?"

"We're OK," Noah said. "Look, it's Friday, so why don't you come round tonight? We'll..."

"Do something," Harry smiled.

Noah tried to read Harry's face, but there was no

cheeky raised eyebrow or dirty smirk, it was just open and innocent.

"Huh. Do something, yeah," Noah said.

"THE GODDAM THIEVING BASTARD FROM HELL!"

Noah watched in alarm as Gran pulled the final drawer of her bedside table out and emptied the contents all over her bedroom floor.

"SEE!" she said. "GONE! STOLEN!"

"What is, Gran?" Noah said, looking around at the utter chaos of the room. Everything had been turned upside down. Gran's clothes from her wardrobe were all over the floor. The chest of drawers – ransacked. Even the flowers that Eric had brought her the other day were out of the vase and strewn over the carpet.

"Thieving bastard, no-good crook!" Gran was muttering.

"Gran, what's wrong?"

"Always trying to screw me over!"

"Gran?"

"Never done an honest thing his entire sorry life!"

Noah edged into the room, feeling the crunch of something under his foot as he did so. He gingerly lifted his foot to find the fragments of a porcelain mouse, dressed up in an apron.

"Don't worry about it," Gran said. "Piece of shit

anyway. Who wants a mouse dressed up like a cook? Fucking nonsense."

"Is everything OK, Gran?" Noah asked, shifting a scented lavender pincushion out of the way and perching on the edge of the bed.

"No, Noah, everything is *not* OK. My tiara. It's gone."

"You mean..."

"Yes, Noah. The tiara with the precious diamonds set in it! The one you used to play with. The one meant for your inheritance. That one!"

"But ... really? How can you be sure?"

"Because I was looking for the tiara and now it's gone! How do you think I know?!"

Noah sighed. "OK, look, could you have put it somewhere different?"

"No."

"Where did you last have it?"

"No idea."

"Did you have it out recently?"

Gran shrugged. "I don't know, Noah. All I do know is it's no longer in the place I always keep it."

Noah nodded. He understood Gran was upset and he would have to play along because she wouldn't be told otherwise, but the fact remained: the tiara and the "diamonds" were cheap metal and glass tat that nobody would want to steal, and the story about the Danish princess: bullshit. In all honesty, this was a distraction

Noah didn't need right now. "OK, well, I'll try to find it for you, Gran."

"Well, I'll give you your first clue!" she said.

"Uh-huh?"

"Try your no-good thieving excuse for a father!"

"OK, right, I will."

"He's behind all this! He's the reason I'm in this GODDAM HOME to begin with! Wanting to get rid of me! Wanting to live in my house with his new fancy woman!"

"Do you mean my mother?"

"I love you, Peanut, but that woman is a catastrophe!"

Noah shrugged. Even with her dementia, Gran was sometimes incredibly lucid.

"I'll do my best, Gran."

Gran slumped down in her chair and released a gigantic and incredibly loud fart. Noah screwed his face up in disgust.

"Oh, I'm so upset, I can't even laugh at this," Gran said, pulling a whoopee cushion out from underneath her. "It was a practical joke I'd set up for Dickie." She slung the whoopee cushion on the floor with the rest of the mess. "I'm reduced to things like this to provide some form of amusement in this HELLHOLE."

They sat in silence for a few moments.

"SERVICE!" Gran shouted. "What do you have to do to get a Scotch on the rocks around here?!"

Noah leaned forward. "See, the thing is, Gran—" He stopped because she was crying. "Oh ... Gran. Gran, it'll be OK, I promise."

He didn't know what to say. Or do. He'd never seen Gran cry before. He had cried about a billion times in front of her, when he was little. And she would always be there with a plaster, a comforting hug and usually some sort of confectionary to help cheer him up. He got up and crouched down by the side of her chair, holding her frail hand in his. "I'll get it back, Gran. Honest, I will."

Gran shook her head. "Everything's going, Peanut. I'm losing it all, aren't I?"

"No, Gran, you're not. You're..." He didn't want to say "you're fine" because she wasn't "fine" and he wasn't going to lie to her. She deserved more than that. "You're doing great, Gran. Me and you – we're a team."

She laced her fingers between his and held them tightly. "You'll help me, Peanut, won't you? When I forget things... When... Always come and see me, won't you? Even if I... Because one day, maybe I won't remember... And I don't want to lose you. Not ever, Peanut. *Noah*."

"You won't lose me, Gran," he said, swallowing hard, blinking the tears back. This was all the more reason why Gran needed to be in Kingfisher Meadows. They could help her. Help her remember, hold on longer. He had to make it happen. In the meantime, he would just have to do what he could to keep her happy. "And I'll get your tiara back."

"What tiara?"

"The one that…" Noah sighed. "It doesn't matter."

Gran shrugged, looking around the room. "They don't clean these rooms properly. Bloody disgrace. The staff are so lazy, you wouldn't believe it."

"Sure." Noah nodded.

Gran was the only person who had believed in him all these years. It was Gran who cheered loudest whenever Noah had won a prize at school. It was Gran who had paid for him to go on the residential trip to France, or to attend Scouts. And when he was being bullied, and thought he was worthless and useless, it was Gran who talked him round and gave him the confidence to believe in himself. And now it was his turn to believe in her and do something for *her*.

He glanced up at her. She looked sad. Eyes far away, someplace else. He needed to change the subject, cheer her up. "So, Gran, let me ask you. If I said to you 'secret meeting at night, Russian money transfers, mysterious holdalls and crates' what would you say?"

Gran's eyes lit up. "That's something juicy!"

"Something bad?" Noah said.

"Well, almost definitely. Almost definitely!" Gran said. "Either that or you've been reading a Hardy Boys adventure. Which is it?"

"I think something bad's afoot — I just don't know what yet. Can't piece it together."

"The clues are always there — you just have to look."

"I know, Gran. I just don't know what I'm looking for."

Gran shrugged, a small smile playing on her lips. "I don't know. Everyone's hiding something, I suppose." She leaned forward. "What about you, Peanut? What are you hiding?"

"Nothing."

"I don't believe you."

"I let Pierre kiss me."

The words hung in the air as Gran took a deep breath and sat back in the chair. "Well, well," she said.

"I didn't ask him to, but I may have inadvertently encouraged him."

"Because you thought you had something to be jealous of."

"Well ... it's true, I was worried that Pierre and Harry might be getting it on."

"And yet ... they weren't."

"I don't know. I guess not."

Gran nodded, deep in thought. "Like in *Othello*," Gran said after a bit. "Jealousy destroys all in the end."

Noah's mouth went dry. "That can't happen. I need to tell Harry and sort it out." He looked at Gran for some indication that she thought that might work. Her face was neutral. "I mean, would that be a good idea?"

"Who knows?" Gran said.

"You think he might take it badly?"

"Generally speaking, people you are seeing romantically don't take it well when you tell them you've kissed someone else. How would you take it if Harry told you he'd kissed Pierre?"

"Well, I wouldn't like it, but the point is, I didn't kiss him. He kissed me!"

"It's a subtle difference."

"But—"

"Would you call it an assault?"

"No."

"Then a kiss is a kiss."

"But—"

"The point is, the conditions of a kiss happening were in place. That's true, isn't it, Noah?"

Noah thought about it. The picnic, the lantern . . . the damn melted cheese. Yes, the conditions for a kiss were in place.

"I don't deserve someone as nice as Harry," Noah said, surprised to hear himself saying his thoughts out loud.

Gran heaved herself up and came to sit next to him on the bed, putting an arm across his shoulder and pulling him into her. "Now, less of that sort of talk. You deserve to be as happy as anyone else, Noah. Which isn't necessarily that happy, truth be told, but you deserve a shot at it, like anyone. Listen, it's not easy. Nothing in life is. Do your best and try not to screw up too much, that's what I always say. Sometimes we all make mistakes. But the biggest one you appear to be making right now is believing you're not worthy. He likes you, Noah. He's told you that. Why would he lie?"

"Will he always like me, though? Or will it just be until someone better comes along?"

"There is no one *better*, Noah. No one will ever be like you. There is only *different*. And in the future, everything is different. So you can choose to live in the anxious misery of what might be, or you can choose the glorious comfort of the here and now. I would pick the now. Tomorrow could be anything."

Noah nodded. "OK, Gran."

"Now find my tiara."

Noah ambled towards the exit, mulling over Gran's words. She was, as ever, right. Tomorrow could indeed bring anything. But right now, Harry loved him. And he loved Harry. What was the point in worrying about what might be?

Noah walked up to the small desk where the visitors' signing-in book was and jotted down his leaving time. His eyes roamed across the list of visitors over the last few days.

And then he froze, a tingle running up his spine.

A name that should not have been there. That had no business being there.

Pierre Victoire.

CHAPTER TWENTY-FIVE

For once, the house was empty. No Eric, no Dad, no Mother . . . just Mick, sitting on the sofa like it was *his* sofa, painting his nails, feet in a portable electric foot spa and a mobile phone crooked between his shoulder and neck. "Babes, that is such amazeballs news!" Mick was saying, confusingly using Bambi's voice.

Noah coughed and crossed his arms, waiting for Mick to finish.

"Bambi's back and she's gonna be bigger than ever before!"

Noah rolled his eyes and snorted. Mick looked up at him.

"I've gotta go, babe," Mick said, narrowing his eyes at Noah.

"Yes, you have," Noah said, under his breath.

"Love you lots, and Bambi's gonna see you tomoz!"

Mick released the phone and it dropped on to the sofa. He hadn't even pressed the "end call" button – relying on the other person to make sure they had ended the call. *Selfish*, Noah considered. Making others do everything. Relying on their charity and hard work.

"Good news, babe!" Mick said. "Bambi's show in the big smoke is already nearly half sold out!"

Noah raised an eyebrow. "Oh?"

"And now my flyers have arrived, that number's only gonna go up." He extended his arms, like some sort of showgirl. "London, babe! Bambi's doin' what she does best – headin' south!"

Noah wrinkled his nose. Was that some sort of attempt at innuendo? "Well. Congratulations."

"You'll miss Bambi when she's gone!"

"Yeah," Noah said, severely doubting it. "Look, when exactly are you going?"

"Soon."

"Yes, but is it *quite* soon? Like, in the next hour? Or now?"

Mick shook his head. "You and I have never seen eye to eye."

"Well, maybe that's because when I first met you, as a tender and innocent thirteen-year-old, we were eye to gigantic breasts. It scarred me, and the legacy lives on."

"Just a bit of fun, babes."

"Not fun!" Noah said. "And I also don't appreciate how everything you say and do is laced with sexual references and innuendo. It's tiresome."

Mick stepped out of the foot spa, wet feet directly on to the carpet, not a towel in sight. "Well, I'll be out of your hair soon. If Bambi can make the show tomorrow a hit, then there might be more, thanks to my old pals Milly Feuille and Cherry Macaroon! They've got an in with one of the top promoters, see? I'm gonna be the talk of Soho!" He draped a pashmina around his shoulders, whisking out of the room.

"OK. Bye then."

Mick turned back at the door, eyes full of tragedy. "You know, I tried with you, Noah." And he swept out of the room.

Good, Noah thought. Now he had the house to himself.

Noah lit a few tea lights and decanted a grab bag of Skittles into a soup bowl. He wanted things to be nice for Harry. They would talk, and Noah would explain, with full and total honesty, what had been happening in his head over the last week, and how this had accidentally culminated in Pierre kissing him, a trip to the shed to spy, and running into some mysterious agents/police/gangsters because something BAD and WEIRD was happening in Little Fobbing that probably involved MURDER and STABBING and GOVERNMENT COVER-UPS AT THE HIGHEST LEVEL.

And then, maybe, they could do some kissing.

"I just want to put something out there," Harry said, leaning back against one of the sofa cushions and throwing a handful of Skittles in his mouth. He chewed for a bit. "If you're thinking we might play 3D Cluedo, I'm not sure I've got the stamina for it."

"We'll just have a relaxed evening," Noah said. *If you can call revealing to your boyfriend you've accidentally kissed another boy "relaxing".*

"Just chill?"

"Chill, chill, chill. So..." Noah said, immediately trailing off, because despite having planned this next bit, he was now beset with doubts about it. This was actually very tricky when the person concerned was sitting right next to you. There didn't seem to be any good-sounding method of delivery. Example:

1) "Harry, Pierre kissed me." (Sounded like it was a surprise, but not unwelcome.)

2) "Harry, there was a kiss with Pierre that I was not expecting, and I didn't participate as such, my lips were just in the wrong place at the wrong time." (And yet, I didn't stop him! Why not?)

3)   "Harry, I had consumed a glass of red wine and some cheese and was so 'wasted' that before I knew what was happening, Pierre had kissed me." (Sounds too romantic in the lead-up to the kiss and that I would kiss anyone if plied with any sort of food and drink.)

So, there were a few options Noah could go for, but—

"I want to tell you something," Harry said.

Arse. He really needed to think more quickly, so he could get in there first with stuff. "OK, fine," Noah said.

"Pierre made a pass at me."

Noah's eyes nearly popped out. "No way! Me too!"

"What? No way!"

"Yeah! But, I mean – he tried to kiss you? When?" Noah swallowed back the sour taste in his mouth. Harry and Pierre. Were his fears justified after all? He crossed his arms over his stomach and looked down at the floor – if Harry was about to tell him something bad, he hoped he would just say it quickly.

"At the cinema," Harry said. "He started leaning into me and getting, you know, a bit too close? And I could just tell, you know, like you can, that he was going to try and kiss me. Could just … feel it in the air, right?"

"Uh-huh."

"So, totally honest, before he did, I just turned to him and said, 'You know I'm with Noah, right?'"

Noah looked up at him. "You did?"

"Yes, of course I did!" Harry said. "What did you think I was going to do? Let him kiss me? That's not really how this whole boyfriend thing works, Noah. Anyway, he made out like he was all surprised, but I knew he wasn't. You gotta watch him, that's for sure. I wasn't sure whether to tell you, 'cause nothing actually happened and I knew you'd freak out a bit, but then when you started acting weird I wondered if someone had told you something ... like, maybe someone saw us at the cinema?"

"Huh. Sure."

"Like, Jess Jackson?"

Noah nodded. "Yeah, she did mention it, Haz."

"Sure," Harry said, rolling his eyes. "'Course she did. And bigged it up no end to you, I'll bet."

"I guess."

"So, anyway, that's the truth and you've got nothing to be jealous of because I would never do that to you." Harry kissed Noah on the cheek. "So he tried it on with you too, huh?"

Noah swallowed. "Um, a bit, yeah."

"When?"

"Um, you know, when he came round last night, you know, to apologize to me, with the picnic."

Harry narrowed his eyes. "Picnic?"

"He brought a ... a picnic. Little ... picnic?"

Harry looked blank.

"He said you knew about the picnic."

"I did *not* know about the picnic," Harry said. "What sort of picnic?"

Noah swallowed again. "Oh, just the usual … some food in a basket."

"Crisps? Egg sandwiches, that sort of thing?"

"I mean, essentially, that's what we were dealing with. Some … old bread, you know … a bit of dry cheese … maybe a platter of cured meats, I can't really remember."

"A platter of cured meats!"

Noah shrugged. "I mean, nothing much. Some hams, I guess."

"Hams! Wow, he was really going for it, then!"

"I mean, I assumed it was just his way of apologizing to me for that stuff about my quiz night. That's what I assumed. I would not have gone otherwise. No way. I've got his number too, Haz. You gotta watch him."

Harry sighed. "God. You really have. So, some bread, some cheese, a platter of cured meats… What happened next?"

"Um, well … let me think now…" Noah said, blinking rapidly. "So, there was some talking about stuff, blah, blah … bit of food, nibble, nibble, and then he … he…"

"He tried to kiss you," Harry said.

"Mmm."

"Wow."

"I know, right?"

"What did he say when you told him?"

Noah nodded. "Told him, yes. He was ... sad ... but happy that ... our relationship was so strong that things like that, like errant kissing with random boys, just wouldn't happen."

Harry shook his head. "Sneaky," he said.

"So, so sneaky," Noah agreed, trying to breathe normally. Shit, shit, shitty, shit. Now he'd gone and lied. No, not lied as such. Omitted a detail. A ... crucial detail. How had this happened? Was it because Harry was a trustworthy, reliable, entirely *sorted* type of person who never did the wrong thing, and Noah was a weak, pathetic, jealous liar who was two-faced and horrible? Oh God, it was!

"Look, hey," Harry said, putting his hand on Noah's leg again. "Don't feel bad about it. I know you only went on the picnic to be polite and wouldn't have been expecting him to pull a stunt like this."

Noah managed a half smile. That, at least, was true.

"There's always gonna be people who have their eye on you," Harry said, leaning in and kissing Noah softly. "I'm a lucky guy. You're a catch."

Noah felt the tingle still on his lips. "Haz, don't be silly. I'm not a catch. You're the catch. I seriously thought..." Noah put his head down. "I did actually think you liked Pierre."

"I could never like someone like Pierre."

"But why not? He's very good-looking. He's got all the moves."

"He's a player. And there's something about him that... I dunno, there's just something. And I don't want that. I want someone I can trust. Someone I can properly fall in love with. Someone I *have* fallen in love with."

Despite his best efforts, Noah's bottom lip started to wobble. "Huh."

Harry leaned closer in and kissed Noah again. "You're so sweet. And look, something else too. There's no rush for us to do stuff, like... Well, you know what I mean. It's not about that. You know? It happens when it happens."

Noah pressed his forehead against Harry's. "OK. Thanks."

Harry chuckled. "You don't have to thank me. And, I mean, I do want to. Sometime. When it's right. I want... I just want to be close to you, Noah. In whatever way that you're happy with, but in a way that isn't like what you have with anyone else. It doesn't have to mean sex. It can mean like now. Just this. Sitting here, cuddling. I don't mind. Why are you crying?"

He was. He wiped away the stupid tears that were part happiness, part guilt, part sadness that Harry was everything Noah wasn't, and Noah wasn't remotely worthy of this beautiful, kind, adorable boy's love. "I love you," Noah managed to mutter, completely choked up.

Harry smiled. "I love you too." He kissed Noah again

and wiped the last little tear away with his thumb. "Now cheer up because everything's good and pretty much perfect, so there's nothing to be sad about."

Noah smiled, while his heart sank into his stomach. Why couldn't he enjoy a single, pure moment of happiness? Maybe if he hadn't been such an idiot, he would have.

He had planned to say more about Pierre. He had been going to tell Harry about the overheard conversation in the toilets, the spying mission to the shed, and Pierre's strange and secret meeting with Ms O'Malley, all of it. But he didn't want to now. He couldn't. Harry would see how little Noah trusted him.

And he didn't want to spend another moment thinking about, or talking about, bloody Pierre. He just wanted him gone and forgotten. And then Noah and Harry could get on with their lives and maybe, just maybe, everything really would be OK.

"Do you want to watch some telly?" Noah suggested. "I recorded an episode the other day. It's a good one."

"Is Jessica invited to see an old friend whilst on a book tour, and then encounters a murder that the police bizarrely can't solve?" Harry asked.

"Yeah! I wonder who did it?"

"Probably one of the minor characters who doesn't get much screen time initially."

"Stop. Spoiling. *Murder, She Wrote*," Noah said, jabbing Harry in the thigh with his index finger.

Harry laughed. "Go on, whack it on!"

"I'm whacking it on," Noah said, pointing the remote at the Sky box.

Harry smiled, put his arm around him, and pulled Noah towards him, so they were nestled into one another.

"Ooh, look," Noah said. "Some bad guys are meeting in a shadowy alleyway! I wonder what's happening!"

Harry chuckled. "They're setting up the red herring part of the plot."

"*Harry*," Noah warned.

"Sorry, Noah," Harry said, staring at him.

Noah flicked his eyes to the side to look at Harry and then back at the TV again. Then to the side again. "Why are you ... look at the TV, Harry, not at me, you'll miss vital clues!"

"I want to look at you, though."

"Yes, but look! See?! That character has literally just threatened to *kill* the other man! He's as good as admitted it!"

Harry kissed the side of Noah's neck and worked his hand up underneath Noah's hoodie and T-shirt. "Oh, goodness!" Noah said. "In front of Jessica, though?"

Harry stroked Noah's tummy. "Jessica's cool with it."

"But—"

"Nothing's happening, Noah. All I'm doing is stroking your little tummy."

"Uh-huh," Noah muttered, feeling like he might

explode with every exquisite touch and stroke of Harry's fingers, his stomach muscles twitching in little spasms of pleasure. He hoped Harry wouldn't be put off by his obvious lack of abs. "Um . . . oh gosh. . . There's a . . . on the screen now. . . Jessica is meeting her friend and. . ." Noah swallowed as Harry nuzzled into Noah's neck again and then put his other hand behind Noah's head and pulled him into a kiss which was TOTALLY CRAZY right in front of Mrs F, but Harry was probably right, she wouldn't mind and would probably fully approve. And this was nice. So nice. Somehow, now that Harry had said it didn't matter if they actually did anything or not, the usual sense of panic hadn't appeared. "Oh God, I really like you, Harry." Noah pulled away, breathless. "You make me very happy in all sorts of wonderful places."

Harry was still looking at him, breathing heavily.

"Are you OK, Haz? Are you having an asthma attack?"

Harry chuckled. "Idiot."

"Then what?"

Harry fixed Noah with a stare. There it was. You *could* totally tell when something was going to happen with another person. And it totally was now. Words weren't necessary. Noah stared back, swallowed. He wanted to. And he also didn't want to. He didn't know why he was suddenly scared, but he was. What was there to be afraid of? It was Harry. And he loved Harry. Harry had said it was OK to wait – fine. But he would want to do stuff at some point. It couldn't be avoided for ever. The clock was ticking. A timer. Counting down to a ... great, big ... sex bomb.

Noah's phone chirped.

And again.

And again.

At least it broke the moment, so that was good.

And when Noah picked his mobile up, that really was the *only* good part.

CHAPTER
TWENTY-SIX

The messages were from Eric: **Catch us if you can!**

And then: **Me and Dad have the tiara!**

And presumably, just so Noah was totally clear, a picture of said tiara.

Gran's tiara. Noah snorted and shook his head. Seriously?! A crappy fake diamond heist? Were Dad and Eric really so stupid that they thought that thing was worth anything? Normally, if Eric and Dad wanted to waste their time on some stupid scheme, he would have let them. But he'd made a promise to Gran. Noah texted back:

Dear Eric, Thank you for your kind message. How interesting that you and Father have stolen an item of Gran's... My, how thoughtful of you to take an item of sentimental value from a poor old lady with dementia – I must remember to put

you both forward for an OBE for services to humanity. It's of no actual value, but it is to her. Bring it back. Kind regards, Noah Grimes.

"Everything OK?" Harry said.

Noah smiled. "Everything is fine and dandy! Would you like to resume some low-level petting?"

"Yeah." Harry shrugged. "Always up for low-level petting."

Noah's phone chirped. "Sorry," he said, batting Harry away. "I just have to address this small matter, then petting can resume." He glanced down.

Eric: **Cool, cool. Just so you know, the attached image is a screenshot from last week's Antiques Roadshow. Note the special hallmark that matches the one on Gran's. The tiara itself is indeed pretty worthless. But the diamonds in it are valued at twenty grand. Tell me, are you still feeling quite so smug, jackass?**

Noah pursed his lips and opened the image. There was Fiona Bruce, grinning next to a frumpy old man. Noah enlarged the image with his fingertips and froze.

Oh.

Oh my God.

There was Gran's tiara. OK, not exactly, it had slightly different design, but it was really, really close, and the hallmark was definitely as Noah remembered. Noah grabbed the Sky remote, frantically pressing the buttons until the episode that his dad had recorded came up, and

Noah was able to fast forward to the final five minutes – Fiona Bruce and some jewellery expert, and a plan hatched by a Danish princess to smuggle twenty valuable diamonds out of the country so she could start a new life. The story matched the one Gran had told him exactly – the two tiaras, the plan to set the valuable diamonds in the worthless metal, so no one would suspect, and the theft from the jeweller's workshop – only a fairy godmother and some clever mice were not involved, as it turned out. Fiona Bruce's final words: "We've found one tiara, but the other is still out there somewhere – probably posing as another piece of costume jewellery. So do check those toy boxes and backs of wardrobes, because, who knows, you too could be sitting on a goldmine."

The credits began to roll, Noah staring in disbelief at the screen.

Ten diamonds. Twenty thousand English pounds. The sort of money that could solve a lot of problems. The sort of money that could secure Gran a place in Kingfisher Meadows. And, of course, the sort of money that a couple of ne'er-do-wells like Dad and Eric could use for all manner of shady schemes – which was presumably exactly what they were thinking.

"Noah?" Harry said. "Are you sure you're OK?"

Noah nodded. "We'll maybe attempt some mild frottage in a minute," he said absent-mindedly.

"*What?!*"

"What?"

"What did you just say?" Harry said.

"Harry. There's a matter. A thing. A crisis. I don't know what to do."

"Right..."

Noah relayed the tale as efficiently as he could, conscious that every second wasted was time that could be spent ... well, what? He didn't know. Getting the tiara back? How would he even do that?

"You're telling me that stupid cheap tiara you used to play dress-up with is actually *real?*" Harry said.

"You also dressed up," Noah corrected him. "And yes. Apparently it is real, which means it's not stupid or cheap."

"So, call the police."

"I can't do that. The police are still investigating my dad for the shit he got mixed up with the Spanish timeshare apartments. If there's anything else, that'll be it."

Noah stared into the middle distance, thinking. Were the mysterious strangers he'd seen around town already on to his dad? Had they somehow been tipped off? Was—

Noah's phone chirped again, breaking his thoughts.

Would have thought a smart guy like you would have been on to us by now!

Noah scowled and hammered out a reply: **Bring it back at once, Eric. You are BREAKING THE LAW!**

Eric: **No can do. Plan is in motion. Shame you were too slow to stop us. Too busy being gay with Harry, I guess?**

Noah: **No that's not true. We have only been talking not that it's any of your business. You will not get away with this!**

Eric: **Oooh. Really scared. Please don't make any more scary threats. Might do a classic "you" and piss my pants.**

Noah (furiously): **Right, that's it! Just wait! Also, FYI, it's not cool to make fun of someone who had a BLADDER INFECTION I don't know how many times I have to say.**

Noah slammed his phone back down on the table. "He's damn well baiting me! He's enjoying this! He's such a little shit. Perfectly happy to make off with Gran's tiara, without thinking how she might need the money! I've got to get it back, Haz. I've got to. For Gran."

"OK, that's fine," Harry said, "but they could be literally anywhere. I mean, they're planning on selling it, I suppose?"

Noah shook his head. "Highly unlikely they'd try to sell the whole thing, as is – it would be too identifiable if it's reported stolen. Too risky. They'll just take the diamonds out and sell them separately, since they're the valuable bit."

"Well, there's a jeweller's in Little Fobbing, should we go there?" Harry said.

Noah got up and started pacing. "No, they'll take the diamonds out of the area. That way, they'll arouse less suspicion. Plus, Dad will need one of his dodgy contacts to sell them on their behalf. Someone who doesn't ask too many questions, or require documentation."

Harry actually looked impressed, a smile creeping across his face.

"What?" Noah demanded.

"Nothing. You're just quite sexy when you say things about stuff you know."

"Well, you didn't say that when I gave my presentation about wind farms, and I know quite a lot about them!"

"Yeah, but this is *criminal* underworld stuff. It's ... I dunno, naughty, isn't it?"

"Harry, there's nothing sexy about being a crook. It's bad and wrong. And as non-existent God is my witness, I shall get Eric banged up in a borstal for bad boys for this. That's where he belongs!" Noah smacked his fist against his other palm. "Anyway, that's all for later. For now, we must take action."

"All right, *Velma*, I'm all yours."

"Why am I Velma?"

"From Scooby—"

"I know what you're referring to!" Noah said. "I just always saw myself more as Fred."

"Oh, of course. The gay one."

Noah gasped. "Fred's not gay, is he?"

"Noah, he wears a *cravat*!"

"Well, I don't think cravats are indicators of sexuality! They're sophisticated! And ... argh! We don't have time for this! We can talk it through later. What shall we do? Phone Eric?"

Harry laughed. "Yes, because he'll definitely pick up and definitely tell you exactly where he is."

"Sarcasm doesn't suit you, Harry."

"Althoooough..." Harry continued, "he's just texted you, so his phone is *on*, which means, if you can access the 'find phone' function on his laptop, we should get his approximate location."

Noah slapped Harry on the back. "Brilliant! Brilliant! I mean, the idea of touching his laptop is rather *eww*, because we all know what its primary function is, but I guess with some rubber gloves on we could give it a go?" Noah was already up the stairs, retrieving Eric's laptop from the cupboard in his parents' bedroom where he left it between visits, along with some disposable plastic gloves from his mother's hair-dyeing supplies. He gingerly bought everything back through to the lounge. "Here it is. The things this poor screen will have displayed!"

"Open her up."

Noah snapped on the gloves and did so, the password box immediately flashing up. Noah looked up at Harry. "Thoughts?"

"OK, put yourself in Eric's head."

"Grim," Noah said. "But OK."

"What comes to mind?"

"Harry, let's avoid using words like 'come' when we're talking about Eric's laptop."

"Maybe that is the password!"

"What, *come*? Are you serious?"

"Try it."

"No! We'll only have three attempts and we can't waste one on trying 'come'."

"I think we should try come."

Noah looked up sharply, straight into Harry's grinning face. "Right, fine, OK, we'll try 'come'. Here we go. C-O-M..."

"Wait!" Harry said. "He'll spell it 'c-u-m', you know, the *porn* way."

Noah swallowed and typed it in. The little password box shook. *Incorrect.*

"Well, that's two attempts left. I mean, this is pointless. He's not going to have made it easy," Noah sighed. "Think, damn it!"

Harry shifted on the sofa. "Sorry, I'm trying to focus."

"OK, well, good. That's good. I'll be honest, Haz, I'm not sure all this talk of 'porn' and 'come' is helpful. I think it's *unhelpful*. It's distracting, because all it makes you think about is ... well, you know..."

"Right," Harry muttered.

"OK, well—"

"So," Harry said.

"OK."

"So..."

"All right, then." Noah nodded. "OK, so maybe we go back to just one, final, *quick* bit of kissing first, OK? Just to put a full stop on the events. Is that—"

Harry was already locked on to Noah's lips before he could get to the end of the sentence. Harry really was a tremendously good kisser. And Noah was pretty sure he was getting better at it too.

"Show me that pic again!" Harry said, suddenly breaking away. "The one Eric just sent of the tiara."

Noah pulled his phone from his pocket and handed it over. "It's definitely Gran's tiara," he said.

Harry shook his head, fingers enlarging the photo. "It's not that. Look." Harry handed the phone across, the screen zoomed in on the background of the photo. "What do you see?"

"Looks like a menu," Noah said. "So, this photo was taken in some sort of restaurant, specifically –" Noah zoomed in a little more "– an establishment calling itself 'Route 66', strapline, 'The All-American Dining Experience'."

Harry nodded, eagerly. "I know that place! It's on the A46, just south of Newark. We went there once on our way back from Nottingham – they do amazing milkshakes with totally batshit-crazy toppings. They must have stopped off there for some food, but it's a start. Maybe someone there will have seen them – a waitress or something."

"Ohhhh. You're good. That's good," Noah said.

Harry's smile grew wider. "Are we going to follow them?! Like, in a movie?"

"A *film*, Harry. And, well, yes. Yes, we are, I just don't know quite how. If only one of us were seventeen and had a vehicle."

"It's very sexy. The chase, I mean, not our inability to drive."

Noah blushed. "Don't be mentioning sex again because we haven't got time for any more kissing or heavy petting even though..." Noah checked his Casio digital watch and set the timer. "I mean, maybe just, like, a minute?"

"Sounds good," Harry said, plunging right in, so Noah fell back against the sofa arm, Harry on top of him.

Sixty seconds of epic-ness followed, which Noah found highly enjoyable and nice... *Beep beep, beep beep, beep beep...* There, his watch was going off, the minute was up. Already! They really needed to stop this now ... just a second more ... just a... OK, five seconds more is fine... No, that didn't count because he was thinking about allowing the extra five seconds so couldn't actually enjoy them, so it would be a further five seconds, starting in five seconds' time and—

"Hallo, boys!"

Noah twisted his head to see Mick standing in the door as Harry sprang back from him. "I thought you'd gone?!" Noah squealed.

"Takes a girl time to get herself ready!"

"Right. Well. We were just ... having a lie-down."

"I can see!" Mick said. "Looks like a very nice 'lie-down' too."

"Yes, it is a nice lie-down, thank you," Noah snapped. "Will there be anything else?"

"Just wanted to say goodbye, Noah. Maybe you'll never see me again."

Harry turned his flushed face towards Mick. "Where you going?"

"London, babes. Seeking my fortune on the streets paved with gold, following after Dick!"

Harry giggled.

"Harry, that's not funny," Noah said.

"It's a bit funny," Harry said.

"I'm just gonna get the van checked out at the garage, and then I'll be on my way! Gonna drive up tonight so I can spend tomorrow in London," Mick said. "Don't bother getting up – I can see that might be awkward for both of you."

"Wait!" Harry said. "You've got a van?"

"What did you think that huge pink monstrosity parked in the driveway was?" Noah asked, flabbergasted.

"Yeah, I got wheels, babes, what of it? Wanna ride out of this no-good town?"

Noah and Harry locked eyes.

"Come to think of it, yes! We do!" Noah said. "Please. I know we've not always seen eye to ... eye,

Micky, but now, now I need you. I need your help. I need your help to right a terrible wrong and prevent an injustice from occurring. My father and Eric have stolen Gran's diamonds, you see? I need to track them down and get them back. They're somewhere near Newark now. What do you say?"

Mick crossed his arms and took a long, hard look at the boys. "I have a proposal," he finally said.

"We're listening," said Harry.

"This show in London is important to me. It's Bambi's chance to hit the big time."

"And you'll be *great*." Noah nodded.

"But there's so much competition in London. The shows, cabarets, the bars and clubs..."

"The Science Museum," Noah added.

Mick ignored him. "And so little money for marketing. I mean, the promoter went fifty-fifty on printing the leaflets for me, but there's nothing for distribution. Unless I have a little help, of course." Mick smiled. "Unless I have a couple of Soho Flyer Boys to hand them out!"

"Us?" Noah said.

"That sounds awesome!" Harry added.

"Does it?" Noah frowned.

"Noah! It's London. It'll be ace. We'll have a great time!"

"If you agree," Mick said, "I'll help you get those diamonds back on the way down, then you help me for a night in London. You scratch Bambi's back, Bambi will scratch yours."

Noah wrinkled his nose. He didn't want Bambi scratching around anywhere near him; not with those nails. Harry, however, nodded along, his eager face all smiles, like this was all fully amazing. "OK, let's not do anything rash," Noah said.

Harry rolled his eyes. "*Noah.*"

"No, hear me out!" Noah insisted. "What about the geography homework? I was going to tackle that tomorrow!"

"We'll be back on Sunday, do it then!"

"Well, *maybe*, but OK then – what about Timothy the Fish? If I'm away all weekend, who will care for his needs?"

"Ask your mum," Harry said.

Noah gave a mocking little laugh. "*Trés* funny, Harry, *trés* funny. Despite the pretence of respectability my mother is currently putting on, with the house to herself she will doubtless be downing Echo Falls Summer Berries and doing a pole dance before we know it. Timothy will perish under her care – it's a miracle I have survived as long as I have."

Harry sighed, but was clearly determined not to let this opportunity for a trip to London be jeopardized. "OK," he said, "we can take Timothy to mine. My mum can look after him, if that'll make you happy."

Noah chewed his lip. "Mmm, well…"

"Noah, there are literally no more objections you can come up with to this plan. And you want the diamonds back, don't you?" Harry said.

"THE GREAT BRITISH QUIZ OFF!" Noah squealed. "It's tomorrow night! OH MY GOD!"

Harry put a reassuring hand on Noah's arm. "Noah, you do realize, fantastic though the quiz sounds, that two of the three people who will come to it are in this room now."

Noah sucked his cheeks in.

"Because," Harry continued, "*great* as the quiz will surely be, literally everyone else is going to the club night on Saturday. And while they're at some shitty club in Lincoln – your words! – we'll be at a real London gay club!"

"And what of our French wards?" Noah asked.

Harry shrugged. "Probably be good to have a couple of days away from Pierre, after everything, right? Besides, he can look after himself, he's a big boy."

"In all senses of the word," Noah muttered.

"What?"

"Nothing. And Eva seems to hate me anyway, so I don't suppose she'd be bothered."

"Exactly!"

Noah sighed and looked at Mick. "I guess you have a deal."

"YES!" Harry said, punching the air.

"Then get yourselves packed up and ready to go. Bring some camping gear because we'll end up kipping overnight on the way down, and I only have the cash to splash on a London hotel on Saturday night." Mick paused dramatically at the door. "The hunt *is on*."

CHAPTER TWENTY-SEVEN

Noah threw his old camping rucksack from the Scouts into the back of the pink van, next to the case of protein shake he'd stashed in there, in the hope that out of the saturated Little Fobbing market and away from nasty Year Seven boys, he could sell some before the house of cards came crashing down. He narrowed his eyes at the sight of his mother coming down the drive with a carrier bag of shopping.

"What's going on?" she demanded.

"Did you know about my father and half-brother's plans for a diamond heist?" Noah asked.

His mum laughed. And then her face fell as she looked at Noah and realized he was serious. "Noah, really? Brian and Eric have gone fishing, I told you!"

"Lies!" Noah sang. "I'll bet you too are into this up to your saggy neck, Mother!"

His mum put the shopping bag down. "Noah, your dad is a changed man. He's wanting a fresh start. For us to..."

"*Be a family*, I know, Mother!" Noah grimaced. "But the truth is very different. He and Eric have stolen Gran's tiara."

His mum frowned. "That old piece of tat you used to dress up with?"

"Yes, well, it turns out it's studded with diamonds, not glass, and rather valuable."

"This is ridiculous." His mum shook her head. "So, where are you all going?"

Noah eyeballed her. "I am going to track down Father and Eric. Mick is kindly providing the transport, in return for us helping market Bambi's glamorous new show in London Town."

"Mick?" his mum said.

"Don't worry, I'll take care of him, Lisa," Mick replied, throwing the box of flyers in the back of the van.

"I'm sixteen. I can take care of myself now," Noah told them.

"Can I have a word, Mick?" his mum said, pulling Mick over towards the front door.

Noah walked round to the front of the van, as Harry's mum pulled up in her car. Noah smiled as

Harry hopped out of the passenger seat with his bag and unloaded a couple of tents ... and then he frowned as he saw Pierre get out of the back, with his bag too. *Damn it.* He and Harry could really have used a bit of quality time together; now the cause of all the trouble was clearly coming along too.

"Mum was funny about him not coming," Harry whispered quickly as he scooted up to Noah. "Said she didn't know what she was going to do with him all weekend."

Noah nodded. "Fine."

"But we'll both keep an eye on him and if he starts any nonsense, I'll say something."

"Or *I'll* say something," Noah suggested, keenly aware that Harry didn't know everything that had happened, and he didn't want an upset or humiliated Pierre to spill the beans out of spite.

"Yeah, cool," Harry said. "Anyway, I've filled him in on what's going on."

"Maybe we have a picnic on the way?" Pierre grinned, walking up to them and dropping his bag on Noah's drive.

Noah stared at him. "Maybe."

Pierre nodded. "Nice."

"Nice, yes," Noah agreed.

Noah glanced at Harry, who glanced back at him and raised an eyebrow slightly. It was a good moment to make it clear to Pierre how things were going to work, in a firm *but pleasant* manner. "Pierre," Noah smiled, "you have been afforded the pleasure of sitting in the front seat, where you will enjoy maximum countryside views. Harry and I will sit in the rear seats."

"I sit in back too," Pierre said.

"No," Noah said. "You sit in front."

"You sit in the front, Pierre," Harry added.

"Fine." Pierre shrugged, taking his bag and throwing it in the van.

The appalling roar of a motorcycle indicated the arrival of Eva, riding as a pillion passenger with what Noah could only assume was some sort of Hells Angel.

Eva jumped off, shook her blonde hair free of the helmet, and meandered down the drive towards them.

"You are going somewhere?" she said.

Noah raised an eyebrow. "London," he said.

Eva's eyes lit up for the first time since Noah had met her. "Cool. I'll be five minutes."

Noah ran his hands through his hair. "No, Eva! No, you see—"

But in just a couple of strides of her endless legs, Eva was already through the front door, having given a thumbs up to the Hells Angel, who revved the motorcycle and screamed away down the street.

"Argh! I knew I should have had her sent back!" Noah said to Pierre and Harry. "Been nothing but trouble and refuses to engage with me about French matters."

"I am happy to engage on 'French matters'," Pierre said, with a slight smile.

Noah breathed at him. "How kind. Get in the van."

"In back, yes?"

"IN FRONT!" Noah screamed. He strode over to where his mother and Mick were standing. "We need to go."

"Er, you'll go when Mick's ready to go, mister!" his mum said. She turned to Mick. "Don't take any of his shit, will you?"

"I can handle him," Mick smiled.

"EVA?! EVA, WE ARE GOING! GET YOUR SORRY GERMAN SELF DOWN HERE AT ONCE IF YOU'RE INSISTING ON COMING!"

Eva appeared with her guitar case.

"Where's your bag?"

"Travelling light."

"With just your guitar? What about a face wash, at least? Or a simple pair of knickers?"

Eva shrugged. "Just need this." She ambled into the van.

"She's going to smell. We'll try and hose her down at a car wash somewhere. Farewell, Mother. When you next see me I will have thwarted a criminal endeavour and been to London. I will be a changed person. Take a long hard look at the boy, for he will return a man."

"Do you need the toilet before you set off? It's miles to the nearest service station!"

"No."

"I think you should try to have a wee."

Noah chewed his lip. "I'm totally fine. Don't need one. Pretty confident I'm old enough to know my own bladder."

"Make him eat at least *some* fruit and veg, else he gets constipated." His mum shrugged, going inside.

"Mum!"

"Well, it's true!" she shouted from within.

Noah growled in the general direction of his mother, then strode up to the van, hopped inside and slammed the sliding side door shut.

"Where to, then?" Mick asked.

"The inappropriately named Route 66 Diner on the A46," Noah said. "They were there earlier."

"ROAD TRIP!" Mick shouted.

Noah clamped his mouth firmly shut, worried that if he didn't, some sarcastic little remark would likely pop out. Mick was doing them a favour. Noah would just have to suck it up.

Mick reversed the van out of the drive, swinging it round to face forward and zooming off down the road ... just as Noah glanced out of the window and saw two familiar strangers, one holding a camera, sitting in a black Vauxhall Astra.

CHAPTER
TWENTY-EIGHT

Noah's chest was so tight, every breath was a struggle. Pierre and Eva were happily chattering away in French, and Harry and Mick were discussing something to do with Mick's show, but all Noah could do was stare out the window and run through scenarios of what those people in the black Vauxhall Astra wanted and who they actually were. The trip to London was starting to feel like the best thing. The big city promised crowds and anonymity. It felt *safe*.

Ten minutes into the journey and other more pressing matters presented themselves – to Noah, anyway. "It's no good," Noah said, "we're going to have to stop at a service station. I require bathroom facilities."

"Mate, like your mum said, there isn't a services for miles," Mick said.

"Then what will I do?"

"Wait?" Mick suggested.

Noah sighed. He hadn't anticipated needing a wee quite so soon – perhaps it was all with the excitement of the journey ... or those two cans of Cherry Coke he'd downed before they left. But this was fine. He would be fine. He was sixteen now, so he would just wait like any other adult and not piss his pants.

He needed to take his mind off matters.

Aha! Of course! Noah pulled several A4 sheets out of his rucksack. "OK, everyone. We all know journeys can be tedious, so I always bring along my home-made Travel Bingo to help pass the time!" he said, leaning forward and handing Pierre and Eva a sheet each, then passing one to Harry. "Now, as you can see, there are thirty boxes, each containing something you may see on the journey." He handed some pens out to the group. "When you see the thing, just draw a cross through the box. If you manage to cross out all thirty boxes, you shout 'Travel Bingo!' and that means you've won. OK? Pens at the ready... On your marks... Get set... GO!" Noah said, immediately crossing off "Electricity Pylon" as they drove past one.

"Red car!" Pierre said, crossing off that box.

"No, Pierre, don't say it out loud – you'll alert others to what you've worked so hard to see. Now we've all seen the 'red car' and so we will all be crossing it off our cards," Noah told him. "Eva? Have you crossed off 'red car'?"

"No."

"Well, that's up to you, but it is a good start, so I would if I were you."

"I didn't see it."

"OK, well, you need to keep a keen eye out. This game is all about observation skills." Noah struggled to cross his legs. "I'm just going to sit like this for a bit."

"Have you pissed yourself yet?" Mick shouted back at him.

"Nope!" Noah said. "No, I'm fine. It would have been nice to stop, but it's fine that we haven't."

"Lorry," Pierre said.

"No! Pierre, no! You must not say all the things out loud. Keep it in your head!" Noah insisted.

"Golden eagle?" Harry said, looking down his list. "We're in the East Midlands, not the wilds of Scotland!"

"Well, that's the game," Noah said. "I can't help that, can I?"

Harry looked glum. "Be hard to win though."

"But not impossible. Who knows what we might see, if we look hard enough!" Noah uncrossed his legs and crossed them the other way. "Actually, you're right. Let's change it. Everyone delete 'Golden Eagle' and replace it with, um, let's see... 'Toilets.' OK? And, this is going to be a special bonus box, and if you see toilets, you shout it out immediately, and you will have won. So, you've all got a great reason to look out for toilets especially, because then you will win."

"And you won't piss yourself," Mick said.

"I am so, so far away from pissing myself, Mick, but thanks for going on about it," Noah replied, smiling weakly and fanning his face with his paper. "Everything's cool, bladder-wise."

"Caravan!" Pierre shouted.

"That's a motorhome," Noah corrected him. "A caravan must be towed."

"What is 'towed'?"

"Pulled by a car," Harry said.

"Eva? Have you seen anything?" Noah asked, trying to be encouraging. Perhaps a fun game like this would pull the girl out of her perpetual gloom?

"The only thing I have seen," Eva said, monotone, face expressionless, "is one shithole town after another."

"OK, well, that's interesting, but it's not on your card."

"Caravan!" Pierre shouted.

"No, Pierre, that's a trailer."

"Pulled by a car?"

"Yes, but a caravan you live in."

"Motorhome?"

"Like a motorhome, but not a motorhome. Because it's pulled by a car. A motorhome operates with its own internal engines. A caravan without a car is just a . . . shed on wheels."

"With a toilet in," Mick smiled.

Noah groaned as they went over a bump in the road. "Huh. OK, right, Mick ... dear Mick..."

"I'm not stopping."

"Yes, but I really need to stop, though."

"You can go when we get to the diner."

"The diner!" Noah squealed. "Mick! That's nearly an hour away! I just won't be able to... Mick, please! Please!"

"No." Mick put his foot down and the van accelerated.

"Argh!" Noah screamed.

"What was that?" Mick said. "Scream if you wanna go faster?! You screaming, Noah?!" He accelerated some more.

"Just to remind you, we're all under eighteen in here!" Noah babbled. "This is a van full of children, so you have to be responsible, else you'll crash and your guilty face will be all over the news. There's a lot of young promise in this van. A lot of hopeful lives could be wiped out!"

"Please wipe us out," Eva muttered, her eyes glazing over.

"We're barely going forty!" Mick said, shifting the van into fifth. "Speed limit's seventy on this road."

Noah shot up in his seat as they flew over another bump in the road. "ARGH! AH! AH! Seriously, your careless driving is traumatizing my bladder! Please! Mick!"

"Mick, can you pull over?" Harry said.

Mick sighed, slowed down and pulled on to the grass verge. "Go on, then!"

Noah slid the door back and leapt on to the grass, battling to stay upright as his foot slid off a grassy mound and into some mud. He flailed about, looking for a suitably dense bush that he could pee behind without being seen. Damn it, why did it have to be winter and nothing have any leaves on? He pushed through the first couple of bushes, figuring that three separate sets of bracken and brown foliage would hopefully be enough to shield his nether regions from perverted eyes. And it wasn't just the occupants of the van he was worried about. All manner of passing vehicles would contain perverts and predators who would just love to see his willy, he was sure of it. In today's world, you couldn't be too careful.

He found the perfect spot, unzipped and sighed with relief. After this, they could really get on with the journey. Make up for lost time. Gather clues, work out their destination and head them off!

BZZZZZZ!

Noah glanced up to see a most unwelcome visitor. Some manner of black-and-yellow FLYING INSECT with a malevolent attitude about it and definitely some sort of ARSE DAGGER. In winter!

BZZZZZ!

It was taking a keen interest in Noah and his tender and vulnerable boy parts – parts that he would ideally put away immediately, were it not for the stream of pee he was releasing and couldn't now stop.

BZZ! BZZZZ!

Noah wafted at the air as the creature dived nearer, trying not to splash his trousers as he did so, and now having to focus on:

(A) where he was peeing

(B) the arse-dagger-enabled insect

(C) the occupants of the van and whether they could see him

(D) the many perverts elsewhere on the road, and beyond.

BZZZZ!

The creature began a dive-bomb attack, heading directly for Noah's willy. Noah swerved violently and—

"ARRRRRRRGHHHHHHHHH! AH! AH! AH! AH! ARRGGGHHHHHH! AHHHHHHH! HELP! HEEELLLPP!"

Harry was first on the scene, as a stricken Noah covered himself with his hands, eyes watering, lip wobbling. "I've stung it on a nettle!" Noah wailed.

"When you say 'it'?" Harry said.

"My WILLY!" Noah squealed. "Get help!"

"What sort of help?"

"Get the first-aid kit from the van."

Harry nodded and hurried back to the van, while Noah examined the afflicted area. "Oh no!" he cried. "A red

spot has come up on it! WE NEED ANTIHISTAMINE!"
he shouted back towards the van. "I'm flaring up!" This
was all he needed. How much poison was in a nettle sting?
Enough to kill your boy parts?

Harry blundered back through the foliage. "Mick says
he hasn't got a first-aid kit."

Noah blinked at him. "Hasn't got one? *Hasn't got one?!*
Then what am I supposed to do?"

"Maybe we can suck the poison out?" Pierre said,
poking his head up behind Harry.

"Ahh!" Noah said, turning away from them both. "Go
back! Stay back! There's nothing to see here!"

"Shall I look for a dock leaf?" Harry suggested.

Noah nodded. "Yes, try that! Quickly, though, before
the poison takes hold!"

Harry started foraging around in the undergrowth as
Mick arrived on the scene. "What the hell?" he said.

"*You!*" Noah snarled. "How dare you not have a first-
aid kit! Suppose one of us severed an artery and required
a tourniquet? I mean, I'm not expecting a defibrillator, but
not even a cold compress and some sterile dressings?"

"No." Mick shrugged.

"Here!" Harry said, holding up a bunch of dock leaves.

"Right," Mick said, "well, when you've done, we seem
to have another problem."

"What's that?" Noah scowled.

"Van won't start. Dead as a dodo."

"For fuck's sake. Of course it won't. Right, well, first things first, in a breakdown situation, you need to get your warning triangle out of the van and place it a hundred and forty-seven imperial feet from the scene, to warn oncoming traffic."

Mick stared at him.

"Oh, dear Christ alive. You haven't even got a warning triangle! Oh God. We're dead. We're as good as dead."

CHAPTER TWENTY-NINE

Noah breathed a sigh of relief as the police car pulled up just ahead of him. What luck! Now they would all be saved.

"What the hell are you doing?" the policeman said, getting out of the passenger side and walking along the verge towards Noah.

"There is a broken-down vehicle not one hundred and forty-seven imperial feet ahead," Noah explained.

The policeman nodded. "So why are *you* standing here, waving around a pair of red boxer shorts?"

"The owner of the vehicle doesn't have any warning triangles," Noah said, through gritted teeth. "As a result, we had no way of warning oncoming traffic. This was the best I could do to prevent a major accident ... you know? Like in *The Railway Children*?"

Of course, it wasn't ideal. And of course the person who had packed the provocative red underwear had been Pierre, but needs must. And surely Noah had averted some sort of massive disaster through his actions? Maybe his efforts would be recognized… Some sort of community service medal, maybe?

The policeman sniffed. "A teenage boy waving some red pants in the air on the side of the A46 is more of a distraction than that van is. Bloody idiot. Step back from the verge."

Noah lowered his red warning flag and trotted after the officer.

"Have you phoned for assistance?" the policeman called back to him.

"Yes, sir, indeed we have."

The policeman shook his head. "Right. In the meantime, wait up by the fence, not down here where you could get hit. And put those pants away."

Noah tucked the boxers into his front pocket.

The policeman sighed. "Kids today."

Noah watched with a certain amount of awe as a local mechanic, who had introduced himself only as "Ryan", fiddled about under the bonnet of the van, apparently knowing what all the bits did, and not being afraid to touch them.

Ryan was a very capable young man.

He wore some grey jogging bottom shorts, slung low at the waist, so you could see the waistband of his Hollister boxers, along with a white T-shirt that stretched over his ample pecs, that were probably due to lifting car parts about. He also had white socks on and big boots. A good, stout, manly type of boot. Very practical.

"How bad is it, Ryan?" Mick cooed, leaning against the side of the front headlights.

"Battery's dead, but I can fix you up with a new one now."

"Ooh, so there's life in the old gal yet?!" Mick giggled.

"I'll sort her out," Ryan said, and bent back down under the bonnet.

"Mmm," Pierre said.

Eventually, after much fiddling with RANDOM WIRES AND STUFF, and several manly grunts, Ryan slammed the bonnet shut and nodded to Mick, who started the engine with a healthy roar. "Nice one!" Mick shouted.

"Well done, Ryan," Pierre said.

"That's great, Ryan, congratulations on your excellent job," Noah added.

Harry gave him a thumbs up. "Cheers."

Ryan shrugged off all the praise like it was nothing, and he wasn't really SOME SORT OF GOD who knew about stuff and could probably also mend boilers and deal with faulty fuse boxes and things. Ryan was good with his hands. Noah bet he probably made pottery in his spare time, sitting at the wheel, a mound of wet, sloppy clay between his strong hands, gently caressing and teasing the wet... Noah pulled at his collar and adjusted his trousers. That damn nettle sting was swelling.

"That'll just be a hundred, then," Ryan said. "Cash only."

Noah looked expectantly at Mick.

"Lads?" Mick said.

"What?" Noah asked.

"Put your hands in your pockets, then."

Noah stared at Mick. "But..."

"All I have is a credit card," Mick said.

Noah threw up his arms. "But I only have ten pounds! Harry? Pierre?"

Pierre shrugged. "I did not ask to come."

Noah let that go, but vowed to speak to Pierre later about his attitude problem and his disinterest about being a team player.

"I've got thirty," Harry said, ripping his Velcro wallet open.

"So, we have forty..." Noah said.

"Not enough," Ryan sniffed. "I'm gonna have to take the battery away again if you can't pay."

Noah narrowed his eyes at evil Ryan. Like most people who wore Hollister boxers, this was all about him. If he didn't get what he wanted, he was going to turn nasty.

They needed a plan, else they would have fallen at the

first hurdle, just a few miles from home, and Noah's dad would get away scot-free and sell Gran's diamonds. Oh, and Eric would find that very damn funny, wouldn't he?

"Right! Group conference!" Noah announced, huddling Harry, Pierre and Mick together. "We *have* to track down and locate my father and Eric. It's really, really important and it'll make an old woman very happy if we succeed. Now, what we need to do is put our differences behind us, just for the moment, and work as a *team*. We have to pool our resources and—"

"Cool, we're all done," Ryan interrupted. "I'll let you get on your way."

"Huh?" Noah said.

Ryan patted the bonnet of the van. "Sorted. Drive safely now." He sauntered back over to his pickup truck, slammed the door and drove away, tooting his horn as he pulled on to the road and waving.

Waving to Eva, who was just sitting on the fence, waving back at him.

CHAPTER THIRTY

Noah stared hard at the back of Eva's head as they drove along, hoping (for her sake), that his concerns were getting through to her through some sort of telepathy. It was fine, he wasn't going to judge her, she could give her number and whatever promises she liked to RANDOM MECHANICS who she's only known for, like, ten minutes ... except it was potentially dangerous!

Noah cleared his throat. "Eva? I hope, if you do decide to meet up with Ryan again, that you'll at least inform your parents, or some other responsible adult, of your plans?"

Eva turned round quickly. "We got the battery, didn't we?"

"Yes..."

"So the problem is what, Noah?"

He couldn't see her face, but Noah could *hear* the little smile playing on her lips. *Fine, then.*

"Haha!" Mick chuckled. "I think Noah's worried you might like Ryan more than him, Eva!"

"No, that's not true because I don't even care," Noah said.

Eva shrugged. "I have no allegiance to anyone. I'm a lone wolf."

Noah rolled his eyes. *God, it must be great being Eva.*

"Welcome to Route 66," the waitress with a gaunt face and chemically damaged blonde hair sighed as she showed them to their table. *"Where all your American dreams come true!"*

Noah glanced across at the OAPs sitting opposite one another, eating their hamburgers in silence, and then over at the baby in a high chair, which was throwing fries on the floor whilst its mother sat on her phone, texting and slurping on the dregs of a cola.

"Go fuck yourself, Mario!" someone shouted from the kitchen.

Noah peeled a limp piece of lettuce covered in ketchup from his chair and sat down. Harry cocked his head at the menu. "Well, we're in the right place."

"You certainly are," the waitress said, maintaining her fixed smile. "Let's start –" she sounded really bored "– with some drinks. Good news, gang –" it didn't sound particularly like good news "– we do unlimited refills on all our sodas."

"I think we should eat here," Mick said. "Then we can find somewhere to kip for the night."

Noah nodded and glanced at the waitress, who was busy digging a tissue out of the pocket of her stars and stripes tabard. Noah knew he needed to be as charming as possible in order to get this poor woman, for whom the American dream had surely faded, on side. And when it was something he really wanted, Noah was more than prepared to be a total hypocrite. "Howdy, y'all!" Noah smiled at the waitress and slapped his thigh. "I LOVE America!"

The waitress gave him an empty stare. "Drinks?" she muttered.

"I'll have the Mega Choc Super Shake," Harry grinned, eyes all over the manky menu.

"Do you want to go large on that?" the waitress said in a dull monotone. "With extra marshmallows, cream, Oreos, Reese's Pieces, and a whole Snickers?"

Harry's eyes were popping out with all the images. "YES! YES!"

"Make that two!" Noah said. "God bless America!"

The waitress slowly made a jotting on her pad. "Our special today is the Empire State Sharing Plate – ribs, chicken wings, pork belly, loaded skins and shrimp."

"Mmmmm!" Noah said, ladling on the enthusiasm, even though he was *dying* to tell everyone it should be

245

prawns, not shrimp, *because they were not in America*.

The waitress stared into the dark void outside the window. "All smothered in our *famous* Tennessee bourbon glaze."

Noah stifled a smile. Even the inauthenticity was inauthentic. He could only imagine the legal wranglings that had somehow prevented them from calling it a Jack Daniels glaze, although it was presumably because there wasn't a drop of JD in sight.

"Right," Mick said, apparently losing patience, "we'll have the Empire State Sharing plate, three unlimited sodas and two milkshakes, ultimate ribs, spit-roast half chicken – I love a spit roast, me . . ."

Noah rolled his eyes.

". . . sesame chicken strips and the tornado steak." Mick smiled and put the menu down. "Everyone happy?"

"USA! USA! USA!" Noah chanted, nodding excitedly at the waitress, who just stared back at him like he was crazy.

"Excuse me, miss," Noah continued, now adopting his politest tone and most winsome smile. "I don't suppose you noticed a couple of . . . friends of mine in here earlier?" He got his phone out and flashed a picture of his dad and Eric at her. "Maybe a couple of hours ago?"

The waitress looked unenthusiastically at the photo. "Yeah. They tried to make off without paying."

"Yes, that sounds like them," Noah said.

"Then the lad tried to say there was a hair in his sweet and sour ribs, and the older guy claimed his fillet steak was undercooked."

"*Fillet* steak, my, my!" Noah said. "Someone was pushing the boat out! I don't suppose they ... gave any hint of where they were heading?"

The waitress shrugged.

"Any mention of where they were travelling to, after they left?" Noah continued, raising his eyebrows.

The waitress stared vacantly at him for a few moments. "They were talking about a place to stay the night..."

"That's good," Noah said.

"They asked me if there was anywhere near here, and I told them no. Not unless they want to stay at the Deathtrap Motel."

"Wow, they really called it that?" Noah said.

"No," the waitress said. "That's what everyone round here calls it, after a guest caught an STI from the bedsheets. Anyway, they said they would head a bit further south." The waitress shrugged. "I didn't catch anything else. I'll put your order through."

"Surely they're heading to London," Mick said as she walked away.

Noah nodded. "Maybe."

"If you were trying to sell some diamonds, though, surely Hatton Garden is the obvious place?" Mick insisted.

"No," Noah said. "That place is too above board. Dad'll need to sell to a dodgy contact, someone who can get the diamonds out of the country, and who can then maybe take them to someone in Antwerp for recutting."

Harry made a little groaning sound. "Mm, I love it when you talk like this," he murmured.

"Sexy, right?" Pierre agreed. "*Antwerp. Recutting.* He knows all the words!"

Noah gave Pierre a warning stare. "I'm merely stating facts." He turned to Harry. "And like I said before, there's nothing sexy about being a criminal. It's a bad thing. Right!" Noah slammed both his hands down on the table. "We need more info. I'm gonna call Eric!" He got up from his seat. "I'll call from outside – don't want him to know exactly where we are. Information is power, after all."

Eric finally picked up on Noah's third attempt and Noah went right in hard, to show he wasn't messing about. "Where are you, cock cheese?"

"Some place you'll never find us," Eric said. "And I wonder where *you* are, *Jessica*?"

"Don't bring Dame Angela into this!" Noah glanced around his surroundings – by the huge wheelie bins to the side of Route 66, the sound of traffic in the distance, but no way would Eric be able to hear that. "And I'm nowhere. Just at home."

The sounds of the waitress on a PA system suddenly

came blaring across from the restaurant. "WE'RE CELEBRATING A BIRTHDAY. WOOO. SO GIVE A ROUTE 66 CHEER FOR MAVIS – WHO IS SEVENTY-FIVE TODAY."

Noah cleared his throat. "Just hanging around at home."

Eric laughed. "Yeah, I heard that loud and clear, Noah."

"Why are you doing this?" Noah hissed. "Gran needs that money! We could put her in Kingfisher Meadows with it! Have you literally no heart, Eric? Are you, in fact, the very devil himself?"

"Probs," Eric sniffed. "Look, I'm just the monkey in all this. Dad's the organ grinder."

"But you were all too happy to help! Judas!"

"This will all be over by eleven tomorrow morning, so if I were you, I'd let it go."

"Never!"

"Tick-tock, then, Noah. Better come and find us quick, before it's too late. I'd suggest you leave Route 66 sharpish and head, ooh, I dunno, *south?*"

"Right, well, I'm not at Route 66, but that's interesting."

"You're at Route 66. I literally just heard."

"No, I'm not," Noah insisted.

"Whatever," Eric said. "Check your food before you eat – I found a pube in mine." And he hung up.

Noah chewed his lip. *Damn him.* "Head south," he'd said – but what if that was a bluff? What if Eric and Dad were really heading north? Or maybe it was a double bluff, and they really were heading south, or maybe...

"The food is here, so I come get you," Pierre said, appearing at Noah's side. "Although I must say, it is not as good as our picnic the other night! Not like my fine Merlot, huh?"

Noah took a deep breath. Pierre's little remarks needed knocking on the head. Noah had played the whole thing down to Harry, but Pierre risked making Harry think it was a whole bigger deal than it really was. "You told me Harry knew about the picnic, but he didn't know," Noah said.

Pierre shrugged. "He know I came to see you to apologize."

"Yes, but not about the picnic."

"The picnic was a, how you say, a thought after. A special thing I just decide on."

"Yet you told me Harry knew."

"A mistake! Come inside, the food!"

Noah looked Pierre up and down. God, he was handsome. It wasn't just the obvious physical perfection – the chiselled jaw, the defined cheekbones, the carefree hair – Pierre oozed confidence, charm and ... *sex*. It was disarming. It made it very difficult to be cross with him. "All I'm saying, Pierre, all I'm merely asking, is that you back off with the little sexual remarks about me a bit. OK? Just less of 'Noah is sexy' this and 'You make me hard, Noah' that. OK?"

"I see you are still upset by our kisses of passion. Maybe we should just tell Harry everything, so it is all out in the open?" Pierre suggested.

Noah grabbed Pierre's arm. "Let's just leave it, yes?"

"Ha!" Pierre laughed. "I joke with you!"

"Oh fuck," Noah said, staring over Pierre's shoulder.

Pierre shrugged again and walked back towards the restaurant. "Chill out, is not a serious thing."

But that wasn't the thing.

Noah was frozen, staring over towards the far corner of the car park.

A car.

With a registration plate he recognized.

The black Vauxhall Astra.

CHAPTER THIRTY-ONE

Dinner had passed in a blur. All he could think about was that car: why it was here, and why the hell he was clearly being followed? What was it they thought he'd done? Or what did they want? Was it Mick? *Pierre?* Or were they following his father's trail, too?

And by the time Mick had found a random field to camp in – which wasn't even a designated campsite and clearly risked them being shot by the farmer if he found them trespassing – Noah's lack of complaint was clearly making Harry suspicious.

"What's wrong?" Harry said.

Noah eyeballed him. "Nothing. All good."

"Right, well, that's obviously not true – I was watching you out of the diner window when Pierre came to get you for the food, and you were just staring across the car park doing that feet-shuffling, need-a-wee thing. I nearly came out to check, but OK."

"I didn't need a wee. I'm just worried about the diamonds." Noah nodded. "Trying to … piece the mystery together." He tapped his head. "All up here."

"Harry! Come and help me hammer these stakes in!" Mick shouted over.

"Make sure it is nice and erect!" Pierre grinned.

"*Pierre*," Harry warned.

Pierre held his hands up. "What? I say the wrong word?" He reached into his bag and pulled out a bottle of wine. "Everyone needs to chill."

Noah watched as Pierre unscrewed the cap and splashed the wine into a plastic cup. "Here," Pierre said, passing Noah the cup. He lowered his voice. "Not as nice as before, but better than nothing."

"Stop mentioning 'before'," Noah said, downing the cup. "Thirsty," he explained, seeing Pierre's surprised expression.

Pierre refilled him, and glanced over at Harry, bashing a tent peg into the ground. "I lost my virginity in a tent."

Noah took another gulp of wine.

It was going to be a long evening.

But alcoholic oblivion was definitely better than living in fear that a black Vauxhall Astra was going to come screaming into the field any moment, with masked and armed heavies bundling Noah into the vehicle so they could...

No. Don't think about it. It's FINE!

It wasn't fine.

He drank some more wine.

"What the hell are you wearing?" Harry said, watching Noah struggling to take his chinos and hoodie off inside the tent.

"This is a ribbed thermal long john," Noah explained. "With matching vest top. I know it's not particularly sexy, but it's practical." Noah giggled. "Now my willy won't get frostbite."

"How much have you been drinking?" Harry said.

"Oh, for shame! What makes you think I've been drinking?"

Harry sighed. "I've literally seen alcohol pass your lips."

"The merest soupçon," Noah shrugged. "The slightest hint of wine, that is all."

Harry grinned. "You're tipsy."

"No, no, no," Noah said, attempting to pull the right leg of his trousers off, which were caught up in his hiking socks, "no, because alcohol is very damaging on the immature liver, so." He hiccuped. "Mmmm, ver, ver, nice here –" he hiccuped again "– sausages," and giggled.

Harry leaned up on his elbows, already in his sleeping bag. "Need a hand?"

Noah giggled again. "Naughty! Naughty, Harry! 'A hand' indeed! La!"

"Literally just offering to help, but—"

Noah toppled over and collapsed in more giggles and a snort.

"Jesus," Harry said.

"Gaaahhh!" Noah said. "These clothes."

"What about them?"

"I'm too ... mmm..."

"What's the matter? Are you too hot?" Harry said,

"Too ... hot ... yes. Hot. Am hot. All the clothes."

"CAN YOU KEEP IT DOWN IN THERE?!" Mick shouted from his tent.

Noah flailed around on the floor. "I am quiet, though! These walls ... are paper thin! I remember when houses were made of bricks and ... wood!"

"This is a tent, though," Harry said, getting out of his sleeping bag and crawling over to Noah. "Come here."

"I want to be just in my boxers and a T-shirt, like you," Noah said.

"Well, that's fine..."

Noah hiccuped. "No, but, the long johns ... they're too complicated to take off... I wish I'd never... Awww, your nose is so pretty," Noah said, pressing Harry's nose with his finger. "Beep, beep! So cute."

"Thanks."

"SHUT UP!" shouted Eva from the tent she was sharing with Pierre.

"SHUT YOURSELF UP!" Noah shouted back.

"Noah!" Harry said. "SORRY ABOUT HIM, I'M SORTING HIM OUT!"

"WE DON'T WANT TO KNOW!" Mick shouted.

Harry grabbed hold of Noah's trouser leg and pulled the trousers off, along with one of his socks and then, on Noah's insistence, turned his back, closed his eyes, and put his fingers in his ears whilst Noah removed the long johns and put on his normal boxers.

"Am ready!" Noah declared, tapping Harry on the back. "Now, cuddles."

Harry was barely back in his sleeping bag before Noah had wrapped his arms around him and was snuggled into his neck. "Nom, nom, nom," Noah said.

"What was that?"

"Good enough to eat, you are, mister man." Harry's face was so close to his. They were almost kissing. Pretty soon, they would be. "Mmm, Hazza?"

"What?"

"Mmm ... if we ... one day, if we lived together... You know, in a house, or apartment, or villa, or flat, or ... yeah? If we did, OK, would we ... do you think if we had a Nespresso machine, it would be one of the ones that had its own integrated milk frother? For cappuccinos and the like?"

Harry exhaled, clearly thinking about it. "I wouldn't worry too much about that right now, Noah."

"No, but, I do. Would we?"

Harry stroked the back of Noah's head. "Probably."

"Mmm. Good. That's nice."

They lay in silence for a bit, their breathing the only sound.

"Mmm, Harry?"

"Yeah?"

"Why ... why is your ear so cute?"

"IT'S JUST HIS FUCKING EAR, SHUT UP!" Mick shouted. "FUCK'S SAKE!"

"Ver, ver *rude*," Noah muttered. "Such ... foulness. The drag artiste doth not appreciate your fine, fine, ear, Hazzaroo. But I know! 'Tis the finest ear I have ever seen, my liege."

"Maybe try to sleep," Harry suggested.

"No, but another thing," Noah said, "I was wondering what our ship name should be because should it be 'Narry' or 'Norry'?"

"Or 'Hoah'?"

"Hoah!" Noah giggled. "That's so..." He hiccuped again. "Mmm, need a Pepto-Bismol. Mm. Mm, Harry? Harry, can I ask you a thing?"

"Sure."

"I want ... with my finger ... to ... put it here," he said, placing it on Harry's nipple. "On your teat."

"Nipple. Fine. That's fine, Noah."

"Yes."

"OK."

"Is that nice?"

"Er, yes."

"OH FOR CHRIST'S SAKE!" shouted Mick. "CAN YOU PLEASE JUST SCREW AND GET IT OVER AND DONE WITH!"

"Ignore him," Noah whispered. "He is only jealous of our young love and that everything is unicorns and sparkles for us. Mm. Now I just move my finger like this a bit," Noah said, delicately making small circles on Harry's lovely pert nipple.

Harry exhaled unsteadily.

"I read about this in a ... *hiccup* ... book my mother has called ... *hiccup* ... *Foreplay for the Over Forties*, subtitle: *New sexual excitement for jaded lovers.*"

"Uh ... huh..." Harry muttered, eyes closed, with his head back on his pillow.

"Mmm, *Harry*," Noah said, resting his head on Harry's shoulder, while continuing to make the little circles. This was all so much easier to do after a bit of wine. Noah was feeling so emboldened, he traced his finger down Harry's chest, down to his tummy button, and then lower, down to the waistband of his boxers, gently lifting the elastic and sliding his finger just underneath, running it along under the band. Noah looked back up at Harry, who was still lying back, open-mouthed. Harry was adorable. His adorable boyfriend. How had Noah been so lucky to end up with someone as lovely as him? Noah traced his finger back along the waistband. It felt strange, touching Harry like this. This boy who he'd grown up with. This boy who, he realized now, he'd longed for, for so ... long. Sometimes, in the safe solitude of his bedroom, he had thought about Harry. He had thought naughty things. So it was confusing, because here he was, right in front of Noah now, in just his boxers and a T-shirt, and Noah knew, if he wanted to, he could trace his fingers lower ... he could do that ... and Harry was clearly quite keen for that to happen... And yet ... why wasn't Noah? The thought of doing anything more made his insides quiver. And yet, in his head, he'd done that. In his head, he'd done loads of stuff with Harry. But the reality felt scary and ... Noah didn't even have an erection.

What the hell? That could not be normal. He liked Harry. More than liked ... so what did this mean? Noah took his hand away and looked back at Harry, who was smiling at him.

"Night, then," Harry said.

"Goodnight, Harry," Noah said. "I love you."

"Love you too."

CHAPTER THIRTY-TWO

Noah stumbled out of the tent, crusty-eyed and gasping for water, blinking into the bright Saturday-morning light.

Mick had gone.

But Bambi had appeared, in a shimmery metallic halter-neck dress with cutaway shoulders, high heels and a huge blonde wig.

And she was humming Justin Bieber's "Baby" whilst pushing some bacon around a frying pan.

"Um, is there any water?" Noah croaked. "I'm a little—"

"Hungover?" Bambi smiled.

"*Thirsty*," Noah corrected her.

Bambi rolled her eyes and handed Noah a little bottle of Volvic, which he drank, gratefully. "How come you're Bambi now?" Noah asked as he finished the bottle.

"Takes me hours to get all the gear on, and I'm worried with all this tracking down your dad shit I might not have time later," Bambi said. "I've been sitting in the van doing my make-up since five, 'cause I wanna be ready to hit London with a bang. Bambi's a walking advert, babes. You watch the heads turn as I hand out the flyers! Bet you everyone takes one – very hard to refuse a drag queen!"

Noah nodded, glancing over at Eva, who was unenthusiastically buttering some white baps, like the knife and margarine were completely alien objects to her. Pierre was sitting on a little camping chair in jeans and a hoodie, sipping coffee from a tin cup, looking all rosy-cheeked and healthy from all the fresh outdoor air. Noah didn't dare imagine what *he* looked like right now. Pale and sickly would be a good guess. Decomposing zombie would be another. Noah looked at his phone. *"Where are you, Eric? Why do you not communicate? Damn you!"*

Harry scrambled out of the tent. "Do I smell bacon? Oh God, bacon!"

Noah gave Harry a "good morning" type of nod and dropped his eyes. *My God.* Something could well have happened last night – but not if Noah couldn't even get a boner. What was wrong with him? He'd had the opposite problem in many awkward situations. The time he got called up to the whiteboard in maths to solve an equation – boner. His Year Nine assembly on dying bees –

boner. Really lovely and potentially sexy evening with boyfriend – *no boner.* If Harry knew, he would surely think Noah didn't fancy him.

"Dead things," Eva said, handing Noah a white bap filled with bacon and a fried egg.

Noah took it. "Thank you."

He made a half-hearted attempt to eat it. He didn't feel hungry. He had heard of men suffering from these sorts of "performance issues" before, and, underlying medical reasons aside, it was often due to things like worrying about your mortgage, or being stressed at work. Whilst his finances *were* dire, and GCSEs *were* a nightmare, Noah felt the problem lay elsewhere. Because, try as he might to blot it all out, the strangers in the car, the stolen diamonds, Pierre, Ms O'Malley, the goddam *shed* ... they were all he could think about, and in different ways they all scared him.

He had to put an end to all this.

And that meant getting to the bottom of everything.

Noah's phone chirped. Eric, with a text that simply read: **Facebook**.

Noah sighed, logged on to the app, and was immediately confronted with pictures Eric had uploaded, with classic gloating captions that make you want to punch whoever posted them in the face:

Pic of hotel room. Caption: **My crib for the night**.

Pic of en-suite bathroom. Caption: **#bathroomgoals**

Pic of Eric, topless, lying in hotel bed, lips slightly parted. Caption: **Come and get me, ladies...**

"Damn him!" Noah shouted, throwing the phone to Harry, who caught it with the hand he wasn't eating a bacon butty with. "He's just doing this to provoke me! Lording it around, 'Look at me, look what a great time I'm having, your life is shit compared to mine, I'm so much better than you are!'"

"That's just Facebook, though, isn't it?" Bambi muttered.

"*Cock*," Noah said. "He is such a cock ... *flannel*."

"Also –" Harry swallowed the butty he was chewing "– he's an idiot. Because he's left his location tags on." Harry handed the phone back to Noah. "He was outside Watford when these were taken, which means..."

Noah grinned. "London, here we come!"

CHAPTER THIRTY-THREE

Noah was completely agog. There were cars, trucks and lorries *everywhere*. There were people *everywhere*. London, in all its chaotic, dirty, loud, manic glory, was *everywhere*. It pulsed. It was alive, vibrant, exciting. Mopeds zigzagged between the slowly moving vehicles, as an old guy in a pinstriped suit and a trilby played the saxophone on the street corner, and some prick with a beard and dungarees rode *an actual unicycle* along the actual pavement.

"Where is this?" Eva asked.

"Camden," Bambi said.

"Let me out here," Eva said, reaching back to grab her guitar case with her extendable arms. "Camden is great for me."

Bambi shook her head and clicked the central locking.

"No can do," she said. "Not having any accidents on my watch."

Eva scowled at her. "I'll find you later, at the club. I don't need to come along for this diamonds shit anyway."

"Honey," Bambi said, "I'm not being held responsible if you get yourself in any trouble. Do as Bambi says. You don't wanna get on the wrong side of Bambi, believe me."

"Cool," Eva huffed, refolding her limbs back into the confined space of the seat.

"This place is *crazy*!" Harry cooed, checking the view out of every window, as a middle-aged woman zipped past on a child's scooter. "All these people, like, who are they all? And the shops! And they're all open!" He craned his neck to look out of the back window. "Ha! That place is called 'Buy Curious'!"

"Funny," Noah agreed, knowing damn well that if such a shop opened in Little Fobbing, it would be quickly surrounded by indignant, pitchfork-wielding locals.

"Seems to sell stuffed animals, old hospital equipment and ancient relics that look like they might be cursed, if the window display's anything to go by," Harry said.

Noah checked his watch. Ten o'clock. They only had an hour to find where Dad and Eric were and save the diamonds.

Pierre took a picture of a red phone box. "Classic!" he smiled. "Also, I would like to see the Queen."

"You'll be seeing plenty of queens later on, hun," Bambi said.

"Haha! Queens!" Pierre turned his head back to Noah. "I am excited for the gay club!"

"How will we get in, though?" Noah said. "Surely security will ask for ID?"

"Actually," Bambi interrupted, "Bambi can probably get you in the back way, *oo-er*, since you're technically my *entourage*."

"Going in the back way sounds fun!" Pierre said.

"*Thank you, Pierre*. But Bambi, won't you get in trouble if they find out?"

"It'll be fine," Bambi sniffed, inching the van forward a metre. "I'll just say you're with Bambi and get you all some backstage passes. The rest of the staff will just assume you're old enough. *The power of a lanyard*, huns. *Access All Areas*."

"We like to Access All Areas, right, boys?!" Pierre grinned, turning round to wink at Noah and Harry.

"OK, look, Pierre," Harry said, lurching forward in his seat. "Maybe you're just joking, but all of your little comments are getting a bit ... annoying."

"I say something wrong?" Pierre said, face a picture of innocence. "I just say it is nice to be able to access all areas – like a film star, no?"

"No, that's not..." Harry chewed his lip for a moment. "OK, fine."

"OK?" Pierre said.

Harry sat back in his seat again.

"So are you lot coming to the club or not?" Bambi asked.

"I just worry we're asking for trouble," Noah said. "And we all need to think about how an *arrest* would look on our UCAS applications."

"Ah, come on, Noah!" Harry said. "It'll be ace."

"Well, I'm not sure, I've got a bad feeling about it, to be honest. A foreboding. If this were a book, there would be dark clouds right now, and a thunderstorm. Maybe a raven or something."

"Noah!" Harry said, placing an arm across his shoulders and pulling him towards him. "We're in London. We're young. We should have a good time! You gotta grab life by the horns!"

"Yes, grab the horn, Noah!"

"Shut up, Pierre!"

Pierre held his hands out, palms up. "Now what? You just say you *like* to grab horns!"

"You only live once, after all!" Harry said, ignoring Pierre now and resting his head on Noah's shoulder.

Noah swallowed. He loved the way Harry's hair smelt of rose petals. "Very well, then," he muttered.

"Was that a yes?!" Harry grinned, sitting upright again.

"It's a yes if I get the diamonds back."

"YEESSS!" Harry said, giving Noah a kiss on the cheek.

"Well, OK," Noah said. "I'm sure it'll be a pleasant evening. Is there a dress code, Bambi?"

"It's just casual. Unless you want to go into the BDSM room?"

"The what now?"

Bambi glanced at Noah's puzzled face in the rear-view mirror. "Nothing, mate. Don't worry about it. Casual is fine."

"Good, well, I brought some slacks with me, so I expect I'll—" Noah's mobile rang. "Oh goodness, it's Eric. Eric's on the line! It's him. This could be it!"

"Answer it, then!" Bambi shouted.

"OK! OK, everyone silent! He mustn't think we're on to him. He mustn't know we're in London! OK..." Noah accepted the call. "Noah Grimes speaking, who is this, please?"

"Dickhead," came the reply.

"Hello, Eric. To what do I owe this pleasure?"

"You ain't found us yet."

"That because I'm not looking."

"Sure, sure," Eric said. "Dad and I are just here waiting. Arrived ahead of schedule, just killing time."

"Oh yes, doing what?"

"Oh, Noah. Why would I tell you that? If I told you that, it might give you a clue as to where we were, and then you might come and find us!" Eric chuckled.

"What are you laughing at?" Noah demanded.

"Nothing. Just looking at something. Heh, heh! Too cute."

In the background, Noah heard a strange sound. A sort of *hooo whoooop! Hooooop!* type of noise. "Eric? What is that?"

"Time's not on your side, Noah! Less than sixty minutes now. Wonder if Noah Grimes can crack the mystery or if he's all talk?"

The phone went dead. "Well?" Bambi said.

"He didn't give anything away," Noah said. "But I did hear something in the background – something he was looking at." Noah cleared his throat. *"Hooo whoooop! Hooooop!"*

"What the hell is wrong with you?" Bambi said.

"That was the noise! That's what I heard! *Hooo whoooop! Hooooop!"*

"Gibbons," Pierre muttered.

"Those monkey things?" Noah said.

"Yes, *those monkey things.* Their calls are very distinctive."

"Well, why is Eric looking at gibbons?"

Mick suddenly slammed the van into a breakneck three-point turn. "Because he's at London Zoo."

CHAPTER THIRTY-FOUR

"Eighty Great British pounds!" Noah said for the tenth time. "*Eighty!* Just for us all to get into this wretched zoo!"

The group walked through the entrance gates and into the central courtyard. "Eighty pounds!" Noah continued. "Just to see some, what..." He consulted the map of the zoo he'd been given at the ticket booth. "Ooh! *Butterfly Paradise*, that does sound good!"

"Aw, they've got penguins!" Harry said, peering over at the map.

"We must see the lions," Pierre announced.

"OK, so I will *concede* there are things to see here," Noah said, "but still, *eighty pounds*!"

Bambi had a face of thunder. "Who paid?"

"Well, you did, Bambi, very kindly. And I thank you for that kindness. I'll pay you back."

"Yeah? How?"

Noah swallowed. "You'll see. I have ways. I might be running a business now, you'll see."

Bambi gave him a withering look. "You *might* be? That sounds promising." She looked around the group. "Where the fuck is Eva?"

Noah glanced between Harry, Pierre and Bambi, as though one of them might be Eva "in disguise". None of them were. "Shit," Noah said.

"Brilliant, she made a run for it, didn't she? In the queue whilst I was distracted at the ticket booth and you were moaning about how much it was!" Bambi jabbed Noah in the chest. "I'm not taking any flak for this. She's *your* responsibility."

"She's eighteen." Pierre shrugged.

Noah's eyes nearly popped out. *Eighteen?!* And they'd paired her with him, a barely sixteen-year-old?! Such an age gap was outrageous. He would be having *stern words* with Mr Baxter upon his return.

"She's eighteen?" Bambi said. "Oh well, fuck her, then, she's on her own." She rewrapped her pashmina around her shoulders, put a pair of huge sunglasses on, and clapped her hands together. "Right! Any idea where your dad and Eric are going to be meeting this shady contact?"

Noah shrugged. "No idea. We'll have to split up and

do a sweep of the entire zoo. Pierre – head up towards the lions and monkeys. Haz – take the penguins and butterflies; Bambi – do Gorilla Kingdom, then head across to the Snowdon Aviary; I'll check out Tiger Territory, then do the reptile house and aquarium. If you locate them, send a group text."

"We get an espresso first?" Pierre suggested.

"No, Pierre! No. Besides, based on the entry price, it'll cost *ten million pounds.* Coffee later. Everyone, we need to work fast and leave no stone unturned." Noah paused dramatically. "They're due to meet the contact in T-minus twenty minutes."

Harry grinned. "Mmm – I love it when you talk like that!"

"Haz!" Noah warned.

"Say something else," Harry said. "Say, 'Sierra four-five, Sierra four-five from Mike Whisky, over.'"

"No."

"Go on, Noah, say it!" Pierre said.

"Say it!" Harry insisted.

"Just say it," Bambi sighed.

"Sierra four-five, Sierra four-five from Mike Whisky, over," Noah muttered.

"Mmm," Harry and Pierre said.

"Gahh! Just get on with it!" Noah squealed, striding off towards the tigers.

*

Noah shook his head as he walked along the path through Tiger Territory, which could more accurately be called "area with no animals on it" because the tigers were nowhere to be seen. Eighty pounds! Eighty pounds and no tigers! At these prices, they should be putting on a musical revue...

He rounded the corner and heard the *'Whoooooop! Hooooop!'* sounds from Eric's phone call.

Gibbons. Noah walked up to the edge of the enclosure, watching the beasts as they swung around and did acrobatics using their ridiculously long arms. Amazing, really. Noah couldn't even hit a rounders ball – these guys were in a different league, PE-wise.

He felt eyes on his back.

He turned around slowly, because somehow, he *knew.*

And there he was. About ten metres away, standing at the corner, where the path swung round and down towards the reptile house.

Smirking.

Eric.

And no sooner had Noah seen him, than Eric was gone. Noah hurried after him, scrambling for his phone at the same time, attempting to hammer out a group text whilst trying, in vain, to keep a visual on Eric: **Flu eric head to reptile hotel moo**.

Seeing a flash of Eric's black hoodie ahead, Noah upped his pace, quickly weaving between parents with pushchairs and toddlers as he darted down the path, past the kangaroos, and arrived at the entrance to the reptile house.

Noah spun around. The path here split into three. A group of younger teens were gathered by the grass, chatting away in Spanish. Noah scanned them, but Eric was nowhere to be seen. He *must* be inside the reptile house. There was no sign of the others. Noah checked his watch – five to eleven. He had no choice. This was it. He swallowed and went inside.

Noah stood for a moment while his eyes acclimatized to the dark and his nose grew accustomed to the stench. It was the smell of dirty tricks, and Dad and Eric's operation reeked.

It was times like this, Noah was glad he had a wide collar on his coat to pop. He gave it a sharp tug, so the pointy bits faced forward. He longed for a fedora. If he had any hope of getting to the bottom of this case, he had to look and think like a pro, like some heroic, hard-boiled detective in a pulp novel.

He took in the scene. Tanks of different sizes lined the walls either side of the walkway, light reflecting off the wet glass, illuminating the underbelly of this filthy city. But Noah wasn't scared. He was mad. Real mad. So mad he could taste it.

Noah walked silently along the walkway. The place

was so deserted it could have been "chocolate three ways" on a menu – brownie, mousse and maybe a cheesecake, or something like that.

The trickle of water from one of the tanks...

The sound of his footsteps...

A short rustle...

Noah shot a glance behind him. There was no one there. Maybe the others were lost. Maybe they were dead. Life was tough like that. Tough as a nickel steak with a side helping of cast iron fries.

Noah tugged his collar up again and popped a Haribo Starmix in his mouth. He could so handle this.

The bulbs in one of the tanks to his right flickered a few times, casting shafts of light across the shadowy passage, then shut off.

He walked slowly on, keeping close to the left-hand side. He hadn't started this thing, but he was sure as hell going to finish it.

He chewed his Haribo.

Dad and Eric's scheme was like a cheap bourbon – it made you wince, and Noah was going to put it on ice.

He reached a large tank that stood in the middle of the walkway, forming an island you could walk around.

Noah glanced behind him again, the warm light of the exit glowing in the distance. Had all this been too easy? What if Eric's "careless" mistakes hasn't been so careless? What if they were deliberate? What if there was more to this caper than he'd bargained for? One thing was for sure – this was no Sunday school picnic.

"Oh!" Noah gasped, as he turned back and came face-to-face with a forked tongue flicking in and out at him from behind the glass of the tank. It was a snake. And snakes always meant trouble. Noah didn't like its face. And when he glanced at the sign, he liked it even less:

"Ten-foot king cobra – *the world's longest venomous snake. Subdues its prey with massive quantities of neurotoxic venom.*"

And it was then that a hand was placed over his mouth and Noah was dragged backwards.

CHAPTER THIRTY-FIVE

"What the bloody hell are you doing here?" his dad hissed in his ear.

Noah squirmed under his father's tight grip. "Mmmm! Mm! Mmmm!"

"Don't you dare scream for help if I take my hand away," his dad said, removing his hand from Noah's face.

"HELP! MURDER!" Noah shouted.

The hand was slapped straight back on. "Bloody idiot! Do you want to get us all arrested?!"

Noah made a low-level growl.

Eric gave a wave to someone at the other end of the walkway, presumably a staff member. "It's all good," he shouted. "Just my little brother being stupid!" Eric turned to Noah. "Well, hello there, *little brother*!"

Noah tried to wriggle free from his dad's grasp, desperate to set Eric straight: Eric was *his* little brother.

"OK, just chill out, Noah. Calm it down, buddy," his dad cooed, holding him tight.

It was no good. The more Noah tensed and fought, the tighter his dad grasped him. It was pretty tiring, and Noah was already *dangerously exhausted* from all the exertion. He sighed and went limp. Death may as well just take him.

"Good," his dad said, lifting his hands but keeping them hovering just a few centimetres away, in case they needed to go back on again. "We good?"

"I accidentally swallowed my Haribo without chewing it properly," Noah said.

"Right," his dad said. "Well, that'll teach you not to eat sweets while prowling around, won't it?"

Noah nodded, tight-lipped, flicking his eyes down to the floor.

His dad sighed. "Good, then." He put his hands back in his pockets. "Sorry about grabbing you like that. Just didn't want you messing up what me and Eric have worked so hard to make happen, yeah?"

Noah looked up at a triumphant Eric. Smarmy little git. Giving it all smiles, because he was clearly Dad's little protégé now. His favourite. Fine, then. Whatever. He should have known. He should have seen that Dad had way more in common with Eric than with him. They were both dodgy, just out for themselves.

But Noah was Gran's favourite, and he was doing this for her. He glanced up, over Dad's shoulder, seeing Harry lurking in the shadows by the lizard tanks further back along the walkway. Noah took an unsteady breath, then lifted his chin and forced himself to stare his father right in the eyes. "Your scheme is like a cheap bourbon," Noah snarled. "And I'm going to serve it on ice. I mean, with ice. No ... on the rocks. Bourbon – on ice."

"Bourbon's best served neat, at room temperature," his dad said.

"What? Oh. Look, it doesn't matter. Where's Gran's tiara?"

"The tiara's safe, Noah. We've taken the rocks out of it, and once I've sold 'em, I'll replace them with fakes. Glue 'em back in, and Eric will drop the tiara back into her room when she's not there, and she won't know the difference."

Noah looked at his dad and Eric and gave them his best sneering look. "Why? Why d'you do it? Do you even realize how upset Gran is about this?"

"Noah, mate," his dad cooed. "Here's the situation. That tiara would have been left to me in her will anyway. All I'm doing is releasing the funds a little earlier than expected."

"Why didn't you just ask her?"

"She used to bail us out all the time; she's a good woman, my mum. But since the dementia, it's like she doesn't get it any more. It's like ... she's holding on to everything she owns, because she's scared of losing it, you get me? I asked her for cash. She said no."

"So you took it anyway!"

His dad stepped towards him again. "If I don't sort out our cash-flow problem, we are going down, big time. I just want us to have a comfortable life, Noah. Like, I want us to have a nice family car – a Mazda MX-5 or something – right? For our family."

"*Family?*" Noah snorted. "An MX-5 seats two! So does Mum know about all this, then?"

Eric looked down as his dad cleared his throat. "I don't like to worry Lisa with the finer details of our finances. Understand?"

Noah nodded. "Oh, I understand, Dad."

"So I need you to be a man about this, Noah, OK? Don't say nothing to her. Don't worry her. She's done so much worrying over the years – she deserves a bit of happiness, don't you think? Deserves to sit back in an MX-5 and let me sort things out for us. She's always been there for you, Noah. Now you need to be there for *her*. That's the reason I didn't loop you in on all this before – didn't want you to have to keep secrets from her. Guess you found out anyway, but it'd be good if you could keep it zipped. Yeah?"

Noah shook his head and snuck a glance towards Harry. He was still standing in the same spot. Why hadn't he moved forward? If Harry were closer, it would at least be two against two.

"Here." His dad smiled, pulling a little velvet bag from his pocket and handing it to Noah. "Take a look. They're yours too, after all. These little beauties are going to sort out a whole load of problems for us. And you want that, don't you? I mean, you want what's best for our family, right?"

Noah peered into the bag while he tried to work out what his options were for a next move. Some people would run, but Noah couldn't run. Some people would use kung fu, but Noah didn't know any kung fu.

He became aware of a general hubbub, and glancing briefly behind him he saw the group of Spanish kids being coaxed around the exhibits, none of them really giving a shit...

Some people would use the magician's trick of distraction and misdirection.

But that would only happen if Harry got closer! Why the hell was he hanging back like this?

And in a flash, Noah realized.

He was standing his ground, facing off with his father in a confident way. Harry must assume he was dealing with things OK by himself. He had to show Harry he needed him.

Harry's words came back to Noah: *So that's how I know it's time to come to your rescue.*

Of course! Noah started shifting his weight between his feet. *Like he needed a goddam wee but, to be clear, he*

281

definitely did not need a wee because he was practically an adult now.

"So small, but so valuable," Dad said, as Noah continued to look into the small bag.

"Yeah, they're nice," Noah said, gently shuffling about.

"Damn right they are," Eric muttered. "You starting to see sense finally?"

Noah looked up at Eric. "I'm seeing things very clearly, Eric."

At that moment, a group of the kids pushed by in between them, keen to see the big snake, whilst another group hovered behind Noah, laughing and taking photos. Noah casually dropped the hand holding the velvet bag to his side and slightly behind his back, hoping to hell that Harry had seen Noah's signal and done the right thing.

"*De esta manera!*" the tour guide shouted. "This way!"

About twenty Spanish teenagers swarmed amongst them.

He sensed someone close behind him, a waft of something floral, and felt a tug as someone pulled the bag from his hand. Noah prayed it had been Harry, and not some young Spanish pickpocket whose hair coincidentally also smelled of roses.

"Hurry up!" the tour guide barked.

The teens moved off and his dad held his hand out.

"What?" Noah said.

"Give 'em, then," his dad said.

Noah gave his dad a sweet smile. "Give you what, Father?"

"Don't muck about, give me the diamonds."

"Just give 'em!" Eric said.

Noah sucked his cheeks in, chewed his lip a bit and rubbed his nose, hoping his assortment of facial tics and expressions would give Harry maximum time to get the hell out of there. "Oh, the diamonds? Gran's diamonds that you stole? Those ones?"

Dad stared at him.

"Oh, they're gone, quite gone," Noah said.

Dad sighed. "Eric – search your brother."

"Spread 'em!' Eric demanded, swaggering up to Noah.

"I shall do no such thing!" Noah said.

"Up to you," Eric said, jamming his hands in Noah's pockets. "You can make this easy for yourself, or you can make it hard... What the hell?" Eric pulled Noah's portable nail clippers, compass and spirit level out of his coat pocket. "Shit, man, what is this Christmas cracker crap you've got?"

"Where are the diamonds, Noah?" his dad said.

"La, la, la!" Noah grinned.

Eric frisked Noah's legs. "He's clean – what you done, hid them under your balls?"

"Oh, please!"

"Up your ass?"

"That's pretty unhygienic, Eric," Noah said. "Think you know me better than that."

His dad stepped towards Noah, looking about ready to manhandle Noah to the ground, when Bambi tottered up to them, breathless and sweaty. "Hands in the air, motherfuckers!" she screeched, making a "gun" by holding her clasped hands out in front of her, her index fingers forming a point.

"Jesus Christ," his dad muttered.

"Kidding!" Bambi laughed. "But the diamonds *are* gone. Sorry, Brian, Noah enlisted my help and it did sound like you were up to no good, but hey, you're here in London – fancy a show tonight?"

"I don't know what the hell this is, or how the hell you found us, but those diamonds are mine and you're gonna give 'em back!"

Noah snorted. "The diamonds aren't here any more – what you gonna do?"

"You need to leave *now*," Bambi said. "Looks like you lost this one, Brian."

"Piss off, Mick," his dad hissed.

Bambi squared up to him. "Screw you, Brian. You prefer Mick, do you? You want Mick? Mick who grew up on the mean streets of Stoke? Mick who used to cage fight? Oh yeah, Mick can make an appearance all right. Is that what you want, Brian?"

Noah's dad stared at Bambi and then at Noah,

breathing hard through his nose, the vein in his neck throbbing. "Eric?! C'mon!"

And then Eric and dad slammed the bar of the fire exit down, pushed their way out into the bright sunlight and were gone.

Noah turned to Bambi. "It *was* Harry who got them, right?"

"Yeah, babe. It's all good."

Noah released a heavy sigh. "Cool. Thank God. Thanks, by the way."

"Pleasure's all mine, Angel Cake."

"Did you really used to be a cage fighter?"

Bambi snorted and shook her head. "Did I fuck, hun. Did I fuck. And don't tell anyone, but I actually grew up on the mean streets of Chelsea."

CHAPTER THIRTY-SIX

It was quite incredible, really. Noah stretched his legs out in front of him as he sat on the wooden bench overlooking the boating lake in Regent's Park. Bambi Sugapops was sitting next to him, in her full gear, and no one so much as batted an eyelid. Just a teenage boy and a drag queen, enjoying looking at the geese and swans, on this surprisingly mild January afternoon.

This really was a wonderful city. And to find such a tranquil haven, in the middle of all the madness, was rather blissful. London had it all. Even the sun was shining, glinting off the boating lake, as a young couple splashed by in a pedalo. Maybe, when Harry and Pierre returned from fetching lunch, Noah would take Haz out on a pedalo. It had a romantic feel to it, and now that the diamonds were safely retrieved, ensuring Gran would get better treatment, *and* now there was no sign of the sinister government agents tracking him, romance was very much on Noah's mind.

But what if Noah suffered a repeat of the tent incident? What if things were all lovely and romantic, and the moment for *love* had arrived, and Noah couldn't manage it?

On the other hand, Noah had been *very* distracted last night, and perhaps had a sip or two too much of Pierre's wine. Not only that, the others had all been listening in, able to hear every single word he and Harry exchanged – hardly a recipe for successful intimate relations. Surely it was just a blip? Surely it would be fine?

All those distractions had pretty much vanished now.

And in the privacy of a hotel room. . .

Noah turned to Bambi, who was finishing retouching her nails. "Um, this hotel situation. . ." he began.

"Oh, *hun*," Bambi smiled. "I got such a *fabuloso* deal on the website. We're upgraded to executive rooms and breakfast is thrown in free."

"Oh, that's . . . *fabuloso* indeed!" Noah agreed.

"On-site spa too, if you fancy a steam or massage."

"Huh. Maybe," Noah said. "But in terms of the sleeping accommodation, how will that work?"

"I've put all you kids in one room – there's two twin beds, a fold-out sofa thing and a put-me-up – you can fight it out amongst yourselves." Bambi handed Noah the little bottle of nail varnish. "Do that back up for me, babe."

Noah tried not to show his disappointment – it was kind enough of Bambi to pay out for the hotel anyway – but it did feel like this would be a huge missed opportunity. He needed to find a way for Pierre and Eva *not* to be sharing a room with them. Because if something was to happen, it would be amazing if it happened in an executive room. No desperate fumbles on top of all the coats in someone's mum's bedroom for them! Instead, tea and coffee-making facilities, complimentary hand soaps, a sign you could hang on the door saying "Do not disturb", and probably a free packet of shortbread. An opulent setting that most teens planning on losing their virginity could surely only dream of!

Noah looked up and saw Harry and Pierre approaching along the path, bags of lunch in hand. "Is that lunch?" Noah said. "How lovely! Do sit down and let us eat this fine London food! Mmm!"

Harry chuckled. "Someone's in a good mood!"

"Yep!" Noah beamed. "And that someone is me, Haz! At last, something has gone right!"

Harry grinned and perched down next to Noah, pulling some packs of sandwiches out of his bag and handing them to Bambi and Noah.

"Finally, decent coffee," Pierre said, sipping an espresso as he sat on the end of the bench.

"Do you want your baguette?" Harry asked, holding it out for Pierre to take.

"*Merci.*" Pierre took a bite of it and grimaced. "Your English bread is so ... *interesting.*" He tore a piece of bread off and threw it in front of him for a passing goose, then necked the rest of his espresso. "So, Noah, let us see these precious diamonds that we have come so far to receive!"

"Well, OK," Noah said, pulling the little velvet bag out of his pocket with his free hand. "Be careful, though, Pierre."

Noah watched like a hawk as Pierre opened the little bag and peered inside. "Small," he said.

"But *valuable,*" Noah told him, keeping his eyes fixed on Pierre as he took another bite of his ham-and-cheese sandwich. The goose looked up at him and honked, clearly interested in whether Noah might offer some of his sandwich too. "Shoo, shoo, goosey," Noah said, and then looked back at Pierre. "Don't take them out of the bag!"

"I don't," Pierre said. "I only look."

"Crisps," Harry said, passing a bag of ready salted to Noah. "Crisps, Pierre?"

"Sure."

The goose honked again. It appeared to want some crisps too.

Pierre put his baguette down on the bench so he could take the crisps.

And the next thing Noah knew, the goose, frenzied

and fierce, charged towards them, apparently desperate for a bread fix. *HOOOOOONK!*

Pierre gasped and jumped as the violent goose flapped into him, baring its serrated teeth and smacking its wings into Pierre's face like a cricket bat.

Wings!

Flapping!

SLAP!

HONK!

"ARRGH!"

THWACK!

HOOONK!

Pierre flailed, his right arm bashing against Harry's left.

And somehow, he lost his grip on the bag of diamonds...

Which went flying into the air...

Noah watched in slow motion as the bag spun, turned upside down, and ten twinkling diamonds fell out....

They bounced on the ground...

Noah reached out...

But before he could get to them...

The goose had pecked up the lot.

CHAPTER THIRTY-SEVEN

For several silent seconds, everyone just froze, staring at the goose, wondering what the hell was meant to happen now.

"Shit," said Bambi.

"Shit," said Harry.

Pierre nursed his bruised cheek. "Shit."

Noah stared, unblinking, at the goose, that was now finishing off Pierre's baguette on the ground.

"Noah, it's fine," Harry said. "Don't lose your shit. We'll do something."

Noah kept focused on the goose. "Uh-huh. Like what? What are we going to do?"

"Well..." Harry floundered. "We'll ... *think* of something."

"OK, OK, there's no plan, so I'm totally going to lose my shit," Noah babbled.

"Noah, *no*! Do *not* lose your shit!" Harry insisted.

"GAAHH!" Noah squealed.

The goose honked and padded a few steps away, apparently upset by Noah's outburst.

"Shush!" Bambi said. "Just stay calm. Stay chilled. We need to keep it here." Bambi grabbed the rest of her sandwich from the bench, tore a bit off and threw it to the goose, who stepped back towards them and pecked up the food. "There you go, gal! Tasty, huh?"

"OK, so once we've used up all the food, what then? You think the goose will just stick around because it likes us?"

"We kill the goose?" Pierre suggested.

Noah gritted his teeth. "Pierre," he hissed. "You cannot simply kill a goose in a royal park!"

"It's illegal anyway," Bambi said, throwing another chunk of bread at the goose. "There's that ancient law, isn't there? They're all legally the property of the Queen. Killing one is actually treason."

"That's swans," Noah muttered.

"So geese are fair game?" Bambi said.

"We're not going to kill the goose," Noah said.

"I'm out of sandwich," Bambi said, throwing the last piece down.

"Harry? What you got?" Noah said.

"Red velvet cupcake."

"Sacrifice it."

Harry nodded and got the cupcake out of its bag, throwing some icing down for the goose.

Bambi cleared her throat. "Can I just say, we need to be out flyering in Soho in about two hours, so..."

"Can I just say," Noah snapped, "there's currently twenty thousand pounds' worth of diamonds in that goose!"

The goose honked and padded away again.

"Stop shouting!" Bambi hissed. "Every time you raise your voice, you scare it!"

"Throw more cake!" Noah demanded.

Harry threw it down, but the goose looked away and started waddling off down the path.

"Damn it!" Noah said.

Noah stood and crept up behind it. "Come on!" he hissed, beckoning to the others.

The goose continued winding its way along the path, with Noah bringing up the rear, Harry out in front, and Pierre and Bambi flanking it at either side, all trying to act TOTALLY NATURAL and not like they were trying to GET THE GOOSE or anything like that, just in case any of the lunchtime crowds now entering the park were wondering.

"This is your fault, Pierre!" Noah muttered.

"I did not ask for it to attack my face!" Pierre snapped back.

"Shut up!" Bambi hissed. "If we can just get it to stay still..."

"Yes? What?" Noah demanded.

Bambi glanced back at him. "One of us can grab it."

"I go nowhere near it," Pierre said, still rubbing his cheek. "I hate that fucking goose."

The goose took a few hops on to the grass bank by the side of the lake and sped up its pace, the others breaking into a fast walk to keep up.

"I need to take these heels off!" Bambi said, hopping along as she removed each shoe, watched by a couple of OAPs who were sitting on a nearby bench, looking mildly concerned at proceedings. Bambi slowed down and skipped over to them with a flyer. "Fancy a show tonight?"

Noah glanced back. "Bambi!"

"Coming, hun!" she said, cantering back up to the group.

"OK," Noah puffed, "So, suppose one of us does grab it ... *what then?*"

"We have foie gras," Pierre said.

"Call the RSPCA, or the police," Bambi suggested. "They probably deal with this sort of thing all the time—"

Noah snorted.

"...and even if they don't, it's a simple and honest story. We didn't do anything wrong, the goose just ate your stuff!"

"The goose has *diamonds* in it — questions will be asked, it looks dodgy!" Noah said, sucking on his asthma pump as the pursuit continued. "And with Gran back home talking about them being stolen, it'll all come crashing down on my dad, and as much as I —" he clenched his jaw, trying not to scream "— hate his goddam guts, I can't see him sent to prison!"

"Then we kill the goose!" Pierre said.

"SHUT UP!"

HONK! The goose flapped its wings and leapt into the boating lake.

Everyone came to a halt, staring at the goose as it paddled around in the water.

"Oh no," Harry muttered. "It's in the lake!"

"No shit!" Pierre said.

Bambi grabbed Noah roughly by his upper arm and pointed at the small jetty ahead. "We need to commandeer a vessel, hun!"

"Or just pay to hire one?" Noah said. "Harry and Pierre — stay on the bank and keep eyes on the goose. We'll get in the water and try to encourage it back over to you."

"If you have a chance, grab it quickly, wrap your hands around its wings and hold it close to your body," Bambi said.

"Then strangle it," Pierre added. "What? I hate that goose."

"If you harm that goose," Noah shouted back as he

and Bambi ran towards the jetty, "then I will harm *you*! Be. Warned!"

Pierre shook his head, flopping down on the bank next to the lake. "You English are totally crazy."

A beefy man with tattoos, and a scar from the side of his mouth to his ear, eyed Noah and Bambi as they hurried up to the jetty.

"Please, sir," Noah began. "How much for a pedalo?"

"Fifteen pounds for half an hour," the man sniffed, holding his hand out. "Cash or card."

Noah stared at him. "Fifteen? *Fifteen?*" Had the man misheard? He'd said "pedalo", not "luxury yacht"!

Bambi put a manicured hand on the man's arm. "How about I trade you a pedalo for a ticket to my show, hun? You look like a good-time boy."

Noah took a sharp intake of breath. Did Bambi actually want to be the victim of a drag-phobic attack? He glanced over to the bank of the lake where Harry was standing, keeping his eyes fixed on the goose, then back at the man, who was staring at Bambi's chest.

"Yeah, OK, darlin', you can take this one out," the man said, taking a flyer from her and pointing to a yellow pedalo that was parked up on the launch ramp.

"You're an angel!" Bambi said, blowing him a kiss.

"Yeah, yeah," the man muttered, holding his hand out so Bambi could steady herself as she climbed in. He turned to Noah. "In you get, then, mate."

"How does it work?" Noah asked as he struggled into his damp seat.

"Pedal with the pedals and steer with the lever," the man said, giving them a gigantic push as they swept into the boating lake. "Enjoy the ride, girls!" he shouted.

"Don't we need life jackets?" Noah wailed as they shot out into the lake.

But the man appeared to have gone.

"Pedal, then!" Bambi said. "You gotta pump those little legs, Noah!"

"I'm trying! I've got to steer as well," Noah said, pulling the lever and putting them on a direct course to collide with a swan.

"Pull it right!" Bambi shouted.

"It won't go!"

"Damn it, come here!" Bambi grabbed the lever and pulled them back over in the direction of the bank where Harry was now making big pointing gestures towards the goose. "Faster!"

"Bambi, just to ... huh ... remind you –" Noah tried to gulp in a big lungful of precious air "– I'm (a) not yet fully grown and (b) not very good at PE—" He gasped again. "And (c) suffer from mild asthma and am prone to ... huh..." Noah wheezed and gasped. "...bronchial infections, made worse by ... cold ... weather ... and..."

"Stop talking, then!"

"Let me steer a bit," Noah said. "I can do it now."

"*Fine.* Steer. They're your diamonds, what do I care."

Noah took control of the lever, as they lurched too far right and rammed straight into the concrete side of the lake – SLAM! They both lurched forward in their seats.

"Well done." Bambi smiled at him.

"It's over here!" Harry shouted from the bank.

"I know!" Noah said.

"WHAT?!" Harry shouted back.

"I said, I ... gah!" Noah tried to stand up so Harry could see him, the pedalo lurching dangerously left and right as he did so.

"SIT!" Bambi said, pulling him back down, as the pedalo rocked around. "Bloody idiot."

"WHAT'S HAPPENING?" Harry shouted.

"WE'VE RUN AGROUND!" Noah shouted.

Bambi sighed. "We haven't run aground."

"LIKE WHEN THE TITANIC HIT THE ICEBERG!" Noah shouted.

Bambi shook her head. "There's not one friggin' parallel to that situation." She looked at Noah, her eye twitching slightly. "Can you please just peddle backwards so I can steer us back round the right way? If that's OK with you, Noah?"

"WE'RE PEDALLING BACKWARDS NOW!" Noah called across to Harry.

A couple of guys wolf-whistled at Bambi, filming the scene on their phones.

"AHOY, BOYS!" Bambi called out. "Hoist my jolly roger and swab my poop deck, this boat is full of seamen and we're coming for you! You fellows fancy a show tonight?"

Noah gritted his teeth and pedalled furiously. He didn't know what he must have done in a past life to deserve being stuck in a pedalo with reckless drag queen, but it must have been pretty bad.

"Slow up!" Harry shouted across to them from the bank, pointing at the goose. "It's that one – just ahead!"

Bambi steered the pedalo gently behind the goose, giving it the tiniest nudge up the backside, so it flapped, honked and started paddling towards the bank to get away.

Noah stopped pedalling, using the break to flex his cold and wet feet a bit. There was nothing worse than a wet sock. And a wet shoe. And an increasingly damp bottom, and...

Noah glanced down at the bottom of the pedalo and whimpered. "Water!" he babbled.

"Just another few metres!" Bambi smiled. "Working like a dream!"

"Water!"

"C'mon, goosey!"

"WATER! WATER! We're SINKING!" Noah screamed.

Bambi looked down, eyes wide as she took in the

scene that Noah was looking at. The bottom of the pedalo was swimming in a good four inches of water.

Noah threw himself at Bambi, shaking. "I can't SWIM!"

"That bastard on the jetty gave us a dud boat!" Bambi hissed. My *shoes!*"

"I never learned! If I don't have armbands, I'll sink!"

"Noah, it's fine, we're metres from the bank, just pedal some more and—"

"HEEELLPPPP!"

HOOOONK! HONNK! The goose flapped about, spread its wings and launched itself out of the water, hopping up on to the bank, and starting to peck at some crumbs on the grass.

Pierre was right behind it with a big stick.

"Don't you dare!" Noah shouted over to him. "Just grab it!"

"You grab it!" Pierre said.

"I CAN'T, I'M SINKING!"

"Pedal towards me," Harry said, squatting down on the edge of the bank and reaching an arm out. "I'll pull you in."

"I pull you, Noah, if you like?" Pierre shouted from where he was standing near the goose.

"Right! That's it!" Harry squealed, running over to Pierre and launching himself at him, so Pierre toppled backwards on to the grass, Harry on top of him. "Stop it!

Stop saying suggestive things about Noah! ARGHHH! You're driving me CRAZY!" Harry straddled Pierre, pinning Pierre's shoulders down with his knees.

"Oh my God!" Pierre said. "All I do is repeat the same words you are saying, you are the CRAZY one!"

"You know what you're doing!" Harry insisted, pressing his finger on the end of Pierre's nose to make his point, which was about as much aggression as Noah had ever seen from Harry.

Noah never imagined he would be in a position where two boys were fighting over him, but he was scarcely able to enjoy the moment, what with his imminent watery demise and all. Bambi pedalled furiously, the boat shifting another metre or so, enabling a quivering Noah to leap out of his seat and splash over the top of the pedalo, leaping to the shore. "Women and children first, Noah!" Bambi said, hoisting herself out of the wildly rocking boat.

"I am a child!" Noah hissed back, pulling Harry off Pierre as he scrambled up the grass bank. "Boys, I don't know what I've done to cause all this sparring, but you must put your differences aside for now and sort all this out later."

Harry brushed himself down and Pierre scrambled to his feet, shaking his head in disbelief. They all turned to look at the goose, which looked straight back at them, honked, and then started running in the opposite direction, flapping its wings ... and then taking off.

"After it!" Noah shouted.

Noah charged ahead, following the goose's low flight path as it glided back along the path they'd just run down and towards where the van was parked on the Outer Circle.

It flapped down on to some grass near the exit gate, as the four caught up with it and hovered a few metres away. "Right then," Bambi gasped, removing the pashmina from her shoulders. "I guess it's now or never."

Bambi crept up behind the goose, which was busy scratching around in the grass. And then, holding the pashmina aloft, and in one swift movement, she threw the pashmina over the goose's body, and wrapped her hands tightly around its covered wings, so just its head and neck were poking out.

HONK! HONK! HOOONK!

There was a brief struggle, as Bambi wrestled with the goose, rolling over on the ground...

A young couple passed by, looking unsure as to whether this was OK, and possibly part of some site-specific theatre experience, or actually something they should report to the authorities.

"Drag queen goose wrestling," Noah told them. "It's a thing now. In London."

"Cool." The young guy nodded.

"Love London!" his girlfriend giggled as they walked off.

Bambi stood up, holding the goose firmly under her

arm, which just honked forlornly, the game clearly up. "I'm going to stuff it in the van!" Bambi said. "It'll shit at some point, and then you'll get your diamonds back, Noah. We'll stop off at Pets at Home for some hay and seed, make the damn thing comfortable, but after that, we really have to check into the hotel, then get to Soho and flyer. Job done, boys, now get back in the van – we've got work to do."

Noah let out a huge breath and closed his eyes for a moment. *Thank God.* OK, he didn't have the diamonds back yet, but when nature had taken its course, he would. And if that meant sifting through bird poop for the next twelve hours, then so be it. It was the least he could do, for Gran.

He glanced quickly around him, and froze.

There she was.

The woman.

His mouth went dry.

The woman from the car. The woman who took the photos. Who asked him the time.

There she was. In Regent's Park. On a bench. Looking at her phone.

CHAPTER THIRTY-EIGHT

The van was parked in the hotel's underground car park, which at least was out of sight as far as Noah's dad and Eric went. They'd shifted all the luggage out of the back compartment of the van, leaving space for the goose, some hay, seed and a pile of prunes that Noah hoped would encourage the bird to shit both copiously and fast. The sooner the diamonds were out of it, the better.

But all this was small comfort. Noah sat wide-eyed in the front passenger seat, panic-eating a Costa Coffee chocolate tiffin. *He was being followed. Someone was after something. And he didn't know what or whom he could trust.* Damn it! So much for having a clear head so he could properly focus on *sensuous matters.*

There was a tapping at the window. *Harry*. Noah wound the window down.

"Secretly eating a brownie, I see," Harry said.

Noah shook his head. "It's a chocolate tiffin. It's my second. I may have three, I don't know."

Harry narrowed his eyes. "What the matter with you? Everything's OK now, isn't it? I mean, I know the diamonds are—"

"The diamonds, the diamonds, yes," Noah said. He looked at Harry. If there was one person he *could* trust, it was Harry. And if he couldn't trust Harry, he may as well abandon Earth and be the first to colonize Mars. "We need to talk."

"Uh-oh."

Noah opened the door. "Get in."

Noah shuffled along the front seat so Harry could hop in next to him. "Shut the door," Noah said.

Harry pulled it closed. "Look, if this is about what happened with Pierre, I'm sorry and I'm gonna apologize to him. He was just doing my head in with his constant little comments."

"Oh, no, he deserved that," Noah said. "I was quite taken by your efforts to defend my honour."

Harry grinned. "What's up, then?"

"OK," Noah said. "OK, so this is going to sound crazy weird. I mean, you probably won't believe me, which is partly why I've waited until now to tell you, but as my boyfriend, I think you should know. Are you ready?"

"Yes?"

Noah nodded. "Right. I think I'm being followed, Harry. There's this woman, and sometimes a man, and they have a black Vauxhall Astra, and I keep seeing them. I saw them in Little Fobbing. I saw the car at Route 66, and I saw the woman again this afternoon, in the park."

Harry stared ahead and nodded. "You ever seen them before? Do they live in Little Fobbing?"

"No."

"OK, but *why*, Noah? Why would they want to follow you? I mean, not being rude, you are nice, and you're cute, and there's lots of reasons why *I* would follow you places, but two randoms? It doesn't make sense."

"Harry, I don't think they want *bow chicka wah wah* with me. I'm trying to work it out. Like, is it something to do with my dad? Are they hired thugs, or undercover detectives trying to trap him for something? Or maybe it's something to do with Bambi – I mean, how much do we really know about this drag feud in Stoke-on-Trent? *What's the real truth?*"

Harry nodded. "She could have killed someone?"

"I don't know! I just don't know..." Noah shoved the rest of the tiffin in his mouth. "I just can't work out why they're after *me*!"

Harry sighed and looked out of the window while Noah finished chewing on the tiffin and thought about the fact he could have also mentioned Pierre, and whatever the hell he was up to in the shed with Ms O'Malley, but there was no way of doing that without admitting *why* he'd followed Pierre there in the first place and that might just lead to more fights and then Pierre might tell everything and that would all be very messy.

Harry looked at him. "You haven't done anything wrong, have you?"

"Well, no, of course not."

"So stop worrying." Harry shrugged. "Whatever it is, it isn't *your* shit. It isn't *your* life. It's someone else's."

Noah nodded. Maybe Harry was right. You couldn't spend your time worrying what other people might have done, or were doing. That was them. This was him. And he should focus on *him*. Well, him and Harry. The stuff that made him happy. The stuff that *was* his life. Why care what trouble other people might be in? *He hadn't done anything wrong!*

Noah smiled, feeling some sense of relief. "Maybe, later, after the club and everything and, assuming I can devise some way of getting Pierre and Eva out of the room for a bit, we'll come back here and ... and..."

Harry's eyes lit up. "And *what*?"

"And listen to my Spa Reflections playlist. If you want to? Do that? Might you want to do that, do you suppose?"

Harry nodded and kissed him again, putting his hand up under Noah's hoodie and T-shirt, stroking Noah's tummy. "Yeah, that sounds nice."

Noah let Harry gently work his fingers lower, waiting for any form of below-waist tingling that might indicate things would be OK later.

Shiiiit!

"And I'll stop worrying," Noah said, worrying like crazy that he was never again going to get a boner.

"Good idea," Harry replied, sitting back again. "Was that everything?"

Noah nodded. "Yeah. That's everything."

"What's this?" Harry said, screwing his face up and pulling a tub of protein powder up from between the seats, that Noah had moved there to make space for the goose.

"Ah, I was just thinking about, you know, gaining a bit of mass, maybe, like a footballer, but I've kind of gone off the idea now."

Harry didn't look impressed. "Yeah, good. You're fine as you are. I like you as you are."

Noah nodded. "Cool. It was just a thought. Oh, and *thank you.*"

Harry shook his head. "Muppet," he said, passing the protein tub to Noah and opening the door. "We're all heading over to Soho with the flyers in five, so meet you in reception, yeah?"

"Sure." Noah nodded. "I'll just check on the goose, and see you there."

Harry smiled and headed off towards the lifts, his

words still echoing around Noah's head: *He hadn't done anything wrong!*

And then Noah looked at what he was holding and his blood froze.

He hadn't done anything wrong. . .

Except actively participate in a pyramid sales scheme.

CHAPTER THIRTY-NINE

He'd rammed the five tubs of protein shake he'd brought with him under some black sacks in a huge wheelie bin near the exit of the car park.

And then he'd pulled them out again because how would that look? An innocent person doesn't try to destroy evidence.

So he'd put them back in the van and wished he could just tell Harry about it, but of course he couldn't tell Harry because that might *implicate* Harry. That could make Harry an *accessory* to Noah's accidental crimes ... or it might force him into a moral dilemma – to testify in Noah's prosecution or something. Poor Harry.

Noah racked his brains as he walked with Harry, Pierre and Bambi towards Soho. Maybe it would be OK.

He was sure there was no incriminating evidence back at home. There was no paperwork or marketing materials – all Noah had was a few tubs of the powder... And a little shit of a Year Seven who he'd tried to recruit as a rep... Maybe he would have to kill him?

Oh my God. *No.* This was how it happened! This was how people got sucked into a vortex of criminality after just one simple mistake!

But, Noah considered, if it *were* between prison and Jack being pushed down a stairwell, well—

"Look!" Harry said, tugging at Noah's arm and pointing at the Harry Potter signage at the front of the Palace Theatre as the matinee crowd spilled over the street. "Aw, we should have tried to get tickets."

"Next time," Noah said, as they pushed through the teeming crowd and up Shaftsbury Avenue. *Assuming I'm not in a youth offenders' institution.*

His feet ached; it was taking *years* to get to the club, but truthfully, Noah didn't mind. Up ahead, on the right-hand side of the street, Noah could see theatre after theatre, all with signs illuminated by hundreds of little bulbs, twinkling, enticing you in. To his left, Chinese lanterns were hung across the side streets, heralding the start of Chinatown, and as they swung a right into Soho, so many little boutiques and cafés and shops, selling so many weird and obscure things, Noah had to wonder how they turned a profit. One place had tubes of colourful, bubbling liquid in the window – apparently it was some sort of tea. Another sold crisps. *Just crisps.* Albeit in very fancy boxes with dips, but still.

"Finally, the UK has some life!" Pierre said as two guys walked by, holding hands, with no one staring at them.

Pierre was right, and Noah didn't feel like defending Little Fobbing right now. He felt a million miles away from there. Here, he felt lost in the swirling mass, anonymous amongst the thousands; you could disappear here, do what you liked, and no one would know and no one would care.

They stopped outside a shop on Old Compton Street, and Noah turned to look in through the window, coming face-to-face with the sizeable crotch of a male mannequin, trussed up in leather straps with metal studs. "Oh, my!" Noah muttered, feeling his cheeks flush. Oh God. Was this the standard garb for gay guys now?

"Hot," Pierre whispered in Noah's ear as he peered over his shoulder.

"Huh," Noah said. "*Impractical*, you mean. What if you require lavatory facilities? You'd need a pair of secateurs and a hacksaw to get that lot off."

"Listen," Pierre sighed. "After that thing with Harry this afternoon, I think it best that I don't stay in the same room as you tonight. I will get my own room. I give you some space. Plus. . ." Pierre gave Noah a little wink. "We're going to the club tonight, and I'm hoping to maybe get lucky, right?"

This might have been the outcome Noah had been hoping for, but since *he couldn't even get a boner any more*, it all seemed rather academic now. "Oh right," Noah said. "Um . . . have you the money for that?"

"I put it on my dad's Amex." Pierre shrugged.

Noah blew out a breath. *His dad's Amex! Very nice too!* "Well, if you're sure."

"Too good a chance to waste, Noah, huh?" Pierre grinned.

Noah gave a weak smile. He had a definite feeling his chance tonight would end up being very much wasted.

"Right, girls!" Bambi hollered. Noah supposed she was talking to them. It seemed that once they'd entered Soho, Bambi had become even more camp and ridiculous – gaining power like a droid returning to its mother ship to recharge. "Here's some flyers for you all," she said, shoving a pile into each of their hands. "Bambi's off to do a sound check, so she's relying on you to get the punters in. Be at the club by eight and I'll let you in the back entrance – *oo-er*!"

"We won't let you down, Bambi," Harry smiled.

"Thanks, girls!"

"We're boys," Noah told her.

But she had already swept off into the crowd. Noah sighed, glanced at the flyers and screwed his face up. "Really?" he muttered, reading down the leaflet and tutting. "*Sloppy*. Thirty gsm paper stock? This just won't do."

"Shall we crack on?" Harry said.

Noah whipped a pen out of his small leather satchel. "Make a start," Noah said. "I'm just going to correct a few copy errors for them – feel like I should earn my keep, and they'll be grateful for this."

"Okaaay," Harry said. He sighed and looked at Pierre. "Come on, then."

"Really?"

"Yes, really."

"You forgive me?" Pierre said.

"Yes, I forgive you."

Pierre smiled and bounced into the road, which was so full of people no cars could get down it anyway. "Come and receive a flyer, boys!" Pierre called out.

Noah shook his head and seated himself at a small table outside a café, pen in hand, and set to work on the leaflet, his corrections in brackets:

Jason Fuchs Presents *(That's really your surname, is it? OK, cool.)*

GAY BOYZ *(The plural of boy should be spelt with an "s" – is this deliberate? If so, WHY?)*

Soho's BEST LGBT night! *(Says who? Could this fall foul of advertising standards?)*

DJ Ham *(Maybe drop the meat reference and go for*

something more edgy, like "DJ Cool" or "DJ Ace"?) drops SINFUL BEATZ! *(See note about re: plural usage – also, how can a "beat" be "sinful"? Bit confusing. Maybe phrase it like "DJ Cool plays brill tunes" or something?)*

HOSTED BY THE GAY-LARIOUS BAMBI SUGAPOPS! *(OK, so "gay-larious" obviously isn't a real word. Seems too close to "garrulous"? I would just scrap this bit tbh, and maybe just put "A 'funny' drag queen will be here too", with quotes around the word "funny" because you don't want to raise people's hopes.)*

He would give this directly to the club's promoter when they arrived later. This might be London, and it might all be very hip, but they'd forgotten about the one thing that was always en vogue: good grammar.

Noah stood up. *Right, then.* He took a deep breath. If you were going to do a job, you should do it properly, with *enthusiasm* and *passion*.

"ROLL UP! ROLL UP!" Noah shouted. "COME AND GET A FLYER FOR A BIG GAY DISCO!"

For once, nobody mocked him. A couple of guys laughed, but in a kind sort of way, and came to get a flyer. Nobody pointed at him or made a snide little comment to their mate. It was like Noah was amongst friends.

"How old are you?" said a guy, maybe in his late twenties, who came up to him.

"Sixteen, sir."

The guy sucked in a breath. "Jailbait."

"I'm just a boy from the country, sir," Noah said, batting his eyelashes and handing the man a flyer. "And it is *prison*, just FYI, not *jail*, for we are not in America."

The guy ruffled Noah's hair. "Cute." And he gave Noah a hug before slipping back off into the crowd.

Two older guys, who looked so identical they could be twins, both with beards and leather jackets, came over to him and took a flyer. "Is this tonight?" Man with Beard One asked.

"Yes, indeed!" Noah grinned. "A drag queen will be there. Have you seen a drag queen before?"

Man with Beard Two chuckled. "You ever seen a drag queen, Jim?"

Jim screwed his face up. "Ah, I'm trying to remember..."

"OK, sorry, I get it," Noah said.

Jim smiled warmly at him. "Don't ever change."

"What do you mean?" Noah said.

"Just that. You're sweet."

And they clasped hands and went on their way. "Might see you later!" Jim called back as another guy walked by, pointed at Noah and said, "I LOVE GUYS IN GLASSES!"

"Mild astigmatism," Noah confided.

"Sexy!" he shouted, walking on.

Noah shrugged. Maybe the guy was drunk. Or high.

Maybe both.

"You're popular," Harry commented, coming over.

"Everyone seems nice and friendly," Noah agreed.

"Hugging various guys..."

Noah smiled. "Would you like a hug, Harry?"

"I was maybe feeling a bit jealous." Harry shrugged.

"Come here then, Haz," Noah said, wrapping his arms around Harry and pressing himself into him. He immediately recoiled. "Shit. Shit! Shit, shit, shit!"

"What is it?"

Noah flapped about, patting the empty inside pocket of his coat. "I've been pickpocketed! My wallet's gone! Argh! It was that guy! That guy who hugged me! He must have made off with my wallet! Where is he?!"

Harry looked about as Noah spun this way and that, looking through the thick crowd. "I think he's gone, Noah."

"Oh God, think, think, what do I need to do? Cancel my library card! Who knows what that ruffian will do with it! What else?" Noah gasped. "My Superdrug loyalty card! Oh no! I'd built up at least two pounds fifty on there! Damn that cutpurse! Damn him and his wicked ways!" Noah pulled his mobile out and passed it to Harry. "Tell the library what's happened and ask them to cancel my card. I need to find a police officer!"

He bungled the phone into Harry's hands and looked about for anyone in the crowd in an appropriate uniform. Harry dutifully looked up the Little Fobbing Library website and pressed on the phone link.

"Er, hello?" Harry said. "Um ... I'm phoning on behalf of Noah Grimes... He, er ... he's had his wallet stolen, you see—"

"By a CUTPURSE!"

"Yes, by a cutpurse, and needs you to cancel his library card... Well, I think he's worried someone might try to borrow books with it, you know?" Harry listened whilst the librarian spoke to him.

Noah jumped up wildly, trying to see over the crowd. But alas, there were no lawmen in sight.

"OK, that's great," Harry said at last. "Oh? Oh yes? Oh, OK... I'll let him know... It's called *what*?!" Harry looked aghast at Noah, who just held his hands out – *what's the matter?!*

Harry handed Noah his phone back. "Everything fine?" Noah asked.

"Uh-huh."

"You seem weird."

"Nope."

"Huh. Good. I haven't been able to find a police officer."

"Your book's arrived."

Noah nodded. "Right. What book?"

Harry swallowed. *"The Joy of Gay Sex – Junior Edition."*

Noah blinked at him.

318

Harry looked back at him, open-mouthed.

"My mother!" Noah squealed. "She did this! It's probably all part of her crazy attempt to be a 'good parent'! The no-good CRONE! Argh! I promise you, Harry, I did not order that book from the library!"

"That's fine," Harry said.

"Arghhhh! It's NOT FINE! DAMN HER! Arghhhh! MOTHER!" he screamed. "She actually thinks I want to have this discussion with her! She can't find time to get herself a proper job but she can find time to make my life HELL on a regular basis!" He took Harry by the hands. "I have no interest in *The Joy of Gay Sex*," he told him. "I do solemnly swear that to you."

"No interest?" Harry smirked.

"Mmm . . . mm. . . I mean. . . Oh God. . ."

Harry hugged him and kissed him on the lips. "Let's find a police officer – can you give a description?"

Noah was about to answer that, yes, of course he could, but his phone started ringing. "An unknown number!" Noah announced, holding it to his ear. "Noah Grimes speaking, who is this, please?"

"*Grimes!*" Ms O'Malley snarled down the phone. "It has come to my attention that you have fled Little Fobbing with two exchange students in what amounts to an *unauthorized* absence! Where are you?"

"Where?" Noah asked, his brain spinning. "We're . . . we're, no it's fine, I'm sure the school would fully approve, because we're actually just on a luxury weekend coach trip to 'the enchanting Cotswolds'."

There was a silence on the other end of the line. "Right," she said, and hung up.

What did that mean? Did it mean she believed him?

"Noah?" Harry was looking at him expectantly.

"Hello, Harry, everything's fine, no problems."

"I'm not even going to ask," Harry said.

Noah nodded. Was that a hint of irritation in Harry's voice? A little feeling of exhaustion with the constant drama bubbling through? Oh God, was that what Harry thought of Noah? That he was high maintenance and annoying?

Maybe he was! And that certainly wasn't on most people's lists of "qualities to look for in a partner".

Light and happy! He had to keep everything light and happy! After this whole diamonds escapade with his dad and Eric (that wasn't even over yet), Noah's pathetic insecurities, and now all the shit he had told Harry in the car park – who could blame Harry for just wanting a nice, normal life, with a nice, normal boyfriend, not a FREAK who always attracted DRAMA and CHAOS.

Light and happy. Light and happy.

"Haz, let's get rid of the rest of these flyers, go back to the hotel, get our glad rags on, and head out for a lovely, relaxed evening in a gay club."

Harry looked doubtful. "What about whoever was on

the phone?"

'Screw 'em."

"And where's Eva?"

"She'll turn up!" Noah shrugged.

"The goose?"

"...will poop when the time is right."

"And what about your stolen wallet?"

Noah released a breath. "The wallet's gone to a new home – maybe a better home, who knows? Anyway, it's just a *thing*, Haz. *Things* don't matter – people do. The wallet may have gone, but you haven't."

He didn't know quite where that had come from. He'd managed to dredge up some actually *quite good* words from deep within his brain somewhere. He hoped it wasn't a popular social media meme that he'd just plagiarized – he didn't want to seem insincere.

"That's sweet," Harry said, taking Noah's hand.

"Mmm, *yes,*" Noah said. "Um, although actually, can you lend me, like, maybe twenty pounds? I need to get a couple of *things* from the shop."

"What sort of things?"

"For tonight!" Noah winked.

Harry's eyes widened. "Twenty pounds' worth?"

"Special night, right?" Noah smiled, hoping to hell it would be.

Harry blew out a breath and handed Noah two tens. "Special night," he agreed.

CHAPTER FORTY

The bass vibrated through Noah's very soul.

He'd only ever been to a school disco before, featuring six portable disco lights and what amounted to a Fisher-Price "My First MP3 Player" as a sound system. Mr Baxter usually DJ'd, and the food technology department provided non-alcoholic punch and a buffet of sausage rolls and sandwiches.

But this place, *this place*, was real big-boy stuff. Noah had never seen so many insanely beautiful people in one room, rammed together, and apparently having the most orgasmically epic time of their lives. He'd never seen an entire rig of moving lights like they had in this place – not outside of a theatre anyway. And the banks of speakers! Like it was huge gig at Wembley Stadium or something and the glitter balls and the confetti cannons and the—

"I go to bar and get us all drinks," Pierre said. "My surprise!" He pushed his way through the sweaty crowd, looking like some sort of homosexual angel in his tight white jeans, tight white shirt and white trainers. It was all fun and games wearing all white, Noah considered, until someone spilled a Coke over you, or you accidentally sat in some ketchup. Noah's combination of his black-and-white-striped top and black chinos might have had the accidental effect of making him look like a mime, but he could at least be assured the outfit would wear well.

Noah squinted through the stage smoke and shafts of coloured lights, aware that Harry was speaking words at him that were totally lost under the remix of ABBA's "Dancing Queen", which was currently being pumped out at ear-shattering volume. Of course, Harry had got his outfit totally right. Floral-print T-shirt, jeans and Converse – cool, fun, and ... aww, he looked really cute, anyway.

"Right?!" Harry said, grinning at Noah.

"Right!" Noah agreed, blinking back at him.

Harry laughed and stepped in towards Noah, putting his mouth close to Noah's ear. His breath smelt minty. "You've no idea what I just said, have you?"

"Not entirely."

"What?"

Noah placed his mouth against Harry's warm little ear too. "NOT ENTIRELY, NO!"

"JUST SAYING, I'M FASCINATED TO SEE WHAT BAMBI'S ACT IS LIKE!"

"Oh! Huh, me too," Noah said, watching as a boy not much older than them with cat whiskers painted on his face walked past and gave Harry a wink.

"BOYS AND GIRLS!" a voice over the PA system boomed over the track. "IT'S SOHO'S BEST LGBT NIGHT!"

Noah rolled his eyes. They really needed to heed his advice on false advertising claims.

"SO PLEASE WELCOME YOUR HOST, SHE'S GAY-LARIOUS..."

Noah shook his head.

"SHE'S DRAG-TASTIC!"

I mean, this was nonsense now...

"SHE'S HERE AND SHE'S QUEER..."

And she's crap, but let's not split hairs when we can embrace hyperbole instead...

"MS BAMBI SUGAPOPS!"

There was what Noah could only assume was an alcohol – and possibly drug-induced – frenzy of clapping and whooping as the stage lights swung on to Bambi, wearing a full-length, shimmering gold number, huge blonde wig, and the most extraordinary silver and bright purple eyeshadow, which contrasted spectacularly well with her rich, brown skin. She did a little turn around the stage to her entrance music, before striking a pose in the middle.

"Did you like my entrance?!" Bambi shouted into her microphone. "Ooh! I bet you did, naughty!"

Noah winced. Despite their differences at times, Noah felt a strange loyalty towards Bambi. He hoped her crass, provincial, out-of-date drag jokes weren't going to bomb with the sophisticated London gay crowd.

"I had a plumber round to fix a leak in my bathroom the other day," Bambi was saying, going right in with her routine.

Noah glanced over towards the bar, interested to know if there was any danger of a drink sometime soon. Apparently there wasn't. Pierre was sucking the face off some indie-looking guy wearing a trilby. Huh. Pierre certainly didn't waste any time.

"Lovely lad he was, told me my flange was buggered and my nuts needed tightening..."

The crowd laughed. It seemed there was always a market for smutty innuendo, even in sophisticated, cultured London. Noah mouthed along to the punchline, knowing damn well what was coming:

"I said, you can tighten my nuts any time, darlin'!"

Harry had his hand on Noah's back. "Bambi's doing OK!"

"Against all odds," Noah agreed.

"This plumber, he takes one look at my flange and shakes his head. 'I'm gonna need a *really long screw*,' he says. 'Darlin', you might just be in luck,' I tell him..."

Through the crowd, Noah spied the back of a toned lad, strapped up with shot glasses and bottles, and quite naked expect for some tight, white underpants and some silver trainer boots, handing out shots of *some sort of alcohol*. Why queue at the bar when the bar can come to you? How very perfect.

The lad turned around.

Those abs looked familiar...

Noah's jaw fell open.

Oh my good God...

"I said, I like my coffee how I like my men – hot, strong and full of cream. He said, 'If you add steamy and instant to that, we might just be compatible...'"

"Noah? Bro?"

Noah shook himself back to reality as Josh came up to them. "Josh?"

"You've discovered my little secret, then!" Josh said, actually looking a tiny bit sheepish for the first time in his life.

Noah swallowed and did his best to look totally cool about this. Josh Lewis. In a gay club! "Josh, my goodness. You're a member of the LGBTQ plus community? Er... Congratulations!"

Josh held his hand up. "Hold up there, Noah. Hold your horses. I just work here. Freelance basis. I'm a tequila shot boy."

"Oh. But. . ."

"Yeah, got chatting to Bambi one night down the Red Lion – she put the wheels in motion, and here I am. Guess how much I can make a night?"

"Fifty pounds?" Noah shrugged.

Josh laughed. "Higher."

"Seventy?"

"Four hundred quid *a night*. Four hundred! Just for pouring out some shots. The pink pound is where it's at, man."

Harry looked impressed. "Can you get us jobs too?" he laughed.

"You shouldn't even be in here, little dudes. Too young!" Josh put his finger to his lips. "But I'll keep quiet if you guys do."

"Right." Noah nodded, doing his level best to keep his eyeline totally on Josh's face and not anything lower down.

"Jess is on at me the whole time, man. Baby this, baby that. This place is my escape. My fun time. Plus, it pays me good dollar. These days, you gotta *di-ver-si-fy*! You gotta have fingers in so many pies to make some coin." Josh whipped two shot glasses out of his holster and poured a couple of shots. "Truth is, being a PT at the gym doesn't cut it, cash-wise. And Jess's dad, he is *rinsing* me for money to support the kid." Josh shook his head. "Most of what I bank from the protein-shake business goes on to Jess, but she don't know about my little *side*line." Josh winked and handed Noah and Harry a shot each. "Here you go, my good dudes! Drinks on me tonight, as many as you like – on the condition we keep this between ourselves. I don't need Jess and her parents finding out."

Noah eyed up the shot glasses. "Um, is this—"

"On three!" Josh shouted, sprinkling salt on Noah's hand. "ONE, TWO..."

"Josh, you've spilled something on my hand! What is this?" Noah said.

"It's salt. Lick it, neck the shot, then bite into the lemon I'll have ready for you," Josh grinned.

"That's A LOT OF THINGS to do in quick succession!" Noah said. "Why's it so complicated?"

"Why's life so complicated?" Josh replied, which was a good point.

What the hell, Noah thought. This was London. The music was loud, the lights bright, the atmosphere electric. He licked the salt, raised the shot glass to his lips, threw the liquid down his throat and—

BLEEEUUUGGHHHHHHGAAHHHH!

...spat it straight out on to the floor. "OH MY ACTUAL GOD I THINK MINE HAD BLEACH IN IT!" Noah squealed.

"Duuuude!" Josh said, handing Noah a lemon wedge.

"Bite down on this!"

"GAAAHH!" Noah said, recoiling from the sour taste as he crumpled over in agony. "WHY? WHHHYY?!"

From somewhere Noah heard Josh say, "I'll be back in a bit. Don't wanna get you dudes too drunk, they'll boot you out." Ha. There was small danger of that. This stuff was so toxic, it was impossible to keep down. Noah stared hard at the floor, hoping the focus would cause the wave of nausea to pass. In the background, Bambi was still prattling on ... something about a hammer-action screwdriver and lubricating a driveshaft...

Noah straightened himself up. Kitten Face Boy was back and talking in Harry's ear. He couldn't make out what they were saying.

Kitten Face glanced over at Noah.

Noah gave him a brief smile.

Kitten Face didn't return the smile, just went back to talking to Harry.

Kitten Face was an absolute *dick*. Noah crossed his arms and tried to watch Bambi, whilst keeping Haz and Kitten Face in his field of vision. What sort of boy walks around looking like a Snapchat filter, anyway?

Harry nodded, turned away and stepped back over to Noah. "Jeez."

"What did he want?" Noah asked.

"Wanted to know if we were together."

"What did you say?"

"What do you think I said?"

Noah looked straight into Harry's eyes. "Yes?"

Harry smiled. "You are SUCH an idiot. Of course I said yes." Harry glanced over his shoulder, where Kitten Face was still hovering. "He's not giving up, though. I think we need to show him what's what."

Noah's eyes widened. "Challenge him to a duel?"

A smile spread across Harry's lips. "Or, maybe ... just this?" Harry leaned forward and kissed Noah gently. "What do you think?" he murmured.

Noah instinctively stiffened ... a kiss, a public place, other people, what if ... except no one cared. No one was looking or saying anything or ... here they were, just two boys kissing, and it was the most normal thing in the world. Noah gave Harry a kiss back. "I think that's the best idea you've ever had," Noah said as Harry reached his hands around into Noah's back pockets and pulled their bodies into each other. Noah didn't care about Kitten Face any more. He didn't even know if Kitten Face had bothered to stick around and see this. It didn't matter. Nothing seemed to matter, lost in the stage smoke and lights of the club. It was another world. Complete escape. And that felt so good. Harry pressed into him, and Noah pressed back. Breathless.

Hard.

Finally! Thank God! Oh YES! Noah could barely wait to get Harry back to the hotel room and whack on his

Spa Reflections playlist—

"YOU CAN RUN, BUT YOU CAN'T HIDE, SUGAPOPS!"

A gasp went up from the crowd as Noah broke away and all eyes focused on the stage. Bambi looked on, mouth open, clearly aghast, as a tall drag queen, dressed in a mermaid-style outfit, complete with fish tail and seaweed hair, emerged through the dry ice, held aloft by four greased-up muscle boys wearing tiny silver pants. They paraded her around the stage like Cleopatra, before placing her gently down in the centre.

"Mi-Chelle Sea Shells!" Bambi finally spluttered.

"You'd better believe it!" Mi-Chelle snarled, gesturing as two other drag queens entered behind her, who were dressed in multilayered outfits of garish colours. "Of course you know Milly-Feuille and Cherry Macaroon? The Patisserie Sisters!"

"What's this about?" Bambi said, weirdly dropping Bambi's voice and sounding like Mick.

The crowd were agog, enjoying what they assumed was part of the show. But when Bambi's voice became Mick's, Noah knew better. "Something's up," he said to Harry.

Mi-Chelle threw her head back and laughed theatrically. "Oh, honey! This was only ever about getting what was rightfully mine! You wouldn't play ball, so I had to set up a little sting operation!"

Murmurs of interest from the crowd, who now appeared to sense this was an unusual choice of sketch for some drag queens in a gay club.

"Oh, no, it's a trap," Noah muttered.

"YES!" Mi-Chelle shouted, "I got my friends the Patisserie Sisters to offer you the gig here, knowing you would do all the leg work, flyering, filling the place, *sexy go-go boys*." Mi-Chelle lowered her voice. "He's quite a find, hun, I've made him a very enticing offer to stay on."

"Traitors!" Bambi snarled. "You tricked me!"

"The Patisserie Sisters have been friends of mine for years – didn't you know?" Mi-Chelle sneered, her dark blue lipstick accentuating the curl of her lips into an evil smile. "And with the takings from tonight, I'll finally get my share of what's rightfully mine – the van!"

"*My* van!" Bambi shouted. "It was me who made the extortionate hire purchase payments when you'd spent all your money on Botox and that failed nose job!"

An "Ooooooh!" went up from the crowd, who were clearly *loving* this. Noah turned to Harry. "This is going to turn nasty. We have to get out of here. *Fast.*"

"Where's Polly Esther?" Bambi asked. "What have you done to her?"

A sorry look washed over Mi-Chelle's face. "You haven't heard? Polly's dead."

A stunned silence from the crowd and the stage. Clearly matters were more serious than Noah had imagined. Was this what the surveillance team were really concerned with? Bambi pulled her hair off. "Danny's dead?"

Mi-Chelle gave a contemptuous little snort and shook her head. "*Polly's* dead. She won't be performing any more – not after some of her tweets from five years ago mysteriously surfaced, where she'd made some *deeply offensive* comments about the gay clubs in Stoke, and all her bookings dried up. *Danny's* fine. He's having a couple of weeks in Lanzarote with his wife and kids to take stock of everything."

"We've all had beef with the clubs in Stoke, and you know it!" Mick said. "*You* dredged those tweets up deliberately!"

"That's slander, Mick," Mi-Chelle purred, sashaying up to him. "And I'm a *very litigious* girl." She gave Mick's outfit an up-and-down glance. "Fuck me, you look terrible. Talk about ruining the magic."

Mick was right up in her face. "Go to hell, you vile little bitch!"

Another "Oooooooh!" from the crowd.

Mi-Chelle just laughed. "Oh, hun, you're all tired old cock jokes and lame knob gags, like some low-rent panto dame!"

"I give the punters what they want!" Mick countered.

"*Gurl*, they don't want your tired shit. They want, they *need*, hell they *deserve* some serious ... ELEGANZA!"

333

Mi-Chelle did a full three-sixty turn, sweeping her fish tail round with her, as a banging remix of Madonna's "Vogue" started up, glitter guns fired into the crowd, and Mi-Chelle and the Patisserie Sisters began a highly choreographed dance routine, ten backing dancers rushing on stage to join them. The crowd roared their approval, chanting "Mi-Chelle! Mi-Chelle!" before succumbing to the beat, throwing their hands in the air and losing themselves in the music.

Bambi stood at the side, watching forlornly, and then stormed off into the wings as the audience whooped and cheered, enjoying this huge theatrical spectacle that, Noah had to admit, made Bambi's stand-up routine feel lame and amateur in comparison.

"Find Pierre and meet me out the back fire exit," Noah said to Harry. "And be quick! Hell hath no fury like a drag queen scorned."

The back of the club couldn't have been further away from the bright lights and glitz of the front. The ground was wet and muddy and it stank of piss. Industrial-sized wheelie bins overflowing with rubbish lined one wall, along with some fly-tipped wooden pallets and a mattress. And a handful of hard-faced waifs and strays stood against the brick wall, smoking and eyeing the new arrivals with disdain.

Noah swallowed. "Right—"

"Hallo, Noah!" Eva said, springing back from a lanky

lad she appeared to be *canoodling* with.

Noah pursed his lips, taking in the cigarette she was holding between her long fingers and the *appalling state* of the young man she was standing with. He was wearing a black Iron Maiden T-shirt and black skinny jeans – hardly a good sign!

"What are you doing out here?" Noah demanded.

Eva shrugged. "The real action always happens outside the club, Noah." She smiled.

Noah sighed. "Well, not tonight it didn't."

"Cool," Eva said. "I'm hanging with Pax –" she cocked her head towards the lanky boy "– and we're going to a mate's of his in Hackney, so I'll see you tomorrow."

Noah opened his mouth to protest "No, Eva" – just as he realized that arrangement would mean he and Harry would have the hotel room entirely to themselves! – "that's a splendid idea! Simply splendid! I hear Hackney is very lovely. Please enjoy yourself with your equally tall *friend*."

Eva shrugged and Noah nodded enthusiastically, hoping to reiterate the point that Eva should very much *stay out all night*.

Mick burst out through one of the fire exits, wig in hand, make-up still on, but now in very skinny jeans and an oversized jumper, pulling a wheely suitcase behind him. "We're going back to the hotel!" he shouted at Noah, Harry and Pierre. "And first thing tomorrow, we're getting the hell out of Slagsville!"

"Mick—" Noah began.

"I don't wanna talk about it, Noah."

"OK, just, I'm sorry, OK? We all are," Noah said. "You were . . . really good."

There was a loud cheer from inside the club, as the music changed to a dubstep remix of "Under the Sea".

Mick shook his head. "Not sure the crowd agrees with you."

Mick strode off down the alleyway, Pierre, Harry and Noah in tow. Where the alley met the street, Kitten Face was waiting. Noah saw Harry glance at him briefly, probably as surprised to see him there as Noah was, and give him a cursory nod. Noah had no intention of doing the same, but Kitten Face had other ideas, and grabbed Noah by the arm as he walked past.

"He's cute, your boyfriend," Kitten Face said.

"Yeah," Noah agreed.

"So why's he with *you*?"

Noah's heart seemed to stop. London nightlife teemed all around him, but in strange, silent slow motion. He swallowed hard, mouth open, wondering why the hell anyone would be so mean to him. "Dunno," Noah muttered, lowering his head.

Kitten Face smirked and walked back towards the club, and Noah shuffled off along the pavement, wiping his eyes with his palms, hoping the others wouldn't see.

CHAPTER FORTY-ONE

"Are you OK?" Harry said as he pushed their hotel bedroom door shut. "You seem quiet."

Noah nodded and gave a tight little smile, which was probably wholly unconvincing. Stupid, wasn't it? All those guys who'd come up to him on Old Compton Street, taken a flyer and called him "cute" – and yet one unkind word from one person, and that's all he could focus on.

And it was probably all part of vile Kitten Face's plan to somehow get with Harry, but even so, what he said *felt true.*

Everyone in that club had been so ludicrously confident and attractive. Did Noah really think that Harry wouldn't have noticed that too? And now they were going to have a night of *bow chicka wah wah*? Who was he kidding?

"So! What do we have here?!" Harry grinned, opening the plastic carrier bag that Noah had dropped off earlier, after his Soho shopping spree. Noah didn't mind Harry seeing what was inside – the one item he wanted to keep quiet about was safely hidden away in the bathroom anyway. Harry pulled out the scented candle and sniffed it. "Mmmm. Nice."

"Lavender and bergamot." Noah swallowed. "Very sensual, just like it says on the label."

"Very," Harry agreed, pulling out a small gold box. "And what's this?"

"Chocolates," Noah said. "In case we get hungry."

"They say chocolate is an aphrodisiac," Harry said. "Did you know that?"

"No, I did not know that," Noah lied. "Very interesting."

Harry prised the lid of the box open and ate a chocolate. "Want one?" He offered Noah the box. "Feeling horny yet?"

"HAHAHA!" Noah said, picking out a strawberry crème.

Harry smirked, popped another chocolate in his mouth, and pulled a small plastic bottle from the bag. "Gosh, is this *lu*— noignoremeit'smassageLOTION. Hahaha! Massage lotion. That's great!" Harry grinned at him.

"What did you think it was?" Noah frowned.

"Hm? What? Nothing," Harry said, face all innocent. "OK, well, do you want me to give you one?"

Noah blinked at him.

"A massage?" Harry said.

"Er, well..." This was all a bit quick for Noah's liking. He wasn't ready for this stage in proceedings yet. He'd hoped to have time to visit the en suite, *freshen up*. He hadn't even put Spa Reflections on yet... But maybe it would be OK. There would be time in a bit.

"Get 'em off, then, and lie face down on the bed," Harry said.

"Get ... what exactly do you need me to take off?"

"Your clothes."

"OK, but which ones? Like, how many of my clothes exactly? I need you to be really clear right now."

"Hey," Harry said, stepping closer to Noah and taking his hands. "We don't have to do anything you don't want to."

"I know."

"So just relax, because everything's fine."

"OK."

"Have you had a massage before?"

Noah shook his head.

"OK, so it's a nice thing. All you have to do, just take your top off, and your trousers, leave your boxers on if you like, and lie down on the bed. And I'll give you a little massage."

Noah nodded, then flicked two of the light switches so the room plunged into a soft glow. Harry chuckled, and Noah pulled his trousers and socks off, then his top, throwing himself face down on the bed quickly, so Harry didn't have too much time to see his pathetic excuse for a chest and abs.

Noah flinched and caught his breath as an ice-cold squirt of massage lotion dropped on his left flank. "Sorry, cold!" he gasped, jumping again as Harry's warm hand started to smooth it into his skin.

"All right?" Harry murmured.

"Uh-huh."

"I'll warm it in my hands this time," Harry said, squirting some more lotion into his palms and rubbing them together a little before placing them gently on Noah's shoulders.

"Uggg..." Noah moaned, as Harry worked his thumbs into a knot below his right shoulder blade. He was pretty sure Harry wasn't a qualified masseuse, but my God, it didn't matter. This was ... lovely.

But he couldn't just lie here and make Haz do all the work. He needed to make an effort too. "Haz – just look in my bag, will you? There's my notebook in there."

"Really?"

"Uh-huh."

Harry nipped over to retrieve the notebook and handed it to Noah, who propped himself up a bit with the pillows under his chest and flipped to the relevant page.

"Shall I carry on?" Harry asked.

"Uh-huh," Noah said. "I was just going to read you a poem, you know, while you worked away. It's a nice poem, Haz. It's about us. Do you want to hear it?"

"Noah, I would *love* to hear it," Harry said, resuming his stroking motions a little lower down Noah's back now.

"OK. Here we go. It's called 'Love Train'." Noah cleared his throat.

"Love is like a train…"

Harry's warm fingers swept lightly under the waistband of Noah's boxers.

"HOT! and sometimes delayed.
But like a train,
Love can…"

Harry's fingers made a sweeping motion, right over Noah's buttocks.

"TAKE you plaaaaaaaaaaaaaces… Ha! Hahhhhhh! Huh."

"You OK?" Harry asked.

"Huh, yes," Noah said, taking a breath, starting to feel himself press into the mattress. *Well, that's a marvellous thing*, Noah thought.

"Sure?"

"Sure. I'm going to continue the poem now."

"OK," Harry said, moving his fingers in circular motions towards the base of Noah's spine.

"Some love is first class,
With plenty of space and free refreshments.
Some love is standard class,
And that's still OK, but definitely less good overall.
(We are first class, in case you were wondering)."

Harry nodded. "Yes, I agree. First class."

"There's more, so—"

"Sorry," Harry said, squirting a little more lotion out into his hands.

Noah cleared his throat again.

"Some love is a fare dodger,
And they get thrown off."

Harry started to gently stroke the backs of Noah's knees.

"LOOOOVE AH AH *must pay its* aaaaaaahhhhhhh... Wa wa wa... *dues!*

You cannot, oh God, *trick,* huh, *love,*

Or ride ... ri ... ri— Wooo woo woo, huh ha ga ga."

"What's that last bit?" Harry asked, still stroking the backs of Noah's knees.

"Ga goo waa..." Noah sank into the bed, Harry's lingering fingers brushing the backs of his knees, tingling, flooding him with warmth. He cleared his throat. *"Or ride the love train without a ticket,"* he gasped.

"I'm not getting the metaphor there," Harry said, stopping his stroking.

"Well," Noah said, trying to think of his best English

literature bollocks whilst feeling really light-headed, "what I think the poet is trying to say here is that love isn't something you can just have for free. There's a price – not necessarily a financial price, of course, because that might make you a rent boy – but you have to give something... Give of yourself, if you like, for love to work."

"That's a nice sentiment," Harry said.

"Yes!" Noah said. "There's more, though, so..."

"Sorry."

Noah cleared his throat as Harry shuffled up the bed a bit, starting work just above Noah's knees now.

"Some trains are slow trains,
But they get there in the end.
Some trains are express trains,
But speed isn't everything and can be dangerous!"

There was a murmur of appreciation from Harry. Good. It just went to show that doing everything all at once wasn't always the best way. Noah was pleased with that verse. It was good.

Harry squirted some more lotion into his hands and started making small strokes over Noah's inner thighs. Noah shivered, nerve endings on fire, with the most ridiculous erection he'd ever had in his life, hypersensitive to every exquisite touch. "Oh!"

"Are you OK with this?"

Noah swallowed. *Oh God he was.* "Yeah, it's... Yeah, I am, Harry. I'm so OK with this."

Harry went higher, brushing his fingers tenderly under the legs of Noah's boxers. Noah exhaled unsteadily into the pillow. One verse to go – he should probably try to say it quickly before he collapsed into jelly.

"Drive the train straight down the tracks,
Into the tunnel, no looking back!
Drive the train to places new,
I want to ride this train with you!"

Silence, and then Harry's lips brushed the nape of his neck with a delicate kiss. "Did you like the poem?" Noah murmured.

"Yeah, it was sweet and I loved it," Harry said.

Noah smiled and looked back at Harry … who somehow, Noah wasn't sure how or when, had now also removed most of his clothes and was kneeling at Noah's side on the bed, in just his boxers.

And, er … he looked just as ready for action as Noah was.

And yet…

Those perfect guys in the club… Kitten Face's mean words… Everyone with their perfect, toned, groomed, *sexy* bodies.

This had to be perfect. He couldn't take his boxers off, not without…

"Haz? I just need to pop to the bathroom for a minute," Noah said.

"Cool," Harry said.

"OK, so..." Noah slid off the bed, keeping his back to Harry as he scuttled towards the en suite and slid the bolt. He released a breath and stared at himself in the mirror. "You can do this," he muttered. "This is the moment. Just one more thing..."

Noah pulled the tube of Veet he'd bought earlier from his washbag and examined the small print on the back. *Blah, blah, blah*, lots of boring stuff they always say about things from chemists, something about it not being suitable for "perianal" use, whatever the hell that was, must be something to do with women, because Noah was *pretty sure* he didn't have one of those. So that was fine. *Blah, blah, blah ... don't use on genitals*. OK, fine, but why not? What could go wrong? And bearing in mind this was a product marketed at women, it probably just meant *women's bits*, not *boy bits*.

With this product, he would remove all body hair in *those regions*, and be smooth, just like the pictures he'd seen online, and in real life, in the shape of perfect Pierre. Everyone else must do it. How else would you remove that sort of hair? A cut-throat razor near his willy? No thanks! How dangerous would that be?!

He slapped the cream on and lathered it about.

Lovemaking, here we come.

CHAPTER FORTY-TWO

"AAAARGGHHHHHHH! AAAAAAAARRRRRGHH!
ARRRRRGGGGGGGHHHH! GAAAAAAAAAAAH!
AHHHHHHH! AH! AH! AAAARGGGGGHHH!"

CHAPTER
FORTY-THREE

Eyes watering, Noah bit down on the balled-up sock that was in his mouth as Mick drove the van over yet another evil London speed bump. On his back, on the rear seats, legs spread out as wide as he could, totally akimbo, anything, just to provide maximum airflow around the stricken area. Harry and Pierre were somewhere in the front; he didn't really care. A hotel "complimentary robe" barely covered his lower regions, but he also didn't care. With pain this intense, the only thing you could focus on was the MONUMENTAL AGONY.

The last thing he remembered clearly was slapping the cream all over his boy parts.

From there, it was pretty much a blur.

He remembered a tingling sensation that quickly developed into RED-HOT HELLFIRE.

He recalled screaming for help.

Desperately scraping the cream away ... splashing with water ... trying to get into the bath ... slipping, flapping about in the bath ... falling against the hot towel rail ... banging on the en-suite door...

The next thing he remembered was Mick carrying him past reception in his arms, like a dying child, Pierre and Harry following, Mick angrily saying, "Grab all your stuff, after this you're all going straight home!"

Words ... frantic phone calls ... mention of A&E departments...

Someone produced a bag of frozen peas, but they were quickly dismissed.

The hotel car park ... was that a black Vauxhall Astra?

The woman ... she was there...

Then bundled in the back of the van...

The pain! The burning! What had become of his testicles? he wondered. Were they still even there? Or had they been burnt away in the Great Fire of Testicles?

Noah's delirious words: *"Is Kitten Face chasing? Is it a test?"*

And then:

BRIGHT LIGHTS

Doctors

Nurses

A trolley – rushing through corridors...

Voices and faces blending into one big nightmarish TUBE OF VEET with evil horns and red eyes, dancing around Noah, goading him, squirting its devil cream at him.

A voice: "Can someone shut him up, there's a man having a stroke in here!"

Other voices – *laughing*?

"Can we just sedate him, this is ridiculous," another voice, maybe a surgeon or very important doctor who had been urgently drafted in for the case.

The last thing he remembered, as a needle went in his arm and the fluid dripped in, was reaching out to Harry: "Has the goose shat yet? *Has the goose shat?*"

CHAPTER
FORTY-FOUR

Noah stared up into the bright white light as a kindly face, probably the face of God, loomed into view.

"Is this heaven?" he muttered.

"It's St Thomas's hospital," the face said, gradually coming into focus. Not God. *Harry*.

"Harry, um ... good, that's..." Noah stared blankly ahead. "How many years have I been in a coma?"

"You've just been sleeping off the sedative they gave you. A few hours, that's all. It's Sunday morning."

Noah glanced at Harry. He looked shattered. "So, Harry, I wanted to talk to you about the different colour bins for rubbish collection, because, er... So, my mother thinks it's OK to put a plastic tray from an ASDA Thai green curry ready meal in the green bin, but, huh ... it's very clear ... on the sticker on the bin ... that ... that type of plastic isn't currently recycled, so it had to go in the black bin, not the green bin, so..."

"He's just a bit delirious coming round from the sedation," Noah heard a voice say, apparently some sort of nurse. "Hello, Noah," she said. "How are you feeling?"

"Fine, fine, fine," Noah said. "The bins, though, I was saying..."

"Try not to worry about them just now, sweetheart."

"But ... it's collection day on Tuesday!"

The nurse plumped his pillows and settled him back down. "OK, well, I'm sure your mum will remember."

"No! Forgets! Or she puts out the brown one, but brown is every other Wednesday. *Garden waste.*"

"How's the pain?" the nurse asked.

"No pain."

"OK, well, you might start to feel a bit sore in a bit, when the painkillers start to wear off, so just say and I'll get you a children's paracetamol."

"But I'm an adult!" Noah said.

The nurse turned to Harry. "Don't let him get out of bed."

Harry nodded. "OK."

The nurse headed out the door of the small, private room they'd put him in. Noah did his best to focus ... really hard ... willing the fog to clear... "What happened, Harry?"

Harry gave him a withering look. "Don't ask, Noah."

Noah nodded. Fine. It was probably all OK, then, whatever it was. Maybe he had slipped in the shower or something? Maybe he hadn't heeded that warning about using the special non-slip mat.

He wiggled his toes. Yes, they were moving. That was good. Checked both his arms – affirmative. All limbs appeared to be present and correct. He quickly did some sums in his head: one plus two – *three*. Two times six – *twelve*. Hmm. Basic brain function was intact. *What does TTL stand for in electronics?* he asked himself. Answer: Transistor-transistor logic. Huh. Memory circuits seem fine. *Why, then, was he in hospital?*

Think . . . think . . .

French people . . .

Gran . . .

A road trip . . .

London . . .

"OH SHIT, THE GOOSE!" Noah squealed. "THE GOOSE, THE DIAMONDS!" He gasped in horror as everything came flooding back. "MY TESTICLES! WHAT'S HAPPENED TO MY TESTICLES?!"

"OK, don't panic, but—" Harry tried to put a reassuring hand on Noah's shoulder, but Noah shrugged him off, lifting the sheet to reveal . . .

Noah screamed. "OH MY ACTUAL GOD?!"

"You had a little . . . mishap. Remember?"

"ARRGH! WHAT?!"

"Calm down."

"Easy for you to say! I've had a testicle accident! How would you like it? Oh my God. Are they ruined? Are my testicles ruined?"

"They think you'll be fine."

"*THINK?!* They *think* I'll be fine, do they? Oh, that's brilliant." He started sobbing. "I hadn't even got to use them properly yet."

"Grimes!"

"Oh no," Noah muttered, seeing Ms O'Malley standing in the doorway, Pierre just behind her.

"Oh *yes!*" she replied. "This mess is precisely why we don't allow you to do unauthorized activities with the French students! We have a duty of care, you know?" She shook her head. "The head wants to speak to you about this. There's talk of a suspension for you."

Noah's mouth fell open. Suspended? Him? He would never live down the shame! "How did you find us?" he babbled.

"How do you think?" she said, indicating Pierre.

White-hot fury bubbled up inside him. "*You?*" Noah said. "But *of course!*"

"What?" Pierre frowned. "Our trip is not secret, no?"

Ms O'Malley crossed her arms. "We've tracked Eva down to what sounds like an illegal rave in Stoke Newington. Once I've picked her up, I'll be taking her

355

and Pierre safely back to Little Fobbing. Meanwhile, I've contacted your parents and—"

"Not my dad!" Noah said.

"... and *luckily*, your father happens to be in the vicinity, so is on his way here to pick you up. This is one big mess, *Grimes*, and at least your suspension will give you a chance to reflect on that."

Screw that. Screw her! So, the Malley wanted to play hardball, did she? She could hardly get him suspended if she herself was IN PRISON!

"I know about you and Pierre," he said, eyeballing her.

"I beg your pardon?" she said, placing a fist on her hip.

Noah took a deep breath. "I first became suspicious when I returned the football to your office and noticed a wire transfer to your bank account, from Russia."

Ms O'Malley glared at him. "Is that right?"

He gave her a little smile. Her careless blunder had cost her dear! "Sometime later, I overheard a secret phone conversation of Pierre's, in which he arranged to meet a contact at the shed by the school kitchens."

Pierre screwed his face up. "If it was secret, why would I do it in school?"

"It was an error, Pierre," Noah said. "You made an error. It's the little slips that provide the clues, you see! Now, I hadn't planned to –" Noah glanced briefly at Harry

"– but I hid in the bushes that evening, covertly monitoring the shed."

"And what did you see, Noah?" Ms O'Malley said.

"What I witnessed was the unloading of several boxes from your car, and the contents of a holdall of Pierre's, as well as a further conversation you had on the phone – *in Russian*. So!" Noah said, triumphantly. "With all that in mind, I wonder whether I'm still being suspended?!"

Ms O'Malley looked at him with stone-cold eyes. "Yes, you are. And then some."

"But—"

"Noah," Pierre said, looking hurt and disappointed. "All you saw ... was some boxes of cheese."

"Drugs cheese!" Noah squealed. "A cover for the drugs! Drugs hiding inside cheese!"

Pierre shook his head. "No. Just cheese."

"Then it's illegal cheese! You've smuggled illegal, unpasteurized cheese into the country!" Noah declared.

Pierre shook his head again. "No. Just small amounts for personal use."

"Personal use!" Noah scoffed.

"Yes, although it must be said, you have also had some of this cheese."

Noah stared at him and swallowed.

Pierre continued, "It is my plan ... to arrange a 'thank you' event to our host families and Little Fobbing residents. At the end of our stay – an evening of cheese, wine and music. An end of exchange prom!"

Noah breathed heavily through his nose, mouth clamped shut.

"The boxes just contained cheese, wine and crackers for the prom," Pierre explained. "We put it all in the store that evening because Ms O'Malley had netball practice until late, so she couldn't help me before. In my bag – some pickles and chutney I had brought over from France."

"And, but... And you... But you visited the Willows!" Noah said.

"To invite some of the old people too. It is a ... *community* celebration. Bring everyone together – that is the point of these exchange programmes, I think? Unity. Togetherness. Different cultures, different ages, all as one?"

Noah swallowed again. "But ... the Russian! I heard Russian! On the phone!"

"You did," Ms O'Malley said.

"Some sort of drugs overlord?" Noah said, hopefully.

Ms O'Malley shook her head. "I'm arranging for my partner to come over from Russia. She's decided she'd like to take the next step and come and live with me. I've been arranging tickets and visas for the past few months," Ms O'Malley said.

"*She?*" Noah said. "So, you're ... you are ... you're a member of the LGBTQ plus community?"

Ms O'Malley looked quizzically at him. "You're telling me this is the first time that thought has occurred to you? Aren't you supposed to be one of the clever ones?"

Noah's eyes lit up. "We could form an LGBTQ plus club at school! You could be senior treasurer."

She snorted. "I'll pass, thanks."

Fine, Noah thought. He was all wrong, then, was he? In that case, he'd hit them with the one fact he *did* have. The one single, irrefutable FACT: "Prom, indeed!" he said. "I mean, excuse me while I just sit on the *bleachers* and eat a *Twinkie*. It's a PARTY! Party! We're not in bloody goddam AMERICA!"

There! That showed them!

Pierre shook his head, sadly. "All this is plainly ridiculous. And, I think, all because you do not like me. You do not trust me. And so, your mind, it goes crazy!"

"I can assure you, I am fully *compote mental!*" Noah hissed. "I'm *fline. Flan! Gah! I'M FINE!*"

"You've never liked me from when we met because you thought I was in love with Harry," Pierre said. "And even after we kiss and I tell you I am in love with you, even then, you still hate me!"

Noah took a sharp intake of breath and looked at Harry. "Those are lies."

"Not lies!" Pierre said, turning to Harry. "I am sorry, Harry. I kissed Noah."

Ms O'Malley raised her hands. "That's my cue. We'll talk later, Grimes." And she walked out.

"He..." Noah pointed at Pierre, trying to find some words. "Ignore everything!"

Harry flicked his eyes from Pierre to Noah. "Noah, I kind of guessed."

"You're not taking this seriously?" Noah howled. "I mean, why? I'm not! I'm ignoring his words for the lying words they are!"

"It was all rather obvious," Harry said. "I can read you like a book."

Noah looked at him, open-mouthed. "But... OK, but I didn't kiss him back."

"That's fine." Harry shrugged. "I believe you."

Noah stared at Harry. "So...? You're not going to storm out and break up with me over this ... misunderstanding? Because that's what it was. A misunderstanding that I handled badly."

Harry shook his head. "Not over that, no."

"OK, good. Great!" Noah smiled. "Thank you."

Harry fixed Noah with a stare. "But I do think we should split up," he said.

CHAPTER FORTY-FIVE

Pierre must have made a swift exit, because it was just the two of them now. Noah stared at Harry in disbelief. "What do you mean?" Noah said.

Harry sat on the edge of the bed, angled towards Noah, head hung. "I dunno. I keep wondering, shouldn't a boyfriend be a good thing for you? Shouldn't a boyfriend make you feel good about yourself? I don't think I make you feel any of those things, Noah. In fact, from what I can see, I just make you insecure and jealous. I make you feel bad about yourself. Don't I?"

"No! You're not doing that. It's not your fault, it's me!"

"It's this relationship, Noah. You know, I'm not bothered – genuinely, I'm not – about not rushing into anything. And I've told you that. And I don't want you to look or be any different to how you are, because that's what I love, however hard you find that to believe. But you seem convinced that I want something totally different. And it's making you miserable and you're doing dumb shit as a result – you *followed Pierre to the shed*?! That can only be because you thought he was meeting me! I mean, God, do you think I would ever do that? But, Noah, bottom line, *you should not be in a relationship with someone who makes you feel bad about yourself.*"

"But, Harry—"

"I'm not doing it deliberately. I don't know how you got this idea, that I would ever like anyone other than you, but somehow you have. And nothing I can say or do seems to make a difference. So what's the point?"

Noah swallowed down the blind panic and went for damage limitation. "I'm sorry, Harry. I should have trusted you, and I know you'd never do something behind my back. It's all me, and I promise you, I'll change. I'll stop trying to have a perfect body. I'll forget all the stuff they say on websites and how people look in clubs..."

Harry shook his head. "Don't you see? You don't have to forget all that stuff about 'having the perfect body' because you already *have* the perfect body!"

Noah couldn't help but grimace at that obviously ridiculous line. That was just Harry being nice.

"What? Only certain magazines and websites are allowed to define 'perfect', are they?"

"No, but... I mean, *come on*, everyone knows that 'perfect' means... You know, well, it doesn't mean a skinny little runt whose vest hangs off him. Hollister are never gonna hire boys like me to sell their clothes."

"Fuck Hollister. Fuck them. *Dicks.* Who cares what they think?"

"But people, Harry, that's what most people think. That's why those brands use those people, because other people like it. They see perfection. Something to aspire to."

Harry nodded and got up from the bed. "When I kiss you, that's perfection. When I hold your hand, that's perfection. When I just spend time with you, and we talk, and we laugh, and you look at me with those stupid, cute, innocent eyes, *that's goddam perfection*!"

Noah felt the tears bubbling up inside him. It all sounded so right. So why had he been feeling so wrong? "I know, Harry," he said.

Harry stood by the window, looking at him. "Actions speak louder than words, though, Noah. And that's not how you've been acting."

"Maybe I could try."

Harry watched him. "Why did you kiss Pierre?"

"No, Harry, *I didn't*! He kissed me! I admit, I was slow to realize what was happening, but as soon as he put his lips against mine, I moved backwards."

"I think part of you liked it."

"What? *No!*"

"I think part of you felt good that a boy as fit and, as you would have it, 'perfect' as Pierre would want to kiss you."

"No, Harry, see—"

"I mean, from my point of view, of course he wants to kiss you. You're ... you're the best, bloody, damn, stupid dork of a boy I ever met and I can't imagine ever falling for anyone like I've fallen for you. But *you* can't see that. You think you're some sort of substandard human being because some stuck-up prick of a magazine editor won't ever put you on the front page of their pretentious little shit rag, and presumably, since I also don't look like that, you don't think I'm perfect either."

"Harry, you are *so* perfect. You are... You're so... You are."

Harry was crying. Noah reached out for him from the bed, but Harry backed off, wiping his eyes with the palms of his hands and sniffing. "I'm fine."

"Haz—"

"I'm gonna go back to Little Fobbing with Ms O'Malley. I think you should think – really think – about who you are and what you want. And maybe I should too. And there's no point, Noah, no point in any of this, if we don't make each other happy. If being with each other isn't so utterly fucking brilliant, that no one else and their stupid opinions matter."

"Harry! No, wait, please don't—"

But Harry was already through the door and gone.

CHAPTER FORTY-SIX

Noah stared straight ahead at the wall opposite him, painted in a pale hospital blue. An A4 sign instructed him what to do in the event of an emergency. He doubted "boyfriend splitting up with you" was one of the ones it advised on.

Harry was, of course, right. As usual. Why should some self-appointed knob get to define what "looks good"? Who is "hot" and who is ... not. Everyone likes different things. Why couldn't Noah sort his head out? Why was he so stupidly insecure? The gym, the protein shakes, how he looked... NONE OF IT MATTERED. It was all just crap. Meaningless. If he didn't have Harry, if he wasn't with Harry, then he had nothing. And all the supposed good looks and money and right clothes wouldn't ever make up for the gnawing emptiness.

Tears streamed down his face.

Why had he been such an idiot?

Why, when he had it all, had he gone and lost it?

"Bingo!" Eric said, pushing through the door with Dad behind.

"It's over, Noah," his dad said. "I want them back. Oh, and how are you, by the way? Hear you've had some sort of accident?"

Noah urgently wiped the tears away and stared at them both. He was in *no mood* for this. "You both disgust me. Stealing from Gran."

Before Dad could issue any sort of rebuttal, Mick was in the door, holding a plastic carrier bag. "Right, I'm done," he said. "Your dad's here now, he can deal with you. I've got bigger fish to fry. Got a career to get back on track. *Stoke Drag Awards, 2008,*" Mick said, pointing to himself. "Done it once, I can damn well do it again. If they want *eleganza*, they're damn well gonna get it!"

"What's in that carrier?" Noah asked.

Mick cocked his head and smiled. "It's a bag of shit, Noah. *A bag of shit.*" He dumped it on the end of the bed. "Spent the last forty minutes clearing out the van. The goose has flown off – if the diamonds aren't in there, you ain't ever getting them back, Sunshine."

Dad's eyes lit up. "The diamonds? *In there?*" He snatched up the bag and looked at Eric, the cogs in their heads obviously turning, as they tried to work out what the hell could have happened.

"Oh, good one, thanks, Mick," Noah said. Oh, what was the point? He'd done his best. Dad had still got the diamonds, and all he'd ended up with was being trailed by a surveillance team, pickpocketed, suspended from school, burning his bollocks and . . . losing Harry.

The rest, he could take. But not Harry.

Never Harry.

He started crying again. "Just go," he told Mick.

Mick turned to Noah's father. "Well, good luck with this carnival of fuckuppery!" he said, before walking back to the door. He paused in the doorway, then shook his head. "You know, Noah, after everything last night, I was ready to throw the towel in. But then I got to thinking – *who am I? Who really am I?* Not a quitter, that's for sure. And when the going gets tough, only thing you can do is buckle up and ride that motherfucker till you get to calmer waters. So ask yourself this: *who is Noah Grimes?*" Mick raised his eyebrows, stared at Noah, and walked out.

Noah rolled his eyes. *A dickhead*, that's who.

He looked at Dad and Eric. "I don't care. I tried. What you're doing is wrong because Gran needs the money from those diamonds. We could get her in a better home, and keep her with us – really with us – for longer. But I did what I could. You do what you want."

"Take 'em, Dad," Eric said. "I'll stay here and make sure he doesn't come after you."

Noah shook his head. "Like I could anyway? I'm in a hospital gown. I don't even have any underpants on."

Dad plucked the carrier bag up. "Nice one. And good thinking, Eric. Noah – I'm sorry, yeah? I don't mean any harm. And I hope, one day, you'll see that. Maybe when you're old enough to take our Mazda for a spin?" He nodded at Eric and walked out with the bag.

There the diamonds went. Taking Gran's chances with them. *Gone.*

He sobbed silently, engulfed in tears. *Who was Noah Grimes?* He was a disaster area, that's what. He was a messed-up idiot of a boy who had gone and lost it all.

"Cheer up, mate," Eric said, sitting down on the edge of the bed.

"Sod off, Eric."

Eric smiled and handed Noah a tissue. "Dad hasn't got the diamonds, though."

"What do you mean?"

"You have," Eric said.

"I'm not interested in any more of your games, Eric," Noah said. "Just go."

"You think you hate me, and I get that," Eric said. "But you need to hear me out here."

Noah shrugged. He didn't care. He just wanted to get

out of here and sort things out with Harry. He had to save the situation.

"OK," Eric said. "So, Dad told me about his plan with Gran's diamonds a week ago, after he saw that *Antiques Roadshow* episode with a similar tiara. Believe it or not – and I know you're firmly in the 'not' category right now – but still, believe it or not, I knew the plan was wrong. I wasn't gonna let Gran get screwed over like this."

Noah waved the words away. "Please, continue with your lies. Very interesting, I'm sure."

Eric ignored him. "So, I visited her and I swapped the diamonds in the tiara, replacing the real ones with some fakes, while she was rehearsing with her band. That meant that when Dad paid her a visit the next day and nicked it, he nicked a tiara with fake diamonds in it. So far so good, right?"

"Yeah, just great, Eric. If you like LIES!"

Eric shook his head, sighed and persevered. "The plan was simple: Dad was gonna meet up with his contact in London, and try and sell what he thought were real diamonds. And obviously his contact's gonna take one look at 'em and tell him they're worthless. Dad will be disappointed, sure, but will just put it down to tough luck. And Gran gets to safely keep the real diamonds 'cause Dad thinks that old tiara ain't worth anything."

Noah looked at him. "So why did you want me to find you? I could have stopped your plan – I did, in fact!"

Eric shrugged. "I have to admit, I kinda underestimated your chances of success. See, as a little bonus, I saw this as a chance to prove to your mum what sort of crook Dad really is. A few months ago I was all set on being Dad's apprentice – work on some business schemes together, you know?"

"Sure, whatever, Eric."

"But, turns out the old man's not as clued up as the son! Turns out he's a chancer who's flat out of chances. And everyone round Little Fobbing knows his game anyway, so it's like, *why am I wasting my time?* I needed to cut him loose and get rid of him somehow. Also, you know I can't stand their new 'ain't love wonderful' vibe, and man, you must have heard them shagging at night? Kid can't get his shut-eye, right?"

Noah grimaced.

"Plus," Eric continued, "with your mum playing all happy families, she's all up in my business the whole time, poking her snout in, when I need to be left alone, right? I got stuff to take care of. Big stuff."

"And how does me coming after you achieve that?"

Eric smiled. "'Cause she's not gonna believe you when you tell her what Dad's done. But I recorded the whole confrontation in the Reptile House on my phone. I'm gonna send the file from an anonymous account to your mum. When she's opens it – boom! She'll hear the whole thing. Hopefully, it'll be enough to prove to her Dad's not changed, and she'll say bye-bye. And no one will know it came from me, so I don't make an enemy of Dad. Things'll go back to normal and I'll be a one-man band again, left to me own devices."

Noah nodded. "Assuming this is true, which time will tell, then I . . . suppose I congratulate you."

"Eric saves the day again!"

"Don't get too cocky," Noah said. "Where did you put the real diamonds?"

"They're safe!" Eric chirped.

"Where are they?"

"Safe where nobody will think of looking," Eric said. "In the gravel at the bottom of your fish tank."

Noah's face froze. A fish tank that was now at Harry's house. Harry who had just broken up with him. Harry, who, regardless of the diamonds, he really needed to sort things out with. "We need to get back to Little Fobbing," Noah said. "Now."

"No sweat," Eric said. "We'll get a couple of train tickets. First class. I'm treating you, 'cause I do feel a bit bad for you, truth be told."

"First class? Where d'you get that sort of cash, Eric?"

"See!" Eric said. "This is what I mean! All up in my business. Know when to keep your nose out, Noah! Let's just say, if things keep going the way they're going, I'm gonna get us all out of the financial pit we're in."

"Legally?"

"I mean, whatever 'legal' means."

"It means in accordance with the laws of England and Wales, Eric."

Eric threw Noah a pile of clothes from his bag. "You worry too much."

CHAPTER FORTY-SEVEN

Noah sighed and attempted a half-optimistic smile, having told a bemused Gran and Dickie all about it – his dad, Eric's plan, the chase to London, the goose, Harry splitting up with him ... and finally the diamonds being safe in the fish tank, which was at Harry's house.

Gran shook her head. "Screw the diamonds."

Noah's eyes widened. *"What?"*

"Don't want 'em," Gran sniffed.

"Gran, you *do*. If we sold them, I was thinking, we could move you in to Kingfisher Meadows!"

"Where the hell's that?"

"It's in West Fobbing, Gran! It's lovely there – it's brand new, they've got a spa and everything. And they do special care for people with ... you know, for people who are..."

"Losing their marbles?" Gran said.

"That sort of thing, yeah." Noah nodded.

Gran took his hand. "But I like it here, Noah. All my friends are here."

Noah stared at her. "Should I quote you directly about Matron, or Vera? And, um ... it might be nice there. And if you've got the money..."

"What's the point, Noah?" she said. "What's the point of having money or nice things if you don't have the right people to enjoy it with? Like Reginald here."

Dickie furrowed his brow. "Dickie!"

"Dickie?" Gran said. "You're Dickie?"

"Dickie! That's right!"

Gran turned to Noah. "I don't know," she whispered. "I think people are changing their names to confuse me!"

Noah shook his head. "But Gran, that money is yours."

"Money? I don't need it. I'm fine as I am, Noah. Any money I have is for you and young Eric, that's what. But I tell you now, you can have all the money in the world, you can have the five-bedroom car and the fast house, you can have the clothes and the bling and the—"

"Nespresso machine?"

Gran nodded. "All of that! You can have it all, and you still won't ever be truly happy if you don't have friends. And I don't mean the type of friends that magically appear when times are good and you're successful and you've got a bit of cash. I'm talking about 'thick and thin' friends. The ones who are there *no matter what*. The ones who don't want you to buy them fancy cocktails in trendy London bars, but who are happy with an Ovaltine and a digestive."

"Like Harry, you mean?"

Gran smiled. "You worked it out for yourself, Noah."

"If you were me, how would you make amends?"

Dickie cleared his throat. "I recall, I must have been nineteen, I think, and I'd upset a charming young lady by the name of Edith. And do you know how I won her back?" Dickie leaned forward in his chair. "Bought her a horse."

Noah rolled his eyes. Even just a fish had backfired. And anyway, Harry had a fairly big garden, but not really big enough for a horse.

"Dickie, that's ridiculous," Gran said.

"I can't buy him anything," Noah said. "My wallet was stolen, and even if it hadn't been, all I had was a few quid on my Superdrug loyalty card, so at best I could have got him a pack of own-brand antiseptic wipes."

"Well, like I was saying," Gran said, "before Dickie interrupted with his conspicuous consumption, *it's not all about the money*!"

"Then what?" Noah said.

Gran put her finger in the air, like she'd suddenly had the best idea.

Noah waited with bated breath.

"No, it's gone," she said.

"What do young people like nowadays?" Dickie said. "Avocados?"

"I'm not going to get Harry an avocado," Noah said.

"*Two* avocados?" Dickie suggested. "In the fifties, I bought a young lady a Johnny Cash long-playing record, and two months later, we were married."

"And six months after that she'd run off with an ex-RAF officer!" Gran said.

"Damn flyboys," Dickie replied, shaking his head.

Noah sighed. "OK, well, thanks for your—"

"Sit your little tush back down right now!" Gran said. "I have the solution, and it's this: you must show him both how you feel and that you've changed, by making *the grand gesture*. If we've all learned nothing else from romantic comedies over the years, we've learned this."

"Gran, Harry's not into all that showy stuff, and I'm certainly not."

"Blah, Noah, blah, I'm sure. It'll work. Everyone's a sucker for it. Trust your old gran." She smiled at him. "Oh, put that sullen face away, else the wind will change and you'll stay like that!"

"What am I supposed to do, though?"

"You'll think of something," Gran said, raising herself unsteadily to her feet. "You're a perfectly bright boy. Now! I must get to my rehearsal! Got to lay down some *bare* bangin' tracks with ma squad." She waddled out of the room.

CHAPTER FORTY-EIGHT

"Good morrow, Mrs Lawson," Noah said as Harry's mum opened her front door. "Is Harry within?"

"He doesn't want to see you."

Noah nodded, swallowed and did his best to smile. "And I understand that. Yet I am here to make amends."

"Go home, Noah, I'm sorry," she said, closing the door in his face.

Noah stared at the polished chrome knocker and stained-glass panels. *Fine.* Be like that. But he would not be giving up that easily. He walked round the side of the house to the back garden, looking up at Harry's bedroom window.

"Haz? Harry? HARRY?! HAZZA?" he shouted up. "Please!"

The back door opened. Harry's mum again. "Noah! I just told you, he doesn't want to see you!"

"But I want to see him!"

"And what the hell are you wearing?" she asked.

"This is the hoodie that Harry gave me," Noah said. "It's so nice, it's my favourite thing."

"I don't mean that. I mean on your legs."

"A woman's linen culotte," Noah explained. "They're the only item I could find that was ... roomy. I had an accident, see. But not that kind! Another ... accident."

Harry's mum shook her head. "I'm sure Harry will call you, if and when he's ready to."

Noah sucked his cheeks in. "How's Timothy?"

"Who? Oh, the fish? I'm sure it's fine."

"No, but is he OK? Maybe ... he is *my* fish, so maybe I should take him back?"

"Noah, the fish is fine. Harry changed the water and gravel over earlier."

Noah froze. "What do you mean? What do you mean 'changed the gravel'?"

"No one told me I was supposed to turn the tank light off at night, so the whole thing had become infested with algae. But it's fine now, it has new water and new gravel."

"WHERE'S THE OLD GRAVEL?" Noah bleated.

Harry's mum screwed her face up. "In the bin, I expect."

"Bin? What bin?"

"The green bin."

"Green? Green bin for recycling? Why would you, oh never mind, oh ... God ... oh shit. Pardon me. OK. Um ... I need some of that gravel back. It's precious to me. I have to get it. I need permission to get it out of your bin, Mrs Lawson? Please?"

She shook her head as she went back inside. "I can't even."

That was, he supposed, a yes. He darted back round to the side of the house where the three bins were kept, and narrowed his eyes at the green one. He chewed his lip. It might be bad if Harry were to come out and find him rummaging through the rubbish. It would be weird. Noah glanced back towards the garden, then back at the bin again, then reached out and very quickly lifted the lid a bit, just like he was popping a bit of litter inside or something. No alarms went off. No sign of Harry. He glanced around again, lifted the lid, heard a noise, slammed it shut.

OK. It was OK. Just a crow.

He turned back to the bin. Reopened it and cast his eye over the contents. It was very different to Noah's bin. Noah's recycling bin had sleeves from ready meal cartons and pizza boxes. Harry's had empty glass bottles of extra virgin olive oil, jars of something called "chorizo jam" and a paper bag from a takeaway sushi place. La-di-bloody-da! But where the hell was the gravel? Would it have worked its way down to the bottom? Or would it be lodged in amongst all the other detritus?

Another quick glance towards the garden, and Noah gingerly lifted an empty plastic pot of what once contained "coconut milk yoghurt" from the bin and shook his head. "This type of plastic is not currently recycled in this area," he tutted, checking it thoroughly before sorting it into the black bin instead. "What is wrong with people, it isn't hard!"

"What the hell are you doing?"

Noah spun around. "Harry! Hello, Harry!"

"Why are you going through our bins?" He crossed his arms and gave Noah a cold stare.

"Um ... no, I was just ... a bit bored, passing the time, hoping you might come out." Noah glanced at the bin, then back at Harry. "I came to talk to you. I'm not here about bins."

Harry just stared.

Noah swallowed. "I'm wearing the hoodie you gave me, Haz. I was missing you, so I wore it."

Silence.

"OK," Noah said. "So, the thing I wanted to tell you, firstly, is that I'm sorry..."

"I'm not looking for an apology, Noah."

"No, but −" he glanced at the bin again "− I have made a mess of things, and for that..."

"This won't work if you don't trust me."

"But I do, see, because..."

"No, Noah, you don't, *because* you didn't trust that I

wouldn't cheat on you with Pierre, and you don't trust that I love you for who you are, and you don't trust that it's you I want and no one else. What, do you think I'm just with you because there's no one better right now?"

Tears welled in Noah's eyes. "I don't know why you like me, though. I just can't see it, that's all. Everything screws up for me, and I drag you down with it, and I'm not good at kissing and I've no idea about … sex stuff. I'm a mess."

"But you're my mess," Harry said.

Noah managed a small smile. "Thanks, Harry."

Harry nodded.

Noah sighed, eyes flicking momentarily to the bin again.

"Why do you keep looking at the bin?" Harry asked.

"I don't."

"You *do*."

"OK, so, quite by chance, and that's not the reason I came here because I would have come anyway because I wanted to sort things out with you, but, turns out that Eric swapped the diamonds. The goose ate fakes. He put the real diamonds amongst the gravel in the fish tank. I didn't know."

Harry stared at him. "You didn't come round here to make up with me at all, did you? All you're interested in is your stupid diamonds? Screw you."

"Ha—"

"No, Noah! SCREW YOU! And get off our property!

Go on! Piss off out of it!" Harry grabbed Noah's arm, pulled him away from the bins, and pushed him towards the front of the house. "You know, this tells me all I need to know. Honestly, I thought maybe you'd come here to actually say or do something meaningful for once. But it's just more of your shit. More stupid drama. I don't care." Harry was actually sobbing now. Noah instinctively reached out to him, but Harry batted him away. "No! Go. Don't come back. I don't want to see you or talk to you."

He gave Noah a final push towards the pavement, tears streaming down his face, then turned and went back in his front door, slamming it behind him.

Noah stared at the space where Harry had once been. If he hadn't screwed things up enough before, he certainly had now.

And he'd underestimated how upset Harry was about everything.

He hadn't fully understood.

But now he did.

And it hit him like a ten-tonne truck as he crumpled to the ground. "Oh God," he gasped, curling up, face in the soft hoodie. "Oh, Harry..."

And the tears started streaming down his face too.

And then he saw the Black Vauxhall Astra parked up the street.

The blood drained from his face.

"Oh fuck."

CHAPTER FORTY-NINE

Noah ran along the pavement, stomach knotted, legs weak, mind spinning.

He stopped dead as he saw the police cars outside his house, up ahead. What the hell was this?

"Keep walking," Eric said, suddenly behind him. "I need you in the back garden. Now."

"What's happening?" Noah bleated, staring straight ahead as they approached the house.

"Just act cool, everything's fine," Eric said.

They walked down the drive and slid around the side of the house into the back garden as Eric unlocked the padlock on the shed.

"Help me out here, mate?" Eric said. "We're in this together, yeah?"

"In what together, Eric?" Noah said, frantically looking between the shed and the back door of the house. "I don't like this, I don't want to be—" He stopped talking as he eyed the contents of the shed. There must have been several hundred plastic tubs of it. *Protein powder.* He looked at Eric. "Explain."

"Long story short," Eric said. "I'm running the protein shake business."

"Oh, Jesus, of course you are!"

Eric sucked in a breath, glancing quickly at the back door. "Thing is, it was going great, but I reckon someone grassed. Found out someone signed up that nasty Year Seven kid, Jack Hooper, to be a rep."

Noah rubbed the back of his neck. "Oh, right?"

"Kid's too big for his boots. He's been trying to get rid of the other reps so he controls the patch. Reckon he pissed someone off and they grassed to get their own back. Must be!"

"I can't be implicated! I'll never be made head boy if—"

"You already are," Eric said. "I know you're one of the reps. There's documents at the back in the folders – shred 'em. And then help me tip the shake down the drains. Gotta get rid of some of it at least, then act like I'm one of the victims who just bought a lot."

"Eric, this won't work!"

"Do it, Noah!"

"Oh!"

"Do it! Christ!"

Noah set to work, ripping up the various documents in the folders at the back of the shed, which had clearly been doubling at Eric's HQ. Great. Now he was destroying evidence in a high-profile criminal investigation. What was next, *plagiarism*?!

Eric was busy unscrewing the tops off the tubs and pouring the contents down various drains. Damn Eric. One minute he was some sort of saviour who had come up with an excellent plan, and then the next, an utter masturbation tissue who was going to ruin everything. Noah slapped his forehead. Why had he even thought this would be a good idea? Easy money? Ha! No such thing.

"Hurry up! The powder!" Eric hissed.

Noah grabbed two tubs of powder, which was about all he could carry without straining something, and walked towards one of the drains, just as a policeman came out of the back door. He froze, tubs in hand, as Eric looked up from the far drain and muttered a single "fuck", which pretty much summed things up.

"Hello, Officer," Noah said, doing a small curtsy, a tub of protein powder in each arm, like some sort of Swiss milkmaid.

"Are you Noah?" the policeman asked.

"Uh, am I Noah?" he repeated, stalling.

"Yes. Are you Noah Grimes?"

"I ... am. Yes. I am Noah Grimes," he said, whimpering as he saw the man and woman from the black Vauxhall Astra over the policeman's shoulder. That was it. All hope was lost. They must have all been working together to gather evidence. He was ensnared. No way out.

"Well, it turns out your young French exchange student has been dealing all the time she's been here," the policeman said.

Noah took a sharp intake of breath. "Dealing? Dealing what?"

The woman walked up to them. "Weed, mainly," she said. "Some pills too. Bit of coke."

"Drugs?!" Noah said, a little laugh bubbling out of him. "Eva's a drugs dealer?!"

The woman nodded. "She's been at it over in France too, and she smuggled a load over here in her guitar case. We've been doing a bit of covert surveillance on her ever since she arrived. Thing was, we didn't know if she was working alone or if any of you were in on it, hence why you may have seen us around." She offered Noah her hand. "DS Carpenter, nice to properly meet you."

Eric put the tub he was holding down and exhaled loudly.

Noah licked his lips. "I had no idea. I mean, I knew she was a bad sort. She used to hang out with people who smoked cigarettes. I suppose the signs were there, when you think about it."

"We're taking her in for questioning anyway," DS Carpenter said.

"If you need anyone to back up your case, I will literally say anything in court to support her prosecution," Noah said.

"Thanks," DS Carpenter said, a small smile playing on her lips.

"Did she have any accomplices?" Noah asked, eyes lighting up. Noah racked his brains, going over everything. "There's a mechanic called Ryan who works for a firm called Garfield Motors near Newark. I now suspect he received drugs from Eva, so you can arrest him, maybe? And there's a load of feral kids who hang out in the park. They too can be arrested."

DS Carpenter raised an eyebrow. "Thanks; like I just said, we've been monitoring her closely, so I think we're on top of things, and we're not really interested in a bit of personal use – not in this case."

"Oh," Noah said. "Seems a bit slack," he muttered.

"What's that?"

"Nothing, Detective Sergeant."

The policeman looked at the shake Noah was still holding. "That good stuff?"

"Fine, it's fine," Noah babbled, stifling a scream.

The policeman eyed it. "All natural, is it?"

"Er, it is. It is," Noah confirmed, struggling to maintain his grip on the tubs with his suddenly sweaty hands. "All good, natural ingredients in this. Anyway..."

"What you doing with it?"

Noah blew his cheeks out, attempting nonchalance as his pulse hit somewhere around two hundred. "Don't ... need it any more... I mean, I've been going to the gym and, um ... reached my goals, so ... was going to bin it, basically."

"It's in date?"

"Yeah..."

"I'll take it off your hands. How much you want?"

Noah's mouth hung open, as he stared at the policeman. "A ... tenner? No! *Twenty!* It's twenty a tub, I ... bought it for thirty, so..."

The policeman took two twenties out of his wallet. "Nice one. This stuff is pricey – I appreciate it." He took the tubs from Noah.

"I doubt you'll see Eva again," DS Carpenter said. "Once we've questioned her, she'll be extradited back to France, where they want a little chat with her too. Wanna say goodbye to her?"

Noah shook his head. "Nah, I'm good."

DS Carpenter shrugged. "OK, then."

The policeman smiled. "Thanks for this." He held up the tubs. "Take care now."

They disappeared back into the house.

"Fuck my life," said Eric.

A moment later the door swung open again and Noah's mum appeared, a glass of wine and a half-empty bottle of Echo Falls Summer Berries in one hand, a cigarette in the other. "Bambi's moving in," she said.

"What?!" Noah squealed.

"And your dad's moving out."

"Have you two split up, ah, that's sad," Eric said. "My sincere condolences."

Noah's mum took a long drag on her cigarette. "Turns out the reason your father is so broke is that he's run up thousands of pounds' worth of gambling debts, playing poker. Stupid dick. And then I receive this weird email, with a recording of what happened at London Zoo. Thanks for that, Noah."

"I didn't send you that," Noah said.

"Well, it came from your email address."

Noah glared at Eric, who just shrugged and said, "You should probably change your password – sounds like you've been hacked. S'funny, I had an alert just on Friday that there'd been some failed attempts to enter the password on *my* laptop. Wonder who did that?"

Noah ran his tongue over his lips.

"Anyway, I've washed my hair of him!" His mum threw her cigarette on the ground and knocked back the entire glass of wine. "Woo hoo! Lisa doesn't need a man. Lisa deserves better! Lisa's gonna rebuild her life – on her terms!"

Noah was delighted – thrilled! – that his mother had also now started talking about herself in the third person, just like Bambi. "Noah's really pleased to hear it," he grumbled.

Mum refilled her glass. "Cheers to that, boys!"

CHAPTER FIFTY

Jess Jackson squealed with delight as she made her entrance into the school hall. "Loving the American theme!" she grinned, looking up at the red, white and blue streamers that hung from the roof. Satisfied that everyone in the immediate vicinity had clocked her arrival, she made a beeline for Noah, who was standing awkwardly at the edge, in his suit and bow tie.

"It's not American, Jess," Noah said.

"Yeah, because it's a *prom*, isn't it? Proms are American!"

He shook his head. It's like she couldn't even see the huge replicas of the Eiffel Tower and Big Ben either side of the main stage, and put two and two together.

"Heard you're getting suspended," she purred, like it was the sexiest thing ever. "You *bad boy*."

"Yeah, well, I'm appealing."

"You *bad boy*."

"You said that already, and like I said, I'm launching an appeal. It's a miscarriage of justice, Jess. It won't happen."

"Bro." Josh Lewis nodded at him as he came up alongside Jess, looking as suave and comfortable in his tux as James Bond, or some other widely admired Hollywood star.

"Josh has bought us one of those three-wheeled buggies for the baby," Jess said, cuddling into Josh.

"That's nice," Noah said. "Lucky you're so successful with your PT and protein shake business to afford it, Josh!"

Josh gave him a forced smile. "I'm gonna share my ... good fortune, dude. Gonna give you a big discount on your next tubs of shake. You'll double your profit."

Noah shook his head. "I'm getting out of the game, Josh. But thanks."

"Oh look!" Jess said. "They've got candyfloss! And it's red, white and blue, just like in America!" She began to push her way through the crowd. "And a chocolate fountain! Maybe Hershey's?" she called back.

Josh nodded at Noah. "You, er ... all good, man?"

"Well, I could be better, Josh, to be honest. See, there was a misunderstanding. With Ms O'Malley. She's got it in for me, and I just feel, if only someone she *respected* put in a good word for me, someone who really excelled in PE as a student here, she might back off?"

"Uh-huh." Josh nodded. "I'm getting you, Noah. I'm reading you loud and clear. You want me to –" he leaned into Noah "– gently lubricate the wheels of justice a bit?"

A little shiver ran down Noah's spine as Josh said the word "lubricate". He did his best not to giggle. "Could you, Josh?"

"I help you … and you…"

"Help you," Noah interrupted. "I mean, no, not *you*, I mean, *I* help you. Not you help you. You know what I mean."

Josh nodded. "Consider it done, little dude." He gave Noah a wink and moved off into the crowd.

Noah glanced around the hall, filling up now with students, teachers, some old folks from the Willows, and parents. A "community celebration" indeed; Noah had to concede that Pierre had done a good job. Along the back wall, trestle tables had been set up, groaning under the weight of French cheese, bread, cured meats … and some pork pies, which Noah supposed was the "British" contribution to this culinary fest.

And then there he was.

Standing in front of the curtains of fairy lights that were cascading down the opposite wall, alone, slightly forlorn.

Harry.

Noah stared at him, his breathing shallow, heart pounding.

"Hello, everyone!" Pierre's voice boomed over the PA system as he addressed everyone from the stage. "If I could have a moment of quiet, please! Thank you. I organized this prom to say a warm thank you on behalf of all the French students to our host families in England. It has been an ... experience. We have tried your local cuisine, we have practised your tongue..."

There was a "Wha-hey!" and general cheer from the students.

"And we have learned so much during our time in your very English town. As we go home, we will have a new appreciation of the many differences between our two countries, and when England appears in the news, or in films, we will think of you."

Applause from the crowd. Noah clapped along too, but absent-mindedly, his focus still on Harry.

"And now, I invite your own spokesperson to the stage to say a few words, I am sure. Noah Grimes!"

Noah looked up sharply as all eyes turned to him and his stunned face. No! No, no, no! What was he meant to say? He didn't know this was the plan! He hadn't prepared anything! He brazened it out, smiling with clenched lips and moving up to join Pierre on the stage.

"Welcome to the prom!" Pierre said, as Noah arrived,

giving him a huge all-embracing hug, which felt to Noah like he was having his ribcage crushed.

"OK, well, thank you, Pierre," Noah gasped, extracting himself. "Um ... as we are in England, I prefer not to call this a prom, as such. Let's call it... a *ball*."

"You like balls!" someone shouted from the crowd, to howls of laughter.

Noah cleared his throat and pretended he hadn't heard. "I just want to say that we have all learned a lot too, so we would like to thank our European neighbours as well. Obviously some of you turned out to be drug dealers who were wanted by the police, but that can't be helped. In any group of people, some will always turn out to be bad. Others good. That's the way the world works." He looked at Pierre and smiled. "But on the whole, I like to think that people are good."

Pierre smiled back and Noah dared to glance over at Harry, who was looking back at him, before flicking his eyes away.

Noah cleared his throat. "As I was saying, it's all been very nice to learn that we have so many similarities. And I just want to finish by saying that I ... I love the Eiffel Tower, croissants and France as a whole."

Pierre led some brief applause and came back on the mic. "Now, we have entertainment for you tonight, including karaoke, and I have had a special request from one of the residents of the Willows to start us off...."

"No, no, no," Noah muttered.

"So, with no further delay, may I present Noah Grime's own grandmother..."

Noah emitted a high-pitched squeak

"... and her band Millie and the Dickheads..."

"Pierre, *no*, she's got dementia, this is—"

"... minus Vera and Babs, who ..." Pierre consulted a scrap of paper. "... have been fired due to artistic differences."

Behind him, much to his surprise and horror, Gran and Dickie wobbled on to the stage, helped by Matron, and took up their positions behind two mic stands.

"Matron!" Noah protested.

She waved him away. "It's fine, Noah. Your gran wants to. And if she wants to, I say go for it. Life's too short! Now get off the stage!"

Noah sighed and shook his head – then he looked at his gran. She was smiling, eyes sparkling, *she was loving this*. And he supposed that was the point. She wasn't suffering *from* dementia – she was living *with* it. *Living*. Making the best of what she'd got and enjoying it while she could. That's what you had to do. *That's all you could do.*

"A one, two, three, four!" Gran shouted, as they started a version of "Go West" by the Pet Shop Boys.

Noah hopped off the stage. Gran could go ahead and pursue her dreams, but that didn't mean the rest of the school weren't a bunch of unforgiving tossers; a low profile would be best.

"TUNE!" shouted Josh Lewis, as he appeared to become possessed by the music and not only start *dancing* but also joining in with the "Go Wests" on the chorus, almost like he *regularly danced to this song in gay clubs OR SOMETHING!*

Whether out of similar enjoyment, or just a desire not to see her boyfriend humiliate himself, Jess Jackson quickly rallied the troops, and pretty soon she, Melissa, Connor Evans and even Mr Baxter were all joining in. From there, the less popular kids quickly embraced it, including the poor girl that Noah had accidentally trampled on during football, who threw down her crutches like the song had magically *healed* her and embraced the campery.

OK, that was something, at least. Maybe he could just disappear to the sides of the room, be inconspicuous and. . .

"This one's for Noah and. . ." She turned to Dickie. "Who's it for?"

"Harry!" Dickie shouted down the mic.

Oh God, this was too much now. . .

Noah gave an embarrassed smile, kept his head down, and headed for the wall.

"Noah?! Go and ask. . ." She looked blank.

"Harry!" Dickie chipped in.

"Ask Harry to dance!" Gran shouted, instead of the lyrics.

Noah glanced back at her, mortified.

"Big gesture, remember?!" Gran shouted.

She should really sing more of the song and speak less.

"Ask him!"

"No..." Noah muttered to himself.

"He's OVER THERE BY THE BUFFET!" Gran shouted. "I CAN SEE HIM NEXT TO THE VOL-AU-VENTS!"

"Gran!" Noah said, through gritted teeth, frantically gesturing for her to SHUT THE HELL UP.

"Harry, Noah may have made mistakes but he loves you, so he does!" Gran shouted. "Who here thinks they should give each other a second chance?" Dickie said.

"YEEESSSSS!" shouted the crowd, in an entirely unexpected, completely unusual and never-to-be-repeated display of Noah acceptance, as they clapped and marched to the beat the song.

"Gahhh!" said Noah, surveying the braying crowd. "Hideous."

A flash of someone moving quickly, and Noah saw Harry push open the fire exit and run outside into the night. Heart in his throat, Noah fought his way through the dancing mob, following him out...

CHAPTER
FIFTY-ONE

"Harry!" Noah shouted. "I'm sorry! I didn't know Gran was even going to be here, let alone do that!" He caught up with him. "Haz?"

Harry turned, eyes full of sadness. "It's fine, Noah. Doesn't matter."

"Can we talk?" Noah asked.

Harry looked down at the ground.

"Please?"

Noah stepped towards him, but Harry stepped back, shaking his head. "I love you so much, Noah, but this is never going to go right, is it?"

"Haz," Noah said. "About all the stuff . . . all the words that have been . . . said. Well, I have thought about it, and the truth is, Harry, you're right. When I was with you, I wasn't happy. I was miserable."

A little gasp bubbled out of Harry, his shoulders slumping, crushed.

"But here's the thing. When I'm *not* with you, I'm even more miserable. Life without you isn't life – it's just kind of existing. I can't easily change who I am, because I am insecure, and I do dumb stuff, and I worry too much and I easily get paranoid, and I'm clueless half the time, but ... I need you. I need you, Harry. You're the only person who can make me feel good about myself. It just took me a while to realize someone could actually do that. Would do that. *For* me. And when so much has gone wrong in my life, I hope you can see that when someone as right as you comes along, it doesn't seem real. And it doesn't seem like it could possibly last."

Harry swallowed and nodded.

"And I hope, one day, that I can be that sort of good person to you too, Haz. And I'll try. I really will."

"You already are," Harry said. "You just don't know it."

Noah wanted to hold him so badly it hurt. "And apart from that, who else is going to ruin *Murder, She Wrote* for me by pointing out that every episode basically follows the same format?"

Harry sniffed and smiled.

"Or eat my lid yoghurt and me not go totally ape at them?"

Harry laughed and stepped closer to Noah. "I've had pretty much the most miserable forty-eight hours of my life too."

"Have you?"

"Uh-huh," Harry said. "But I meant what I said. Let's not be interested in the rest of the world when we're each other's worlds."

Noah smiled. "That's what I thought, too. Gran was on at me about making a 'grand gesture' but grand gestures are all about other people, aren't they? They're about how big and brave it is to admit your mistakes and show your feelings in front of a load of strangers in an airport or something, except that ... none of them matter. No one else matters. Only you and me. So that's it." Noah shrugged. "I love you, Harry. I love you, and I'm sorry..." He reached out and held Harry's hands. "I am so stupidly in love with you and you make me so stupidly happy, that, well, you make me quite stupid."

There was an unmistakable twinkle in Harry's eyes as he extracted his hands, reached into his jacket pocket, produced a small matchbox and slid the little drawer open. Inside were ten glistening diamonds.

Noah looked up at him. "You got them out of the bin?"

"Took me five hours. Mum thought I'd finally lost it, but yeah." Harry nodded. He held the matchbox out for Noah to take.

"Thank you," Noah said, going in for a hug.

Harry smiled, holding Noah gently in his arms and pressing his lips against his. Noah wrapped his arms around Harry too, never wanting to let him go, not ever again, inhaling every last bit of him in.

"Mum's not going to be home tonight," Noah said, breaking away. "She's doing some gig with Bambi in Ashby-de-la-Zouch – they're launching some sort of infernal double act together. I was thinking, you could stay over. Maybe?"

"Maybe that sounds like fun."

"Maybe it does." Noah smiled.

Noah stepped towards Harry, and they kissed again. It was long, breathless, *epic*.

In the distance, the sounds of Josh Lewis singing Shakira's "Hips Don't Lie" filtered through from the hall.

Noah and Harry both looked at one another and laughed.

"Come on," Harry said, pulling Noah back towards the fire exit. "Let's dance."

"Harry – I want to dance with you all night long." Noah grinned. "Even if they play songs by manufactured pop groups with no musical talent."

Harry kissed Noah on the lips. "I love you, Noah Grimes." He reached for Noah's hands and smiled. "This is one of those nights that we'll look back on. I can ... just feel it. In ten, twenty, fifty years' time, we'll look back and remember it as perfect. As special. *Happy*. So let's make it as perfect, special and happy as we can. Let's be part of it. And also, let's immortalize it." He grabbed his phone from his inside pocket and pulled Noah into a selfie. "Let's go with our ship name!" Harry said, adjusting the phone so they both fitted into the frame. "Say, 'Hoah'!"

"Hoah!" they both giggled.

The phone flashed. The moment captured. Noah and Harry. *For ever.*

ACKNOWLEDGEMENTS

A simple "thanks" never feels quite enough for all the people who have helped with this book – so pin me down for a cocktail any time you like, folks... Actually, that's a lot of cocktails – maybe just a Ribena?

Linas Alsenas is my editor at Scholastic and has been nothing short of totally brilliant. Linas, shaping and honing this story with you has been a wonderful experience – thank you for all your ideas, your vision, and for all the laughs. I've loved every second.

Thank you to Olivia Horrox for her PR majesty, and for doing so much to get Noah "out there". I owe Olivia a special thanks because the whole "lid yoghurt" thing was her story and she kindly let me use it.

To the marvellous Roisin O'Shea and the marketing team – huge, huge thanks for all your hard work, support and Noah love. Liam Drane – designer of the awesome covers – you've done yet another cracking job and I bow down to your graphic brilliance. And the rest of the Scholastic Dream Team – thank you for welcoming me and Noah into your world.

Joanna Moult, thank you for all your support, enthusiasm, advice and for being the sort of agent who is always available, even if it's just for a little chat.

Johnny Capps, Julian Murphy and the team at Urban Myth Films – I'm so pleased you loved Noah enough to option it for TV. Working with you on the development process has been a real pleasure.

A massive thank you to all you fabulous book bloggers out there, who have reviewed Noah, interviewed me, and been so lovely and supportive. I really appreciate everything you do. Similarly, to the booksellers who have taken Noah under their wings and really pushed it in their stores, I love you, thank you. Same goes for the awesome librarians and the schools who have stocked Noah in their libraries, invited me in to talk to their students and shortlisted Noah for awards. And to all you readers who have bought, borrowed or who have got in touch – it means a lot, thank you.

To both my fellow CringeFest tour authors, and the Funny YA gang who occasionally meet up for cocktails – hooray! Funny books rock!

Gareth Williams, thank you for my pretty website, and to all my other friends, especially Simon Woolley, Matthew Freeman, and Gregg Mills: thanks for your patience when I'm always promising to meet up and send dates ... and then never do because of vague, book-based reasons.

Paul L Martin, thank you for the years I spent producing cabaret shows with you on the Battersea Barge and in Soho. Working with some of the best drag queens in the business has proved invaluable in the writing of this book. I'm raising a glass to Trinity Million ... and Ashby-de-la-Zouch.

Huge thanks to Sue and Peter Counsell for your continued support.

Mum, thanks for getting me through my teenage years relatively unscathed, unlike poor Noah. This one's for you, with lots of love.

And finally, to Sarah Counsell, my screenwriting partner and long-suffering best friend – whatever I write here won't ever be enough to express my gratitude for the love, sacrifice, kindness and help you have given me over the last year of writing this sequel, so I'll just say this: I could never have done this without you.

SIMON X